Under the biological microscope, fractal geometry reveals itself as the secret structure of Life itself. Like Russian dolls, the closer we zoom in, the more we pass into repeating realms of infinite divisibility. In *Ultrameta*, Douglas Thompson searches for just such patterns in the confusion and social devastation of modern urban life. *Ultrameta* is the metropolis of all metropolises. The city we all live in, wherever we happen to be in the world. London, Glasgow, Athens, New York, Tokyo . . . the 'City of the Soul' that has grown within all of us. The time-span of the text ranges from Ancient Greece to the unnervingly familiar present, leading us to uncomfortable questions about ourselves and the life we live. It encompasses a vast emotional and social spectrum, which we plunge through as we follow the main character, Alexander Stark, through a vivid range of different identities, moving from one time and place to another in a seemingly endless cycle of death and re-emergence.

What is Ultrameta? Visionary horror? Experimental surrealism? Trippy outsider art? Like Danielewski's *House of Leaves*, this is one of those few books that possess a core of something genuinely unusual, both in its ideas and its approach to storytelling. A tale of 'Serial Suicide' – or perhaps of immortality. A circular novel – or is it a story collection? A four-dimensional shadow of, or an enigma modelled on, Life itself? *Ultrameta* represents a striking development in Slipstream writing and a unique way of looking at the world.

to Rachel K

ULTRAMETA

A Fractal Novel

by Douglas Thompson

A Surreal Story or Stories of the City of the Soul

Eibonvale Press

Ultrameta
by Douglas Thompson
Second Edition

Publication Date: November 2011

Cover and Interior Art by David Rix

ISBN: 978-0-9562147-1-3

NOTE: Ultrameta is a work of fiction, and therefore all characters within the text have invented names and are not intended to resemble real people.

Eternal thanks are hereby extended to the editors of the following magazines, who each supported and encouraged the author.

Publication History

Part 13_*Ultrameta* –published in Chapman, Issue 108, summer 2006. www.chapman-pub.co.uk Editor: Joy Hendry.

Part 12b_*Thanatavista* –published in Dream Catcher, Issue 20, autumn 2007. www.dreamcatchermagazine.co.uk Editor: Paul Sutherland.

Part 7b_*Paternoster* –part published (under the title *My Ruined Father*) in Random Acts of Writing, Issue 6, January 2007. www.randomactsofwriting.co.uk Editors: Vikki Trelfer, Jennifer Thomson.

Part 6b_*Scarabolis* –published (under the title *Piranesi In Scarabolis*) in The Drouth, Issue 22, Winter 2006. http://thedrouth.wordpress.com Editors: Johnny Rodger, Mitchell Miller.

Part 7a_*Icarus* –published (under the title *Icarus In Nouvelleville*) in Subtle Edens, An Anthology Of Slipstream Fiction, from Elastic Press, Autumn 2008. www.elasticpress.com Editors: Allen Ashley, Andrew Hook.

Part 12a_*Casamundi* –published in Visionary Tongue, Issue 25, Autumn 2008. http://myweb.tiscali.co.uk/ jamiespracklen/visionarytongue/ Editors: Jamie Spracklen, Donna Scott.

Part 7b_*Paternoster* –further part published (under the title *The Inhabited Man*) in Dark Horizons, Issue 53, Autumn 2008. www.britishfantasysociety.org.uk Editor: Stephen Theaker.

Part 11b_*Telemura* –published in Dark Horizons, Issue 54, Spring 2009. Editor: Stephen Theaker.

Part 11a_*Anatomicasa* –published (under the title *Anatomy Of A Wounded House*) in Theaker's Quarterly Fiction, Issue 28, Spring 2009. www.silveragebooks.myby.co.uk Editor: Stephen Theaker.

Part 10a_*Mortadore* –published (under the title *Madame Mortadore & The Clouds*) in Theaker's Quarterly Fiction, Issue 29, Summer 2009. Editor: Stephen Theaker.

Part 8b_*Bedrock* –published (under the title *The Son Of Yesterday*) in Visionary Tongue, Issue 26, Summer 2009. Editors: Jamie Spracklen, Donna Scott.

Douglas Thompson graduated from the Mackintosh School Of Architecture in 1989, then went to busk on the London Underground and win the Grolsch/Herald Question Of Style Award for new writing, all in one strange summer. Since then he has published short stories in a wide range of magazines and anthologies, including Ambit and New Writing Scotland, and reviewed architecture for The Herald. He won second prize in the Neil Gunn Writing Competition in 2007, and currently works as an architectural designer and computer 3d-visualiser. He maintains the website www.glasgowsurrealist.com with his brother, the contemporary surrealist artist Ally Thompson. Douglas lives in Glasgow with his partner Rona. Ultrameta is his first novel.

Acknowledgements

Inspiration: Dennis Leigh, Ally Thompson, Frank McFadden, Martin Kane, Peter Howson, Hugh Byars, Alec Mather. *Support*: the early encouragement of Joy Hendry at Chapman Magazine and later dedication and skill in proofreading of the entire text, is gratefully acknowledged. *Encouragement*: the remarkable David Rix, Allen Ashley, and all the other editors who got it. *Love*: Rona. *Apologies*: to the many left out. Complain at this website:-

www.glasgowsurrealist.com/douglas

In loving memory of Norman D R Thompson.

Contents

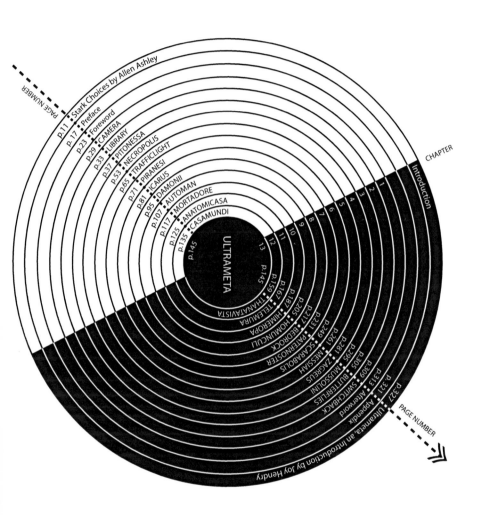

... Alexander Stark, a respected University professor has gone missing, apparently suffering from amnesia. Soon handwritten letters begin arriving at his wife's house, in which Stark seems to adopt multiple personas (a down-and-out, an amnesiac murderer, a nightclub songstress, a paranoid single mother), each suggesting suicidal or homicidal behaviour.

Years later, the professor reappears at his wife's house in a confused state, and together they read over his collected letters. "Ultrameta" (the name Stark gives his private world, his city of the mind) is Glasgow, Edinburgh, Dublin, London, Rome, New York, a restless and haunted place where human identity is constantly being eroded, social division is simmering, and truth is a dwindling commodity. Perhaps Ultrameta is where we all live, and sleepwalking; are each its unwitting guards and prisoners...

2a: _Library

I am ten years old. Polished dark floorboards. The ticking of the clock, a grandfather clock. A real ticking like a heart, like a captured bird whose wings have been sewn or bolted to some Edwardian mechanism. This sound fills the drawing room of this house. A ticking, a clucking, plucking, a sobbing of a tired heart. Around the walls are many books in glass bookcases. I like to read the names on the spines and wonder about the contents. And, from time to time, I slide back the glass, take a volume down and begin reading.

The dark floorboards reflect the summer light outside. It is August, and through the old leaded panes of glass of our window, I see a golden field with rolled-up bales of hay in it, and beyond that the outline of the village: low red clay-tile roofs, a church spire. Each hay bale throws an afternoon shadow, the light is golden on the golden field: shorn texture of clipped straw, hugging the good brown earth.

And I am alone in this house because the family have all gone to the sea: my brothers, my mother, my father, have strolled off an hour ago down the half-mile farm track to the shoreline. The track is dry and dusty and deeply furrowed, with several changes in direction as it skirts the ancient boundaries of fields on its way to the sea. The glorious sea, a broad low band of endless blue always just out of sight beyond the tawny wheat fields, as you follow the track.

So the family are gone for now, except me, and soon I will get up and follow them. But for now I savour this moment and this house with its library and its ticking heartbeat. I sit on a creaking chair in the middle of the room, and I can see through the open door to the hall, and from there through the Sitting Room with its tri-partite window to the garden. The garden with its empty swing, its flowerbeds, and its occasional white butterflies. Sometimes I think these butterflies are my family transfigured – my brothers, my mother and father. That they, like me, are trapped within this moment and can have no life outside this day, this house, this garden. But it is just an idea, a child's day dream in an empty house.

So white butterflies play in the summer garden and my family have gone to the sea. I will join them soon. The echoing pendulum clucks and sobs within the grandfather clock, the locked doors, its little coffin.

I stand up and look again at the names and titles on the spines of the volumes in the bookcase. Some are old and faded, some new and fresh. A wasp collides momentarily with one pane of the window. I am not afraid here, not now, after the changes. The villagers say there is a boy, *the maddy,* who is left to roam by day and night. Who sometimes presses his face against windows towards evening. We have not seen him yet. He is said to be harmless.

I am not afraid here, the owner told us with a knowing smile that the old house had many sounds. It was once a boarding house for farm labourers. One night my brothers and I heard heavy boots coming down the stairs, a commotion of raised voices so real that we stayed by the closed door to the hall, clutching croquet-mallets, in terror for fifteen minutes. But when we finally opened the door, of course there was nothing, the hall empty, all other doors locked. The dead are here with us, but they mean us no harm.

The same night, my brothers and I each slept with croquet-mallets by our beds in fear, and one by one they fell asleep, all except me. And once I was the last, the house came alive atom by atom. Every timber and every pipe began to creak and click with ever-increasing frequency until I lay frozen in a cold sweat, eyes firmly shut, amid a symphony of inexplicable sounds. I finally tried to wake my nearest brother, but, before he came to, he said in a voice not his own: *Do you want me or the blacksmith?*

Through the leaded glass window, the shadows have lengthened just an inch, beneath the hay bales in the golden field, beneath the church spire and the village roofs. And running my fingers across the spines of books, to my surprise, I have come across one which holds my attention, it seems to bear my own name:

Alexander Stark : The Seven Circles

It is a neatly handwritten manuscript, on faded parchment. I take it down, and by the light of the summer window, begin reading:-

Alive again, the hunger returns. This broken body...

~

3a: _Pitonessa

Alive again, the hunger returns. This broken body, no matter how many times I try to lose it, always finds me washed up, spat out by the city after another day's use. And here I am: spread out on my back on the mudflats under a wild blue autumn sky, brought ashore at the estuary, the delta of the wide river where it weeps so blindly, endlessly, into the boundless ocean.

And the sky above me; suffused with softening yellow light, leans already towards nightfall and forgetfulness. Who am I? I have the tattered clothes I lie in, the wind-torn streams of cloud overhead: but what to connect it all with? The puzzle has neither author nor answer, just its own inexorable progress, the cycle of destruction and rebirth, the first drops of blood smearing the clouds, approaching sunset.

I stand up and look about. Behind me the ocean, in front of me the city in the distance, on my right the long rippling estuary, grey and polluted, on my left the brown mud flats leading to distant woods. And there in the distance I see a figure running away. My eyes adjust and I trace their footsteps in the beach right back to this point. They must have been here minutes beforehand. I shout after them, and stagger forward. But they half-turn and run faster, as if afraid of me. Then at my feet I notice they have left a canvas bag. I kneel down and open it up. There is a change of clothing in it, a black suit identical to the one I am wearing but without the stains and holes. I look about again. Without a soul under this sky to see me, I strip and re-dress drowsily, still a little unsteady on my feet.

Like homing pigeons, my new shoes seem to wish to return me to the city of their origin. Across the impossibly long, bleak mudflats, my feet carry me towards those looming shapes in the distance, the tower blocks and cranes. Above me, the sky is like a woven pattern of cumulus, a little too regular to be believed, while the mud below is curiously striated by the retreating tides. And across this I move, exquisitely small like the shuttle of a loom, or a solitary soldier ant, returning home late to the nest.

As I walk, the sky changes and the sunset begins. The bleak open space is strangely comforting to move through; some part of me wishes it to go on forever. And I want to go on walking too, the rhythm greatly therapeutic, but the walking brings the city closer, will bring an end inevitably, to my wilderness.

Eventually, I see the docks looming, cranes and canals, the criss-cross formwork of girders, blackened against the deepening blue of evening. I walk on, my feet encountering cobbles now, and quayside mossy stones underfoot, discarded packing crates, rusting capstans, rotting frayed ropes. And everywhere, puddles, fragments of reflected sky like glass shards, lying dappled on the uneven, neglected pavements. Occasionally, a shipyard, still working, noise of men shouting behind the gates, glimpses of sparks flying to the ground, the sound of riveting and bolting. Huge steel cliff-faces taking shape, reaching upwards to the sky. But mostly the empty spaces; vacant yards, rotting iron hulls of dead barges, stunted tufts of coarse grass growing on the piers, rails of disused tramways criss-crossing my path.

And derelict warehouses: their facades like heartbroken faces, broken windows, empty frames, bolted iron doors below, skirts of meagre weeds where walls emerge from the cobbled roads. Rusting derricks guard lonely pier-heads, their jibs swinging like the hangman's noose. The sky is blood now, punctuated by man's ladders of steel, fragmented rungs reaching up to scrape the emerging crescent moon.

But just who am I? The occasional strangers I pass offer no information: shipyard fitters finishing work, gypsies scouring the wastelands for salvage. I look for clues, further evidence of civilisation. Gloomy brick chimneys smoke like the Victorian pipes of Sunday fathers, rotten timber telegraph poles lean, their wires dishevelled but still gesturing in lines towards lost horizons, speaking in semaphore about distances and emptiness. At last, in the distance, I see a new station perched above the canals and quays, and weave my way towards it, negotiating locks, towpaths and bascule bridges.

The sky is ablaze. I climb the gleaming new metal steps upwards, as if into it all. Above the docks I join an ordered world of timetables and bolted steel junctions, sandblasted green glass, sparkling white louvres. Like some technological animal, the station perches over the wasteland, the steps and lift door like some icy proboscis thrust down into its dying jugular, paralysing the victim in economic stasis. I look along the rails and wires stretching into the endless distance and am enchanted: by the music of technology and schedules, the romance of futurism. The wires rattle gently: the start of an approach. From the gleaming glass tombstones in the distance emerges the nose of a train, some wicked antennae seeking me out. The twilight above and around emerges from behind the fiery clouds, deepening blue ink. I close my eyes and breathe in the white dust of new concrete platforms, absorb the growing sound of approaching carriages, the mundane crescendo of rattling wires and rails, the resonant hum of high voltage. I stand at the edge of the platform with my head and nose to the wind, a student of technology. I wait patiently to be made its servant.

The doors open. I step up and suddenly find myself among the commuter crowds. The warmth, the rush of flesh is almost overpowering. We are forced to press all our bodies together. From no identity, I suddenly find myself with a hundred, all pressing in, all vying for attention. And yet they are all strangers, to me and to each other. Some read papers, others look out of windows, look at the floor, close their eyes, listen to secret music from hidden places. Their clothes are all so different. I see different emotions: tiredness, hope, expectation, despair. Recollections of their days wash over them: I see it in their eyes, like shores where waves of memories break silently. Some feel disgust for each other, some feel attraction, take furtive glances at areas of bared flesh, or where concealed flesh is expressed by the hang or cut of cloth.

Above all, these people that I touch are in motion: have precedence and sequel; an office or a shopping trip they have left, a husband or child they are returning to. They are underway, bound. They have meaning, which they express in their confidence and self-composure, and that they celebrate with ornamentation: patterned ties, sloganned t-shirts, eye shadow, lipstick, swept-back hair, tattoos, earrings, studs. They exhibit chains of personal decisions; they are mobile art galleries of themselves. They are enterprises, open for business, but just what business precisely? Individuation, if we had to put a name to it. And I, who can lay no claim to a name or a personality, envy these shining icons around me who drip with signification.

I wish they would spare me a gesture, a quirk, a trademark or two. Something unique that somebody might remember about me, something I might measure myself against eternity with, something that might convince me that I am alive today, might fool me into thinking I mattered for a second.

But already I know who I am in that respect: somebody who must die every night, who cannot live the sleepwalkers' life, who cannot believe that life goes on unchanging in blissful boredom, secure and content. I envy the commuters their lives, their clothes of unknowing, their blindfolds, their mutual forgetting. But I know the thing that they cannot bring themselves to face. I live their nightmare for them, I swim in it. I burn in the fire and yet, every night I return unscathed, without a single witness to the miracle. That is my fate. But their eyes are warm. They look at each other and imagine laughter, contentment, making love. I look and see exotic animals, doomed to die soon abandoned by their health, discarded by their own kin, deluded as to their own importance, robbed in the end of everything, even their dreams. I see their futures and I weep for them, for myself, and for us all.

The doors open, and without making a decision I am swept outwards with the jostling sea of bodies, I am a fluid with them falling through underground pipes. I flow upstairs, down ramps. I am disgorged into a vast circular hall, spinning out into the middle, slowing down, escaping the centrifuge. There are perhaps six or seven different directions, archways leading away, with obscure symbols and names over them. Everyone seems to know where they are going, but it is all chaos to me. Some queues form in front of various portals, newspapers being sold and tickets dispensed. I stand at the empty centre of this space and turn slowly, my face blank, my head empty, waiting for a sign, for something to make sense.

Gradually, as if drawn magnetically by my presence, various figures separate out from the crowds, and gravitate towards me by circuitous stops, territorial orbits. Do I want a taxi? Do I want Hash, Crack, Heroin? What are they I ask, don't I have them already? Why don't they look me in the eyes? They check over their shoulders, as if stalked by some terrible invisible predator. A woman's hair falls across my face, her perfume is cheap and sweet, overpowering. She whispers in my ear about wanting to do something for me for thirty-five Dollars. *Can't I do that myself?* -I ask. She laughs coarsely, her head thrown back, fake jewellery clattering, a gap in her teeth. *If you can, you should go on the stage sugar...* Is that my name, *is my name: Sugar?* And like this, each in turn roll their eyes, check my pockets, conclude I am crazy, and lose interest in me.

As they clear away, I notice other people further away, watching me. Their attention seems quite different. One pretends to read a newspaper, another to be waiting for someone, but I can tell that they are monitoring me. One returns my stare. He wears a grey suit, similar in cut to my own. I make to walk towards him and he retreats, starts walking, glancing over his shoulder, moving towards a ticket desk. As I catch up, he takes a little writing pad from his pocket and scrawls a note. He tears it off as I reach him, hands it to me, then turns to leave. I grab his arm, saying: *Wait, who are you? What is going on?* His eyes are dead, his expression listless as he looks back at me. Reluctantly, he takes the pad from his pocket again and writes one more note, tears it off, hands it to me, then freeing his arm brusquely, walks off without looking back.

I read the note: *the Keepers protect and guide the Witness. Wait!* -I shout, running and grabbing him again, *-Who is the Witness?* Annoyed, but still patient, he removes my hand from his arm and turns it back to press against my chest. He looks at me meaningfully. He brings his other hand up and points his finger until it touches my chest. Straightening his arm, still pointing, he inches away, his eyes filled with immeasurable tiredness. I move my own gaze slowly down until I look at his finger, my chest. *I am the Witness!?* -I ask, incredulously. With a single gesture, just discernable as an affirmative nod, he turns and leaves. I turn and read the other note: *Ask for a ticket to Pitonessa.*

I take my place in the queue. At the window I expect to be asked for money, but the assistant gives me a long meaningful stare, then asks quietly: *Do you remember your name?* As I say no, he nods as if a code has been correctly answered then hands me a ticket with handwritten directions on which passages to take, signs to follow. I thank him, but he shakes his head once and turns to the next customer.

Soon I am on a train again, this time heading for suburbia. I sit by the window as we emerge from the tunnels, regaining the surface. Now the sky is a deep twilight, the embers of the fire overhead fading to grey. I bathe in the exquisite tedium and order of the commuter life. The fabric of the seats is chequered, the suits are patterned with subtle grains and lines, the newspapers are regimented, held high in discreet broadsheet privacy, resplendent anonymity. Throats are cleared, headphoned music putter-patters somewhere. Occasional conversation may be overheard: strained manoeuvres of polite exchanges avoiding intimacy. Occasionally the rules are breached, a child or a drunk causes laughter to break out, smiles are exchanged, but the breach is usually containable.

Outside, I see suburbia taking shape. Like the pattern of the fabrics on the seats and suits, I love the grain of fences and streets, the apparent sameness, the subtle elaboration, layer upon layer of texture from macro to micro scale. The hedges: tiny leaves flickering in an evening breeze, the grass lawns mowed, unmowed, blades of grass in the wind, lime green then emerald; whitewash render, painted, unpainted.

My station arrives – I see the sign appear outside. I step down onto the platform and feel the rush of air behind me as the train departs. Now I am alone, above what was once a town, now absorbed and subjugated to serve the centre, a dormitory suburb where humanity comes to rest. And sleep hangs everywhere in the quiet air. It drips from the leaf-laden branches, snoozes beneath hedgerows. I stroll down the ramp to lose myself in this green labyrinth, hoping I might stumble on some clue at its heart; some fragment of my identity.

And now darkness has fallen as I wander, aimlessly searching the streets of suburbia, admiring the little parcels of life laid out in neat rows, the gardens, prisons of groomed nature. The grass never gets to grow long. The tree that reaches upwards and strains out, grasps at the sky, will always be cut back in time. If civilisation stopped, how quickly the plants would rebel: does anyone imagine for a second? How the trim golden beach hedge would run riot, become a grove of 30 foot giants, rupture the tarmac path in front of them, twist and buckle even the steel fence, rusting by then. How the unchecked weeds, *horsetails* ancient as the dinosaurs, would slice the tarmac to ribbons with their silicon-armoured fronds, destroying all the roadways? In one blank generation, suburbia would be reclaimed as the domain of nature again. Aided by the cycle of rain and frost and thaw, the neighbourhood would become a jungle with an interesting display of ruins within it.

So everything here is about suppression, repression, denial, keeping nature perpetually in check, maintaining the façade. We shall do our daily grind of work, discard the feeling of gloom and futility each shift leaves us with, tell ourselves it means something, that we will strike lucky, that we will become so magically rich some day to be able to stop and leave. But we will only leave in a coffin. And as we age, our animal natures must be pruned and controlled to accept our fate. We shall die quietly and slowly over several decades, like autumn leaves swept into a pile, maturing, manuring, through the seasons, sad then foul, then finally slightly useful.

I pace the streets and somehow am filled with wonder and reverence for suburbia: it makes a sweet monument of futility, of surrender. With no personality or name, I find this world my perfect counterpart: here the loss of identity is celebrated, accepted. I want to lie down and sleep beneath this hedgerow, to run through banks of rose bushes until I am torn into nothingness, my red blood mingled with inconsequential rain, gurgling into the gutters of suburban avenues under orange streetlights. To leap into the huge fat green heart of this juniper bush and be swallowed up, vanishing there, hunched up in the foetal position, shivering and grey like a rotting walnut, with all that foliage of fronds swaying gracefully around me like flags of surrender.

But everywhere the leaves are falling. A breath of evening wind is picking up, and all the streets seem to weep with exhaustion onto the pavements, onto the lawns. The memory of summer is written, burnt onto every leaf like an elegy, the piles of orange and red and yellow and brown bleeding back to one colour. Over every street I pace, a hundred puddles glimmer: fragments of the broken mirror of reality. I remember this much: that as a child once, I believed these puddles were windows to another world. Like our own world, but upside down, equal in every detail and yet subtly, horribly altered. As a child running home, I grew afraid to look into these windows, more scared still to step into one, lest I fall straight through and become trapped forever in the world below.

And it occurs to me at last that I am in that world now. The world of childhood nightmares, of the streets whose names have been secretly changed, where everyone you know is altered or gone, where you are lost without even the memory of your mother's face to guide you, where your very identity is slipping away, where an unfamiliar environment threatens to cancel you out.

But now the leaves are whipped up into a whirling dervish in front of me: they loom up into a cloud of flickering, panicking little fragments. They re-assemble, and from this cloud, as I cover my face against the breeze, a figure emerges from the orange streetlit haze. A little black dog appears at my feet and begins barking, then whimpering excitedly. He looks up at me, he circles my legs. And at the end of his leash now there stands a woman, her back to the halo of electric light. I move closer to see her, our eyes meet and I see that she has started crying. The dog barks for attention, I kneel to stroke him. I stand up. She is still crying. *Is something wrong?* -I finally ask. *-Can I help?*

She half laughs, half sobs, wiping her eyes. *How can you? Is it possible? After all this time? How can you just turn up like this?*

For a moment I feel ashamed without knowing what for. *Do you know me?* -I ask. *I mean... should I know you?*

She lunges forward and slaps me hard across the face, then holds me by the shoulder, looks into my face, her expression dissolving by the second, then embraces me with a sob, shaking against my chest.

She draws away. *Don't you remember me? Is that what you're trying to say? That you have amnesia? So how could that have happened? When?*

I shake my head, and look down at the pavement. *I don't know the answer to any of these questions. I'm sorry. You seem like a kind person... I'm moved, if you are saying that I mean something to you, but I have no recollection of why. Should I be your friend? Is that possible?*

Moved? -she mouths, incredulously. *You're moved!!? Have you any idea how long you've been away?*

I look into the distance, look into the horizon for assistance, where a red glow persists above the silhouettes of roofs and chimneys. I finally shake my head: *None, a few months?*

Ten years... over ten bloody years, probably eleven by now... Where have you been?

I shake my head again: *I remember only... today, nothing more except a few fragments maybe of what I think might have been my childhood, but they come and go.*

Why are you here then? This is where we lived together. How can you have known to come back here today?

I take a crumpled note from my pocket and hand it to her. *A man I had never seen before gave me this note in a station. There were others like him, watching me from a distance, they're probably watching now. I don't know what this means... unless it's some kind of experiment.*

My God... she says *-It's like you're a mental patient or something. Is there anything else in your pockets, paperwork?*

I turn them out: *-Nothing, I have nothing. I am nothing. I don't even... I mean... would you tell me... What is my name?*

She snorts, it's not even a laugh. She puts her arm over my shoulder and turns around: *-Come with me, I'll show you our house, David. Your name is David Thin. How does it sound?*

I walk with her. She guides me with one hand around my waist: *now do you remember my name, or... the dog's name? Try...*

We turn a corner and begin to walk up a long hill. The roads are quiet here, only occasional cars slide by, their headlamps illuminating us briefly like a couple, like we were always together, I see our long momentary shadows stretch out as each vehicle passes. The dog jumps ahead, seemingly excited by my arrival. One or two stars appear overhead as we climb the long hill. *Do you remember the way, David? Can your feet lead you there?*

At last, near the top of the hill, we turn into a garden, extraordinarily neglected, but beautiful still. Two tall thin yew trees stand either side of the front door. What was once a lawn is now a waist-high meadow of wild grass, swaying and hissing in the night wind. The dog vanishes gleefully into its folds and waves, playing with ghosts. The windows of the house have been closed over from inside with old wooden shutters.

My name is Donna, -she says, -and he… when he re-emerges from the grass, is called Musso. It's short for Mussolini… one of your jokes – your idea I'm afraid. How does it feel by the way, to encounter your own sense of humour?

*Strange, -*I say, *but why is it funny?*

*I never thought it was, particularly, -*she says, opening the door with a rusty set of keys, *But I suppose you thought naming a tiny harmless dog after a great dictator would make the dog seem grand, and the dictator seem ridiculous, I don't know. You tell me… if you can remember.*

I told you, I remember nothing like that at all. But tell me… I mean, I'm curious… please don't be angry. I want to know…

She lights a match and leads the way though the cold darkness of the abandoned house. *Yes?*

Did you love me? Did we… love each other? … Before I left?

In the darkness, I have no idea of her expression. She is fumbling with some candles by the fire, her back turned. But one by one, she lights them; thirteen in all, placing each one about the room in strategic places, on top of bookcases, settees, coffee tables, and as she does this, piece by piece, the room comes alive, is recovered from oblivion, reconstructed before my eyes.

Yes, -she says, as she moves about, carrying the light. *Yes, I loved you, and you loved me... I'm certain of that. But that only made it worse. More painful... the more inexplicable that you should leave...*

But why did I...?

Now she kneels to light a fire in the grate, and Mussolini scrapes past my legs in anticipation. *Can you hold this match here, while I get more wood?*

I take her place, holding the flame and Mussolini licks my other hand, bounces around to look at me. I look back at the room behind us, furniture draped with white dust sheets, fantastical shadows being thrown over everything by our little scene: the dog a lion, and me, a kneeling giant.

She returns and says: *Well you tell me please... because that's the whole issue. You just disappeared one day, with no reason, no explanation, no phonecall, and you never returned...*

A missing person? -I ask, sitting up and taking a place near the fire.

Not quite, -she says, *I could have lived with that, maybe... but you began sending letters... every week... every month.*

Then I explained myself? There WAS a reason?

They explained, you explained, nothing, unfortunately. The police helped me to establish that they were in your handwriting, and of "sound mind and body" as they say, but other than that I wouldn't even have known they were yours. They don't say Dear Donna, they don't even say Hello or Goodbye. They're just diary entries, or stories or something, extracts from some larger journal that never seems to really begin or end or have any purpose… I kept them all.

Do you have them here? -I ask.

Incredibly, -she says, *Yes, I do. That and so many other things about us that would remind me of us and of you. I left them all here in this house, just the way I left it, when I couldn't bear the silence anymore, waiting for you, wondering where you were or what had happened to you. Had you lost your mind? One day I turned this place into a shrine: I left all the things, even the furniture that would remind me of you. I abandoned it all and locked the door, and went back to my mother's house. Ten years ago…*

She turns her eyes on me in the candlelight, sad still, but her expression warmer. *Is it really you?* -she leans closer to look at my face.

Was I unhappy? -I ask.

She turns away and stands up suddenly, her face lost again in the flickering darkness above; her voice bounces around the room as she walks over to a bookcase in the far corner. *-As far as I know, no. You were no more unhappy than any reasonably well-off, gainfully-employed thirty-something. You were happy with ME, put it that way, and that's what really mattered, I always thought. But happy with the world, with your world, now that's another thing again. Happy with your job, happy with the way most human beings turned out in the end? Well now, that depressed you sometimes… I remember that.*

Here, -she brings back a pile of paperwork, handwritten notes, and places them in my hands. *Here's what you posted to this address. We even had police psychologists go through them to decipher why you would send such nonsense to people, but their conclusions were… well, inconclusive. "Possibly suicidal, partially delusional" -I think, was their spectacular verdict, after six months. They even tried to locate some of the places in the letters, in case they were real, but they're all sort of altered, apparently. Addresses that don't exist. Places that are distorted somehow. Then a few months later, they just ran out. No more letters. I missed them then, I suppose. They were all I had by then.*

I pull a candle over close to where I sit, and take the manuscripts onto my lap.

They're pretty weird I'm afraid, I should warn you, she says, -*a bit sick in places. Some of them are written as if you think you are a woman. One of them was even written in Latin and we had to have it translated. I mean why and how would you ever have written it in Latin?*

I shake my head in disbelief, and begin reading:-

I wake up babbling, almost screaming. It happens a lot recently...

~

4a: Necropolis

I wake up babbling; almost screaming. It happens a lot recently. My heart racing, my throat choked with unformulated distress. As if some other life, some other ghost, were trying to take me over. I used to think this effect was some irrelevant detail, a small malfunction in the human machine, like déjà vu. But now I know its real significance: that sometimes the ghosts will win. More often than not these days, in fact: I wake up as a different person.

I sit up bolt upright under a wide blue sky. Only a few white puffs intrude up there to trouble my mind. Fresh air, birds singing, but a chill from the bare ground beneath me. Autumn again. I am sitting down in a large graveyard on a hill. I have been asleep in the shadow of a semi-ruined Victorian tomb. My bleary eyes rest on the blackened peeling stone next to me, bright sunlight blasting its surface. I reach my hand out to touch it: it is warm. I try to stand up stiffly, but fall back down, then crawl around the tomb in curiosity. I touch some moss, and read a faded inscription: *Septimus Ellis, 1740 – 1802.*

Hey... pal... -A voice rings out behind me, a shadow crossing the sun. *Huv ye goat a light there mate?*

A... light, -I mutter to myself, pulling myself up against the tomb, and tapping my pockets instinctively. I shake my head and look at this skeleton of a man who confronts me; unshaven, unwashed, his skin bleached to a weird grey pallor, like a graveyard statue come alive. *There,* he says, and points at my chest, top left. Without irritation, almost tenderly, he leans close and withdraws a box of matches from my chest pocket. He lights a cigarette, a curious homegrown affair, as crumpled as its owner. He sighs and breathes out, handing me the matches back.

How... -I begin uncertainly, running my hand through my hair, *How did you know my matches were there?*

He is turned slightly sideways to me, looking out over the city below. Now he snorts a half-laugh and turns, fixing me with his narrow, haggard eyes: -*Been on the mad-dog again huv we, Malky?*

What?

Yup. Forgoatten yir name as well no doubt. Heard it all a million fuckin times. The fuckin lost spaceman act will be up next...

Where are we? What's this place called?

I notice his shoulders tensing, he is turning away from me again. *Necropolis...*-He says.

Necropolis...-I repeat, -*City of the dead...in a long dead language...how appropriate.*

Appropriate... -this skeleton whispers under his breath then suddenly turns on me, roaring in a hoarse rasp: *I'll gie ye fuckin appropriate...!*

Without warning, he grabs me by the hair and rams my head into the side of the stone tomb. With his wasted yet malevolent limbs, he is kicking the back of my legs while he bangs my head up and down on the cold decaying stone:-

Yir name's fuckin Malky, ya eejit. Ya've been here fur years, ya daft cunt. Ya used ti tak smack n'shit. Yir wasted mate, remember? Yir name's Malky. Is it no comin back ti ye yet?

The repeated blows against the stone are making my head numb. I am growling, crying out, blood coming down from somewhere is beginning to mist my eyes. I spit out a tooth. To my right along the horizontal top surface of the tomb, across the bleak landscape of moss, I can see a half empty bottle of something... cheap wine. To my surprise now, quick as a flash, when I feel my tormentor's grip relax just an inch, I grab this bottle and with one continuous motion smash it against the edge of the tomb then swing it upwards into the area of space above me. Everything goes quiet. My eyesight slowly clears.

I stand up. And as I do, my friend balanced against me falls slowly sideways to the ground, then lies on his back with the jagged broken bottle stuck into one side of his neck. He is making some kind of gurgling noise in some way connected with a red foam emerging from his throat. His eyelids flutter, his feet twitch, his arms make little attempts at movement, up to reach the bottle, but they never make it.

I wipe the blood from my face, and look about. All across the hillside now, as if summoned by the sound of our confrontation, I see other skeletons emerging from their temporary homes amid the tombs of the great and the good –

the illustrious Victorian city fathers. One by one, from little blackened houses of the deceased, I see the bleary faces of these downtrodden ghosts emerge. In curiosity I sense, rather than menace, they drift towards me: an effect akin to standing still amid a field of curious cattle.

Here, on this forsaken citadel of the dead, amid the huddle of topsy turvy tombs, some tumbled-down, some broken-open, a group of ragged men is gathering now, each grey as statues come alive. One kneels down to look at my victim. I look down too. He is still twitching, but less now.

I hated the cunt Malky, nice fuckin joab…

What's happening to him? -I ask.

He's kicking the bucket, mate, another minute or two and he's fuckin history, I reckon. Any last words, Clayso, any last words? -he sneers into the dying man's face.

He's just changing channel I call it, -some other comedian snorts hoarsely -*he'll be better oaf noo – wiz always whinjin aboot hiz mammy's raw deal o a life. Now he can neb her ear instead o oors…*

Someone claps me on the back; -*Christ you always were a vicious shite, Malky. Looks like Clayso tipped ye oar the edge at last eh?*

Another tattered scarecrow kneels by the body: -*He's deid noo… better hide him, before the polis come pokin aboot…*

The whole city spreads out below us, but it cares little for our domestic drama, a dysfunctional family of down-and-outs. Down there, perhaps real people live and die and lament each other's passing. Here, life is a more casual arrangement, cheaply bought and sold, among an army of shadows.

We lay our comrade in an old tomb, and roll a slab closed over the entrance. Scrawl a word or two with a nail onto the surface: *keep out -Clayso (R.I.P).*

No ceremony necessary. The non-people, shadow-men, we drift apart as soon as our purpose has been served. The tyrant buried, we can return to the minutiae of our habitual regime – trawling of bins for leftovers and fag ends, begging at the feet of the shining people, craving small change for the firewater to fuel us – to unlock the chambers of the mind that hold our hope of escape from the wretched game.

I stagger back onto the streets. The sun is going down yet again. It seems like the very moment I get hold of a day, the day begins to escape, tries to abandon me. At least the oncoming darkness will hide my guilt. I have no memory of the day before this one, and yet it seems I have a name, and already a crime to hang on it. The glass shards leap up in front of me; brutal broken crown of this city; the prism of building facades reflecting facades endlessly, and with it the million faces of which I am now only one.

I stumble among the perfect people. I cannot stand as tall and steady as them. My sense of balance, my lungs, my muscles: everything in me feels crushed by something, squeezed out into a hunger which eats me from inside.

Now the sunset is forming: swathes of orange and dribbles of blood well up in the clouds, as if punctured by the glass prism of the city. Then fluid reflection in the thousand faces of this labyrinth. The perfect ones sniff me and walk wide. They hide their eyes in dark glasses; more glass, like the buildings, avoidance, reflection. The human soul is lost here, hidden behind mirrors, or crushed inside the leftover-people like me: the dead ones.

Everything is deflection here, evasion. I beg now, like my comrades, grey arms bared, thrust out into the paths of the shining angels who always move so purposefully compared to us, always in a hurry. They all seem to matter so much to each other, or at least to themselves. The women wear short skirts in gleaming leather, more reflection – show bare flesh of thighs and breasts, and yet the eyes are so often closed with glass or hair or an implacable expression. The beautiful people seem to open like flowers, and yet they seem to close off at the same time, to guard what they are offering up. They are like roses: luscious, dripping with dew, and yet barbed, homicidal, dripping with blood just as easily.

Still, some of them give money. The sunset is ablaze now. It blinds me with its gold in the city's shining facades. I fall back against a doorway mouth. I take a swig of my secret flask of firewater, then fight off the claws of some rival reaching to share it from the shadows. The fire burns down through my chest, then my sight clears for second.

A figure has appeared on the street, who is not moving: he is dressed in black and he stands perfectly still, a few metres away, while the sea of golden vicious angels swim past him. I rub my eyes. I see his face, his eyes are piercing like jewels of white light. He walks towards me, I cannot look away from his face. I want to look away, I feel ashamed in his presence.

He picks me up by the arms and carries me into the shadows. He is whispering in my ears. His voice is not like the others.

So it's you. It's a miracle I found you. I've been searching all day. Don't worry, we'll get you cleaned up. I know, you're confused, you don't remember who you are or what's going on. Don't worry, I'll take care of everything.

We emerge at last into bright white light and tiles and mirrors. A public toilet. He props me forward against a sink and throws water over me. *Look at yourself,* -he says. And forces my face towards the mirror. *Look at yourself, remember who you are. Remember. Drink this.*

He looks around to see that nobody else is about, then produces a vial of glowing blue liquid. *Drink this.* I protest, but he forces me to drink it. I am violently sick several times, while he steadies me. *Now look again,* he exclaims, taking me back to this mirror -*This is who you are.*

My vision clears a little, I wipe the mirror clean with my arm and cough. I look at myself. I wash some blood away. Something familiar is there, behind the worn lined skin, ingrained with dirt, behind the crazed eyes, something familiar is waiting there, hidden.

I don't remember who I am, I say. *Who are you?*

My name is John. I am known as the Reverend John around here. I am one of the Keepers. You don't remember any of this, but I work for you. You hired me once, a long time ago, to follow you, to trace you, to monitor your behaviour, to help you sometimes, to keep records. I am one, but there are others. I think I know some of them by sight now, but the rules prohibit us from talking. It's simpler that way anyhow -we each work only for you, or for the person you used to be.

Why? -I whisper.

We are paid, every week, from accounts you set up. But it's more than that, especially for the ones like me. You saved me once. You revealed The Creator to me, The Knowledge. The same knowledge that you have found a way to forget now. We will protect you from it as long as possible, but in the end it will find you again, if you survive. Do you understand what I have said?

My head is clearing, the world has stopped spinning. I look myself in the eyes calmly, then turn around.

What madness is this? What are you telling me? Is this a game?

Madness eh? Look who's talking. For instance, just what have you done so far today?

I pause to think. *...Killed a man I didn't know and hidden his body. Gone begging, raked through bins, drunk industrial strength alcohol....*

Fascinating... well, this game, as you call it, is what is known as real life, and you are here to record it.

But it's insane. There are people fighting with rats over half-eaten chip suppers out there while people drive by in sports cars that look like space ships. People dying of hypothermia, sleeping beneath shop windows selling suits for over a thousand pounds. What kind of mixed-up nightmare am I living in?

Record it, bear witness... -he says, putting on his coat and hat, moving away from me -*that is all that is required of us... to bear witness, tell the truth, because most people are strangers to it.*

But where are you going? I don't even know who I am. Can't you tell me about myself... even what my name is?

He laughs, smiling for the first time. *Ahh, I see you're sobering up now, that's good. And fear, you're feeling fear again for the first time. You'll find your instructions and a little money in your left hand trouser pocket. Drink only water for the rest of the night... the chemical I gave you will make you violently sick if you touch alcohol. You have no name now, and no fixed personality, you are as I said, an observer. Oh yes,* he pauses, -*and one other thing you might not have remembered...* He stands at the door -*you will probably die later tonight, no matter what you do. Don't be afraid of that. It is nearly always painless, but more painless if you choose and plan it yourself. You'll know when it's time for that. I have to go now. Good night...*

I am alone again. Too tired to run after him, my body sags. I reach into my pocket, and pull out a small white envelope and open it: a latch key falls out along with a handwritten note:

Here is a key to a locker at the station. Go there and retrieve a fresh set of clothes. Change into them. In one of the pockets you will find a key to a new flat on the Riverfront, number 2003 Ocean Street. Go there and shower and rest for one hour. Then write down your impressions of everything that you remember, of what you see and experienced today. Write only in the present tense. Then seal it in one of the envelopes provided and post it to the printed address. Then go to the night club called Zagreus to report for work. Tell them that your name is William Gaunt. Everybody there will remember you from your previous shift which was just last week. Do one shift then leave. You'll know by then what is expected of you.

I make my way through the darkening streets, towards the river. The sky is big and blue now overhead, the clouds dispersing, a few stars appearing. The shoppers seem less in number, and instead a different atmosphere seems to fill the streets. Younger, louder people appear, strutting strangely in little groups, the girls giggling, the men shouting, looking at each other suspiciously. Some of the women seem almost naked, painfully so, shivering in the cold autumnal night. I have difficulty understanding this; they seem to be well-off and yet they do not have enough clothes, if by choice then why? Or if not by choice then what strange accident or assault has befallen them since leaving their homes fully-dressed to end up stripped like this?

I reach number 2003 on the Riverfront and look up at the façade: to reach the door, I must walk across a bridge through a tangled forest of structural steel masts. Behind this rests the obligatory glass façade which at this time of night glows and glimmers with the signs of domestic life within placed curiously on show, as if the inhabitants were zoo animals. I cross the bridge and take the lift up.

Up inside, perhaps because I am a drunk and a murderer, or just a normal human being, I immediately close the thin white curtains.

I take a shower. I collapse onto the bed and sleep for about one hour. I get up and sit at the desk at the foot of the bed. I open the drawer on the left and find a pile of writing pads. I lift one out, switch on the desk lamp and take a pen from the tub in front of me. I open the right hand drawer and find a pile of brown envelopes. Each one has the same post office box number address printed on it with pre-paid postage. I notice that the top envelope has something inside it: but it is not yet sealed.

I lift it out, and carefully shake out its contents. There are 8 pages of handwritten text. I look at the handwriting, then I take the fresh pad on my left and test my own handwriting on it: I write my supposed name on it: William Gaunt. Then I copy out the first sentence of the text:-

I fall with incredible force, face down onto the pavement...

I compare this to the original: they match perfectly.

I look at the time. I put the pen down for a while. I begin reading:-

I fall with incredible force, face down onto the pavement. A woman is screaming somewhere high up behind me, passers-by are gasping and gathering around me...

~

5a: Trafficlight

I fall with incredible force...

I fall with incredible force, face down onto the pavement. A woman is screaming somewhere high up behind me, passers-by are gasping and gathering around me. And behind all this I gradually hear the background sounds of any ordinary busy city day: Horns, brakes, engines idling and groaning, waiting then moving, the music of inconsequence. Reluctantly, I open my eyes. And, a little stiffly at first, rise onto my elbows and turn around sideways, lying on the tarmac. *But there is no blood...* -someone is muttering.

I'm fine, actually, thank you, please, honestly... -I try to say. But they are all babbling, pointing upwards, something about twenty storeys, hundreds of feet, somebody is calling an ambulance on their cell phone. They don't believe me, so I stand up and show them my rib cage, my unbroken arms. A middle-aged woman shows signs of fainting and is caught by a young city executive. Hoping this will be sufficient decoy, I turn and head away, stumbling slightly over the fractured indentation I have left in the tarmac underfoot.

I try to lose myself in the Saturday crowds. It's autumn again of course, that yellow sidling sunlight seeking me out, even down here amid this canyon of highrise glass and steel. It blinds me as I move, and the million passing faces are like a shadow-play, stroboscopic filigree of silhouettes, lacelike, flickering over me like the sprocket-holes of old film pulled rapidly from the spool by a vast and unseen hand.

My life moves on, to who knows what, another chapter underway again, no time to pause or take stock, to look for meanings. Two blocks on, looking over my shoulder, I slip out of the river of bright noise into a shady bar, my eyes adjusting, stepping slowly, a mellow music gradually replacing the hubbub behind me as the door moves shut.

In the toilet, I mop my brow, begin to dust down my torn clothes, checking my face in the mirror, trying to recover my identity. The door behind me is thrown suddenly open, and a man dressed as a cleaner with mop and bucket shuffles in, takes a glance up at me, whistles an idle tune and places a pile of clothing on the counter next to me. His face seems vaguely familiar, but he avoids eye contact. As I comb my hair, he finishes wiping the floor then leaves. I look at myself again then down at the pile of clothes. I inspect them more closely. I open them out, I hold up a jacket, then trousers. I see in the mirror that they are a suit identical to the one I am wearing, but brand-new and unworn. I make to run out after the cleaner, then hesitate, thinking, and turn around. I consult my own vacant expression in the mirror again and then after a moment take the suit into a cubicle to change.

Returning to the bar, I order a drink and take a seat. Mellow jazz and muted lighting resume. Behind the glasses and shelves I can see my reflection lurking. Someone pulls up a stool next to me. She touches my arm, saying: *Who are you?* I start to get up, but she grabs my sleeve -*Wait a minute… I saw what happened back there. The police are looking for you. How come you're not injured?*

Are you one the Keepers? -I ask.

Her eyes widen: -*Who are the Keepers?*

They monitor my progress, they give me fresh clothes, and occasionally tell… -I stop suddenly, noticing she is adjusting a device in her pocket.

You're a reporter, you're recording this.

Yes, she says, defiantly, looking up to face me. -*Don't you think people would like to know about the mystery man who jumped off a twenty-storey building and walked away unscathed? Sounds mildly interesting to me…*

You can't print this… -I mutter, turning away.

Confidential… legal injunction?

No, that's not what I mean. You won't print this, because you won't understand it. Or if you do, you won't be able to handle it, you'll be jumping off the next towerblock with me.

Try me, -she smiles. -*I've covered some pretty appalling stories in my life -can yours be any worse?*

Yes, because it's your story too, you are its victim, as are we all. And it must be lived to be understood, no newsprint platitudes to protect you…

She finally looks truly puzzled, turning her head quizzically, slightly on its side, as if her hearing is failing.

I grab her hand and lead her to the door. She struggles at first against this grip, enraged by its presumption.

Outside in the blinding light again, I hail a taxi cab, but when I stare into the driver's face his expression goes entirely blank, his mind emptied. I open his door and lead him out onto the road, sit him down on the kerb to rest, return to the wheel myself.

Get in! -I say to the Reporter, who is watching the driver's empty expression, waving a hand in front of his face.

Driving off I take a manuscript from my inside pocket and toss it onto her lap.

There's your story. Now read it to me, please. Read it out loud while I drive.

But where are you taking us?

Nowhere of course. There's nowhere to go, as you will realise when you have finished reading. But in a car like this, identical to a thousand others, we might just evade the Keepers for a while, gain an illusion of freewill. -my voice rises, pumping the accelerator and clutch, moving down through the gears.

"November 1778, Via del Corso, Rome. The great artist and architectural polemicist Giovanni Battista Piranesi is dying..." Hey what is this shit? -her voice sounds uncertain and stilted at first, and then as I make her continue: *"His wife Angela Pasquini and son Francesco are at his bedside..."* -with increasing clarity and confidence, as I drive through the maze of city streets. Twisting and turning robotically, in ways I seem to remember automatically like the steps of a combination safe. Like unlocking this city, as if even its gridiron-pattern plan is not fixed, but will gradually change and evolve, shift over, open up, lead us to its hidden heart -If we can only complete these esoteric traffic rituals perfectly, going through lights and roundabouts, approaching enlightenment, enacting a sacred dance.

~

6a: _ Piranesi

November 1778, Via del Corso, Rome. The great artist and architectural polemicist Giovanni Battista Piranesi is dying. His wife Angela Pasquini and son Francesco are at his bedside. His health has been destroyed by years of exposure to the noxious fumes from the acids used in the etching process. These etchings have made him wealthy, world-famous, and yet: despite the warnings he has worked harder than ever recently, inhaling more acid fumes, driven by his mission to show the beauty of the ruins of the classical Roman world to the intellectuals and travellers of the European enlightenment. This is more than archaeology. To Piranesi, this has been the titanic struggle to wrench back the glory of Roman architecture from historical obscurity, to put western civilisation back on track, to pave the way for some new Caesar.

Delirious with pneumonia and opium, he clutches Francesco's hand, touches the calluses at his fingertips, comforted by this evidence of his son's devotion to the etching work. Whispering, coughing, he begins to tell Francesco of the dreams and visions he has been having. A whole new series, he says, of architectural fantasies. He has seen strange new cities, perhaps cities of the future that he must make pictures of. But how?

Francesco and Angela look at each other, they know the old man is hallucinating, is half mad, but that Francesco must go on humouring him, must do his every wish, to soothe and honour the great man and give him dignity in his last days. *You must draw them, these cities...* -the old man spits between coughs. *I will describe them and you must draw them, as I watch.*

But it is impossible of course. At last Francesco convinces his father that he will record in words, as a treatise, each of the cities that his father sees, and produce illustrations of them later, under his guiding eye.

But this last proposal is a lie, of course, that they are both happy to tell to each other to make the coming hours more bearable. Both know that Giovanni Battista Piranesi will never recover, that Francesco may record in words these final visions of his father, but that whatever he does with them thereafter, illustrate or publish or not, must be done in the cold winter light of the days after his death.

As Piranesi begins to dictate, Francesco writes at his bedside, quill scratching parchment, suspecting the words are just gibberish and his father is lost in the madness of fever and death, half-wishing sometimes with a pang of guilt that he is feeling it: that he could be out among the young and living instead.

The candlelight flickers by the bedside, sometimes blown by his father's intermittent breaths, his eyes opening briefly then closing again, his voice starting and stopping. The very futility of the task is what gives it its nobility. It was easy after all, to do his father's bidding when it made some obvious sense, when it was the etching of some magnificent scene, but how much more of a test, the ultimate human test perhaps: to move forward without any hope whatsoever.

Francesco scrapes with the quill as he has done since boyhood with the stylus on the etching plate, exercise after exercise. He is a stalwart soldier of Rome, tireless, unerring, as his father has always told him in moments of encouragement, in happier, more youthful days. The dictating and the writing gives them both comfort as they pass time waiting for death's carriage to arrive. It gives them purpose and gravitas: a homage to the consuming mission and dedication that has been a covenant between them all their lives, the very fibre of the ropes that bind their happy slavery to a great ideal.

Piranesi speaks and his son writes:

Of course I should have heeded my father's warnings and not flown towards the sun, but what sun? What son does not wish to exceed the limitations of his parents and reach out for what is forbidden...

~

Why Piranesi, Martha? -Dundas stands at the summer window, absent-mindedly turning the Venetian blinds to gaze down at the streets and the riverfront below. Geometric sunlight cuts across the hairs on his chest and strikes the white hotel room wall behind him.

Martha sits up in bed, her long black hair falling over her face, as she reaches for her briefcase.

Dundas listens to the hiss and sigh of the traffic for a moment and half hopes, half dreads what Martha might say next. *The Project* as they have taken to calling it, seems somehow to dignify these encounters, but the sex unnerves him. He shivers, and considers lighting a cigarette. His eyes fall for a second onto a family car below: a classic vignette of normality, man and wife on a shopping trip, two laughing kids in the back. He never expected to feel like a deviant for the first time this late in life. Almost the sort he has been tracking down and locking up for the last thirty years.

74

Martha calls him over and opens an Ordnance Survey map on the bed then gets him to help pin it up on the wall. He starts to protest about the pin marks, then stops short as she winces, dreading a familiar diatribe about how staid and conventional he can be. He sits back down on the bed and she throws him a library book. *Ahh…* -he says, opening it and leafing through it.

Page 62… -Martha says, not bothering to turn around, as she draws lines in pen and lipstick onto the map.

A self-portrait, Dundas says, *-an etching self-portrait of Giovanni Piranesi.*

Notice anything? -Martha asks, turning.

Odd ears, or ear… a bit shell-like… the one that we can see.

Also, no facial hair, a full-head of hair unlike some… She smiles, patting his bald patch, *-and quite large breasts for a naked man wouldn't you say?*

Yes bigger than mine I suppose… but certainly inferior to yours. But why's he important to Stark?

He's important to everyone, Walter, whether they realise it or not. Take a look out that window again and tell me what you see there.

Dundas squints and laughs -A *paparazzi from the Daily Record with a telephoto lens aimed right at us…*

Don't joke. I'm serious.

Seriously? Lots of old buildings… and lots of new ones in between. This city transforms itself constantly… I scarcely recognise it from when I was a kid.

Yes, old classical buildings everywhere, and one reason they're classical as opposed to Gothic or Scots Baronial or any other style is Piranesi. He re-sold the Romans to us, he is a link between the ancient civilisation that marched up here from Italy two thousand years ago and the more modern one we built here ourselves after the middle ages, once the European enlightenment got going. Britain's architects were enthralled by Piranesi's exaggerated images of Rome's ruins; they wanted to regain that grandeur.

But what's with the map, Martha?

She turns and half kneels on the bed in her underwear, reaches one arm up to lean on the wall. *This is the Antonine Wall, another of Stark's obsessions, just a few miles from his home. The northern boundary of the Roman Empire, now mostly buried under farmland. Built in 142 AD, but abandoned only twenty years later; not long before the Empire began to decline and withdraw.*

So why did the wall fail?

A matter of conjecture. It was probably under a lot of pressure from unruly local tribes, our ancestors. There is even a theory that the Roman History of this region was talked-up, for propaganda and political gain. The version of events handed down to us was written by Tacitus, who was the son-in-law of Agricola, the general in charge. Think about it, look for a modern analogy. Imagine if the only reporter on the Falklands War had been Carol Thatcher, or if Euan Blair with a camera was our source of footage for the Iraq Invasion. For a Roman General, a good conquest was the usual platform to launch your bid for power when you returned to Rome. But the Emperor Domitian had Agricola recalled to Rome early, and then, rumour has it, may have ordered his forced retirement and eventual poisoning. Hardly the fate of a triumphant conqueror like his son-in-law described him, maybe more like the shabby end of a disgraced politician caught in the lie. So then we're left wondering: what really happened between the Romans and the Picts and who came off worse?

But why was Stark ranting on about this in a letter? -Dundas asks, getting frustrated.

Martha turns and picks up the remote and puts the TV on with the sound down then flicks between News Channels. A reporter addresses the camera from in front of the American White

House, its classical architecture gleaming like a marriage of power and history. Then the visual serenity shatters into scenes of roadside bombings in Iraq, twisted wreckage of smoking vehicles. *Maybe it's a "clash of immortality-projects between civilisations" as Ernest Becker put it,* –Martha muses. *You know, Lincoln against Lenin or Mao, or Jupiter against Cernunnos. It happened then and it's happening now. The Romans revered bravery in battle above almost all else, hence the coliseum: it was entertainment with an almost religious resonance. So why did they try so hard to wipe out the Druids in Anglesey, unless they saw them as the Spiritual Engine of a death cult more potent than their own?*

Why a "death cult"? Where do you get that phrase from?

Group consciousness… it's still the most dangerous weapon on earth because it makes suicide plausible. One man with nothing to lose can achieve anything… and everything.

With the sound still down, the screen image zooms in on a US Army Humvee exploding at a checkpoint in slow motion with Arabic subtitles underneath.

What about the Icarus and Daedalus stuff?

Another link in the chain of our civilisation, Martha mumbles absentmindedly, underlining sentences and making notes in her copies of *Mein Kampf* and Ovid's Metamorphoses. *...War is always based on the unconscious jealousy of the old towards the young. Old men plan it, but young men die -"golden child the world will kill and eat" as Sylvia Plath said, a girl after Stark's heart for sure. Also he's showing us alienation and how easily it can occur. Violate the spiritual heartland of any tribe and you activate their death reflex.*

As she sits cross-legged on the bed, Dundas runs his hand through her hair and admires the freckles on her back. He thinks she is ignoring him but when he stops she whispers: *Keep doing that...*

~

7a: _Icarus

"He gave a never to be repeated kiss to his son, and lifting upwards on his wings, flew ahead, anxious for his companion, like a bird, leading her fledglings out of a nest above, into the empty air. He urged the boy to follow, and showed him the dangerous art of flying, moving his own wings, and then looking back at his son. Some angler catching fish with a quivering rod, or a shepherd leaning on his crook, or a ploughman resting on the handles of his plough, saw them, perhaps, and stood there amazed, believing them to be gods able to travel the sky." -Ovid.

Of course I should have heeded my father's warnings and not flown towards the sun, but *what sun*? *What son* does not wish to exceed the limitations of his parents and reach out for what is forbidden, for what is dangerous, for what is new?

So what if I flew too high and, waxing lyrical, my wings melted and I fell towards the sea? How my poor father flying below cried out in horror but he needn't have worried for the Gods smiled upon me and caught me on a trade wind that carried me in time to distant land. The old fool should have followed me, but he was too cautious and afraid as usual, and as stubborn as a man with a bull's head. Last I saw of him, his cautious wings, safe and dry, were carrying him to safe dry land, while I spun recklessly in the breath of Poseidon to Zeus knows where.

I woke up on a beach, wrapped like a swan in the magnificent ruins of my broken wings, and stood up amid a snowstorm of feathers. Instantly I was met with gasps and cries; a gaggle of young water-nymphs had surrounded me where I lay and must have roused me with their inquisitive proddings. They giggled and screamed and fled up the beach and so it was that as my eyes followed after them, they rose to see the tall stone cliffs at the beach's end, forming the entrance to this new and unfamiliar land. I could see these cliffs were carved out with many openings as if they held the caves of ten thousand hermits.

As I approached, my wings trailing behind me in the sand, two centaurs rode out to meet me, no doubt forewarned by the nymphs of my arrival. They made a terrifying sight, each clad in black armour and helmets that concealed their eyes. Their hooves made a deafening roaring noise, and then, as they looked at me, they each took a silver mechanical bird from their pockets which they then pressed against their ears. As they gazed at me uncertainly, they sang quietly to their little metal birds as if soothing them or sending them to sleep lest these pets panic at the sight of me.

Once the pet birds were safely asleep, the centaurs advanced upon me where I now crouched in a state of fear and submission. They spoke a strange tongue and, when I replied to them in Greek and gestured with my hands, they became alarmed by my flailing arms and wings and put shackles on me and pinned me to the sand. Then a metal chariot roared across the beach towards us, and I wished my father was at hand to witness it. Although he might have been just as afraid as me and no more familiar with this alien tongue, I fancy he would have been greatly enamoured with the inventions of these people, and even a little jealous – an emotion he was prey to.

You see, my father was a great inventor, perhaps the greatest in all of Greece. But that was our downfall, for his boundless ingenuity allied to his desire to please all: led him to assist a great lady in an unwise adventure; to have intercourse with the Gods themselves. Thereby he brought about something unforeseen and unnatural: a minotaur. And to cut a very long thread short: we paid the price, to be imprisoned in our own maze at the King's displeasure, until now – hence the escape plan, hence the wings and now the fall.

I hoped to explain all this at the earliest opportunity to my hosts, if I could master their language or find an interpreter, or draw a map for them of my homeland. But they had other plans for me.

They took me to one of their temples and strapped me down on an altar where I was attended by numerous priests and priestesses in long white cloaks. They shone strange lights in my eyes and performed many esoteric ceremonies, and I became convinced that they were about to sacrifice me to their Gods. I panicked and again they restrained me, this time with poisoned needles.

When I next awoke I found that I was shackled to a soft bed, furnished with many fine sheets. I realised that some time had passed and I had been taken home by one of the priestesses to recuperate, like some exotic pet, and over the coming days I found that she was very kind to me and fed me well.

I noticed that she spent a great deal of time with me, trying to teach me fragments of her language, and it disturbed me to think that she might have abandoned her duties at the temple and fled from her masters just to follow her interest in me. Gradually, as time went on, I began to understand the look in her eyes and recognise the exact nature of that interest: she would often strip me naked and examine my body on some obscure pretext. Finally, after a week or two, she threw herself upon me, and no common language was required then to make me understand that I was supposed to fill her sacred place for her.

Afterwards this became a daily occurrence, and after a few months I used my new phrases of her language to ask if she was not with child by now. She laughed out loud and I was puzzled, and then after some reflection I told her gravely how sorry I was for her that she was barren. She laughed even louder, then explained that Nouvellians have developed magical elixirs that dissolve their babies unless they really want them. I became somewhat distressed at this idea and felt sick each time I remembered it for some time afterwards.

Around now, as her trust in me was growing, the Priestess would loosen my shackles on some days, and take me out for short walks through the streets of Nouvelleville. It was well that they were short, for I found them overwhelming and confusing and afterwards my mind would overflow with questions. The streets were full of silver land-ships that hurtled by on invisible winds at terrifying speeds, the larger ones carrying many travellers. The Nouvellians all wore extraordinary costumes in infinite varieties of random colours without any clear sign of rank or order. Above their heads, sometimes covering entire palaces: there were colourful murals, usually of semi-naked women in lewd poses. I gradually realised from this and from the thousand gazes of people around me that the entire city was preoccupied with dissolving their unborn babies with each other and that the institutions of marriage and family seemed all but redundant to every citizen. I told myself that this should make me feel better, but I could not adjust to it, and while the Priestess saw to my physical needs I increasingly realised that my spiritual requirements lay elsewhere and that she could never imagine how to satisfy them.

I tried to ask her in her language, about worship; and how the ordinary Nouvellians prayed to their Gods, but perhaps I failed to find the right words, because her facial expressions became increasingly blank at this and all she would keep saying were words for *"Work"*, *"Money"*, or *"Famous"* which did not seem to answer my question at all.

The next day she took me to see one of the great temples where she said the Nouvellians *"worked"*, but the people looked very much as if they were worshipping to me. In this huge hall, the hundreds of the devout sat in row after row with glowing books open in front of them, magical books where pages changed and turned of their own volition. At the head of the hall a much larger version of this book was open, and various priests paced in front of it, decanting out cups of the divine wisdom of this book of God to the enraptured masses.

How do they worship? -I asked in my imperfect speech, and my Mistress replied that each Nouvellian must *"Upgrade"* every day or their God *Nouvos* will become angry. They are constantly given *Releases* by their priests to bring their books and themselves ever closer to perfection. *And what happens to those who fall behind?* -I enquired, *to those who fail to stay pious and devout?* She shook her head disparagingly and sighed: *Ahh... you mean The Old...* and I noticed she said the words with distaste as if I had reminded her of an unavoidable pest like rats or scurvy. And it occurred to me then that I had not seen a single old person in all my time so far in Nouvelleville, and so I asked about this. Her metal pet bird became restless at this, but once she had soothed it on her cheek and cradled it on her breast like a suckling babe, she took me outside to see a central courtyard where there were great piles of discarded magic books, discarded metal birds, and discarded clothes. I half expected to see a pile of old people, but for this she led me to a balcony and pointed to the far horizon and said that the Old are taken to the *Palaces Of The End*, beyond the Waste Mountains; a line of jagged peaks in the distance.

Now I was full of confusion and questions. How often do you discard the magic books and birds? When is a person called Old? Do they leave willingly for their new home beyond the mountains? My Mistress smiled kindly as if I was a babbling fool, but as I wandered among the heaps of the discarded treasures and saw their often pristine condition I began to wonder if I wasn't amidst a society gripped by madness, some religious fervour perhaps, and only I could see it clearly.

I asked the Priestess what was wrong with all the things that were thrown away, but she could only repeat that they were Old as if this were a curse, and she became agitated as if I were trespassing on a religious edict that she was forbidden to transgress. I had also noticed that she wore different clothes every single day, and I could not get her to understand the restlessness and pointlessness of this practice. The Nouvellians seemed eager to impress with how efficiently they could dismantle and pile up their discarded things, but nothing could persuade them of the obvious truth that most of these things did not need discarded in the first place.

The Priestess led me through streets where countless stalls sold colourful offerings for *Nouvos*, and the crowds of the devout swelled in a state of enchantment, each eager for fresh *Upgrades* for their prayers and study. Behind each street there were always growing piles of yesterday's discarded offerings, waiting to be taken away by the temple guards.

Occasionally I saw groups of unescorted youths encircling older citizens, not even visibly wrinkled yet, and stoning them for being old. Instinctively I was appalled, for in my homeland the old had been seen as the holders of all power and wisdom, but my Mistress laughed aloud again at this; and I began to understand the depth of the gulf between us.

That night she put me in her sacred place again, but then afterwards as she slept I slipped out of her house and made my way across a deserted waste ground towards where I had seen two silver rails carrying chains of land-ships to and fro. Perhaps I am my father's son after all. Conscious of how little time I might have, I resolved to test a scientific proposition that had been playing on my mind. Hearing a land-ship approaching on the rails, I made a careful pyramid of sand and pebbles by the tracks to see how many would be dislodged by the passing vehicles. There was a swishing crunch as the ship passed by then I crawled back to observe my experiment. As I thought, there would be just enough safe space for a man to lie beneath the land-ships as they passed over.

I was ready. I lay down on the gravel in the darkness as I heard a distant moan from another vessel approaching. Looking up at the stars and moon, I prayed to Zeus and Hera to keep me safe, for if my calculations were at all awry then I knew I might die or lose my hands. As the land-ship approached I threw the chain of my shackles over one of the silver rails and held my whole body as close to the ground as possible. My terror as the metal giant hurtled over me is indescribable. Every hair on my body rose on end in the knowledge that the slightest movement or stray object from the ships would maim me forever. But the moment passed and when I stood up my shackles had been cut straight through as effortlessly as if they had been Ariadne's thread.

Now I knew my escape was willed by the Gods, and my new freedom filled my body with a surge of exhilaration, I felt as if I had wings again. I set out along the rails, and when I heard the next land-ships coming I hid behind some barrels and then leapt onto the rear of the last barge and was thus carried with new speed towards my destination.

And where would that be? Soon enough, the tall buildings and darkened arsenals and granaries of Nouvelleville began to peel away as I was carried on that artificial wind out into the surrounding desert and towards the Waste Mountains, beyond which I hoped to find some wisdom, some clue to the meaning of the madness of this country I had been marooned in, and perhaps even a way back to my own.

As the sun was rising I leapt from the moving barge and rolled along the cold sand. Now I could begin to see that the Waste Mountains were made of centuries of ruined ships and carts and houses, possessions of all kinds, discarded for no good reason by the deranged Nouvellians. I wandered along the base of the enormous cliffs, and occasionally pieces of metal armour reflected the sun's light and blinded me, or some decaying fragment caught by the desert wind would tumble down at my feet.

After several hours I passed around the foot of the waste hills and saw the chain of buildings that my Mistress had described: the Palaces Of The End. As I approached I saw that she had spoken euphemistically, for these were not palaces but prisons of sorts in which the Old were held at bay and subdued as necessary by threats or poisons.

I entered the first building and prepared to give the guards my rehearsed story, in halting Nouvellese, of my seeking employment, but the female overseer immediately assumed I was a visitor and seemed very interested in my foreign accent. She repeatedly asked me to say my name and write it out in her alphabet, smiling in that way that I had come to recognise in women of Nouvelleville; and it occurred to me that because I was young and handsome I was already like a God to her, even though she scarcely knew me, and that she was ready to believe anything I said. Indeed, it wouldn't have surprised me if she had been about to offer to put me in her sacred place.

But now a strange thing happened. The overseer produced a little painting of my father from under her table and showed it to me. I was speechless, and could only babble incoherently in my own language while she led me out to her own metal land-ship and carried us several miles in distance to the next prison along the road.

Here she led me into a central chamber and to my astonishment showed me my father sitting in a room with several other old Nouvellians watching a magic book reading itself on the wall. Our eyes met and the old man stood up in joy; we rushed to embrace and were overcome with emotion.

There was so much to recount and to learn that we made little sense at first, but gradually it transpired that my father too had capsized his wings, in his case through fatigue, and like myself had been washed ashore in Nouvelleville. Being old and wrinkled however, his fate had been markedly different from my own. Immediately uninterested in his rantings; the Nouvellians had simply packed him off to the End Palaces without asking any questions. I began to tell him excitedly, and a little disparagingly, of all the demented wonders I had encountered in the city behind me, but at this my father seemed to grow afraid and to my surprise urged me to speak more quietly.

And then it was that I began to see that I had underestimated my father, the great Daedalus. Here, among all the Nouvellian aged he had chosen not to draw attention to himself as I had, but rather to conceal his knowledge and take time to draw up his plans for escape back to our homeland. He had learned and fully mastered their language in the time we had been apart and gleaned much knowledge from his fellow inmates that put my own foolish wanderings to shame. Now he was ready for his escape bid, and like me he took it as a great sign from Zeus that I had been delivered to him at this moment, that we were re-united and that we would be together in the final stage of our adventure.

He introduced me to a particular friend of his, a fellow inmate, a very old Nouvellian who claimed to have fought in a terrible war many decades before, in which Nouvelleville itself had nearly been conquered and overrun by its enemies from the East. Now the sacrifices of this old man and all his comrades were all but forgotten by the young Nouvellians, and he had never expected that his twilight years would be so sad and bitter as this when he risked his life and had seen his friends die for their beloved motherland. *Now they curse me to my face,* he said, *as if I am a beggar or a leper, but there was a time when I held terrible power...* My father put his hand on my arm at this point, signalling to me that this was the place in the old man's story that I should take keenest interest in.

The old man had been the proud captain of one of Nouvelleville's greatest and most terrible inventions: enormous metal birds that carried people and which they had used to drop fire on the enemies from the East. He had watched whole cities burn beneath him, the old man said, he had been as powerful and feared as a mechanical Harpie and lauded with a hero's welcome upon his return. How he wished he had such power again now: to bend the foolish ears of youth towards him, to make them listen to his story.

As night approached, my father and I and the old man waited until the guards were distracted then hid ourselves in the vaults beneath the prison palace. When the stars appeared again above the desert: we emerged from a tunnel that my father had prepared and hurried on out into that vast amphitheatre of sand beneath the watchful moon. We stole a land-ship and the old man showed my father how to operate its controls and I could see that they had rehearsed the whole thing, the cunning old devils. My father laughed like a child once we were hurtling across the desert, and I was reminded of happier days in the dim memory of my childhood when we had first unveiled his inventions to the King of Crete and been applauded by all his people. That old glow was back upon him and I saw now that he was in his element, a fish returned to its sea.

The old man knew his way, even in the darkness and in such a bleak landscape, and in time he led us to a wide valley where we could see the huge moonlit silhouettes of dozens, perhaps hundreds of abandoned metal birds, some of them rusting, all in various states of disrepair. As we drove, the old man made my father slow down and change direction many times, as if like a farmer inspecting the vines in his orchard, he was seeking to pick only the best fruit.

I wouldn't have believed it possible, but by the time the sun was rising, my father had sucked many buckets of blood from the land-ship and fed it into one of the sturdiest of the big birds and the thing was shuddering into life. We climbed aboard and it moved at growing speed across the sand, and finally glided into the air with a magical ease that made all three of us shout for joy. Here was an invention much greater than anything my father had tinkered with throughout his long life. Our wax and feather wings were but as children's toys compared to this and we knew it.

But what came next dampened our spirits more than a little. We checked the angle of the sun and flew south and low over the thundering blue ocean, back towards our beloved Greece, steering for Athens. What we soon saw below us filled us with woe, and we wiped our eyes with disbelief and cursed all the Gods for making sport of us.

Beneath us we could see Athens, or what was left of it. We spied a great white marble acropolis, many remnants of our great temples, even a stolen Egyptian obelisk, but all around these now was the unmistakable cacophony of Nouvellian civilisation: inhabited cliff-towers, roadways choked with speeding land-ships, dismal palaces filled with the bewitched worshippers of *Nouvos* praying for their daily *upgrades*, enormous street murals of immodest women in salacious poses. Surrounding it all, we flew over the customary mountains of waste, the burning fragments of raped forests. It was all too much. *What devilry is this?* -my father cried, turning the wheel to rotate the metal bird around, his eyes and those of the old captain beside him, filled with tears.

But where is our Athens? -I exclaimed, starting to tremble in disbelief.

Truly, my son... My father lamented, his voice broken and melancholy, *-it is Athens that lies beneath us now...*

But how?! I ran between the portholes, beating upon each glass as if to wipe away the images they held. *How could it have changed itself so in the time we were away?*

Who is to say, Daedalus sighed, *how the Gods may deceive us from one day to the next? Perhaps the ill wind that carried us here bewitched us also, and we have both slept for a thousand years before waking again here. We have been cuckolded by metal birds, our mother raped by alien Gods, and now I am old and tired. I would like to sleep for another thousand years...*

Then I knew what he planned to do, and I wondered if he had always planned to do it somehow, if he had guessed more than he had told me of the true nature of Nouvelleville. I put my hand on his shoulder, as tears came to my own eyes: *No Father, not this... I had everything ahead of me...*

He looked up at me for a second, our eyes met, he clasped my hand, then I understood too. Our beloved Athens was lost, so what was there to return to? What place could there be for us in a world we detested so: where the old and wise and weak were cast aside by young harlots and scoundrels raised up as demagogues before the mindless masses. *-But what good can it do?* -I whispered as the avenues of inhabited cliffs passed by below us. *Our blood,* he hissed between his teeth, *will write in history that we loved Zeus more than them, that Nouvos was a false idol.*

The old war hero, silent until now, took the wheel and aimed our great bird into a long avenue of palaces and towering temples and turned his head to us and said quietly: *I understand little of what you speak of, my friends, but I too scarcely recognise this city. It cradled me in my youth, lured me from my village towards its great promises of romance and endeavour, but now it curses me as a stranger. It has used me up and discards me like litter. It would stamp us all under its feet like cockroaches, but before we go I would like to bite its soft underbelly and see the creature jump a little...*

Thus all our embittered eyes met for a moment in strange bewilderment, and then calmed together into cold resolve. The greatest of Nouvelleville's inhabited cliffs rose up now in front of us as we ploughed towards it. Our three tiny figures, our metal bird and its moving shadow, seemed dwarfed and yet somehow aggrandised before its vast facade, like a temple offering. In my mind I began to hear the music of a song like a distant memory: perhaps of my mother singing me to sleep on her lap long ago, something I had forgotten but which had always been there. It wrapped around me like smoke or a mysterious shawl as the daylight flickered and played through my tears as I approached my God at last and prostrated myself before His altar, repeating this strange incantation:-

Hail Cornelius Priscianus, Governor of Britain...

~

8a: _Damonii

Hail Cornelius Priscianus, Governor of Britain, and all glory to the Empire and the good and guiding hand in which it currently resides in his excellency Antoninus Pius. I send this tablet with some urgency in the care of my most favoured scribe, an emancipated slave of local stock, who will, I trust, best negotiate the perils of these provinces in these uncertain times.

The rumour of your wisdom and fortitude shown in your new tenureship has already spread far throughout the Empire, and the days are not yet upon us, nor shall be soon, when Rome should cease to prize this most northerly of its jewels above all its others. Great are its bounties, in mineral and agriculture, and in terms of its peoples: the furrow has long been ploughed wherein that Rome's fiercest foes once vanquished, within even a generation, become its strongest and most loyal blood.

Such is our hope and, in this great endeavour, yours is the high honour to echo the footsteps of illustrious forebears, not least among whom was the first: the great general Agricola, who, immortalised by his son-in-law Tacitus, first brought fame upon this frontier and the eyes of all civilisation to rest in awe upon the heroic deeds enacted here. Indeed, what Roman citizen, from Milite to Senator, has not heard of his proud victory at Mons Graupius and his routing of the Picti before they withdrew in cowardly droves to their forests and crevasses?

My bulletin, however, concerns another tribe, and one closer to the current frontier bearing our Emperor's noble name. The tribe I speak of are the Damonii and, before I led my legion to this most northern clime, I had already heard their name and wondered at what kind of pun or jest had given them such a moniker just one character amiss from our Latin word for devils.

I surmise now that this was no jest, but an appellation as close to the actuality as the original scholar was best able to devise. But let me proceed in earnest to relating the incident that has brought me to make this communiqué.

For several years now, as you will doubtless be mindful, there have been intermittent skirmishes along the noble wall of Antoninus Pius, forming a pattern in which the Damonii raid and plunder the wall at night, and by day we make retaliatory incursions into their territory, slaying tenfold for all Roman deaths and taking such number of slaves as to render the adventure profitable to the Empire, however diminutively.

Recently, however, while leading such an incursion myself, the Damonii led us by means of a sham retreat towards a large flat marshland where they doubtless hoped to ensnare us and our horses while they retreated to pelt us with stone and spears. But at this point we made pause and secured our position while surveying the bog in front of us.

In the meantime, the painted warriors of the Damonii had melted into the wood and scrubland. As you will have heard, this is their most renowned trait, akin to that of the infamous Picti. The ornate blue and green tattooing of these barbarians' skins lends them a kind of codification that somehow renders them invisible when seen at a distance among the birch and oak and reeds of their wretched habitat. Moreover, they seem able to remain very still, and often choose to do so for hours on end, even in freezing water. This is a technique which, it is said, contributes to their reputation as accomplished hunters, who are thus able to move to within touching distance of the deer or boar that they hunt, without so much as a breath reaching the ears of the beast.

It is a chilling ability when turned upon our legionaries, who it is reputed have, on some occasions on night watch at the forts, found themselves at the very spear-head of the phantoms before an alarm has been sounded.

But what transpired on the sortie I describe, was in point of fact quite different. As we prepared to fell trees to span the first part of the marsh, a small hunting horn was heard to sound; not the dreaded Carnyx as the savages deafen us with in battle, but a lighter and less abrasive sound. And at this signal they sent forward across the marsh a representative of their people to negotiate. But although the emissary was flanked by two painted warriors of the Damonii, this man himself appeared to be of quite a different stock. His skin was very pale, and free of the staining and soiling of tan and paint and dirt that renders the Damonii at times close to African in appearance. In all the months of our stationing here, and among my knowledge of the annals of my predecessor, I find nothing that might have prepared us for this apparition and in truth it begat an air of disquiet among some of my men and more particularly their horses.

And yet, the whole party was so clearly unarmed that, we felt, out of curiosity as much as in deference to the laws of war, we should hear their deposition.

The White One stopped at an appropriate distance, and lifting his right hand, moved it in a slow sweeping gesture over our heads that seemed directed at the horses more than us, who, as his power touched them, fell each one completely silent and remained so until many hours after his departure.

Content thus to have prepared his debut, he turned his cold blue eyes to look directly into mine. The sensation was not a pleasant one, like a white eagle tearing at my heart. Indeed, I felt like Prometheus of legend, bound to a cliff, while my men raised their shields and spears as if his very gaze were a weapon, and yet they too seemed frozen by some invisible sorcery that this warlock was bringing to bear upon us.

Men of Rome..., -he began slowly, in a measured Latin as fine as any I have heard further south among the emancipated Britons ...*I am the high priest of the Druidic Order of Alclyd, assigned to the Damonii as their spiritual leader. We come to offer you terms of a truce. Unbeknown to you, the northern peoples are re-grouping and massing against you. They will not be civilised, will not accept Roman ways.*

As druids, a religious elite, racially pure from generation to generation, we have cultivated the powers of second sight. We have met with the spirits and they have fed our dreams and in these we have seen all that will befall these lands. The power of Rome will recede soon, but the tide of anger you have raised will sweep the current order into the sea, and in this we have common cause, Roman and Druid.

We have given the Damonii their invisibility, their kinship with animals, their endurance and fearlessness in battle. These are religious secrets which only centuries of study of the stars and of the entrails of carrion can reveal. We are the authors of the painted art and language of symbols which adorns their every possession and even their own bodies and those of their animals, the language of the Gods themselves, with which all of Nature's work is secretly constructed. These are the sacred codifications that place these men's souls beyond the knowledge of Rome. These are the songs that are woven into the rhythm of their moving bodies, that holds them closer to life than you, that gives them the implacability of eagles and the speed of wolves.

In your Roman towns, you are sometimes awoken by the crying of wolves prowling your cobbled streets at night. Your domesticated hounds shiver at that sound and retract into their Roman cots, but doesn't each of those dogs also die a little at that sound, containing as it does, the bitter seed of a memory of the free animals they once were?

The Damonii are as the wolves, my friends, and you, men of Rome, are as the hunting hounds, for even as you disdain the wolves, yet is it your fear that speaks and your hidden longing that gnaws at your gut; longing for the freedom that you too have lost, and this is what moves you to anger and cruelty. But was not Rome itself founded by the children of wolves?

There is not a man among these people who would trade his freedom for one second of your wine and olives, your cultured ways. You have each been brought up to believe that you are a master-race, supermen, carriers of civilisation. And yet what do you know of civilisation? What time have you set aside to gather the songs and the art of these men before you annihilate them? Without their knowledge of sacred plants and omens, not one of you would survive alone in the brutal and inhospitable landscapes to the north of here, while among the Damonii, even a child would. So who are the master-race in this land?

You believe in an after-life, in Hades, the Fields of Elysium, reward for those who die bravely. But we have shown to the Damonii that they cannot die at all, shown them the inevitability of reincarnation. We have cut life from the chests of living men and kindled it in the wombs of women, revealed to them the undying fire of their tribe. They have seen the spirits of ancestors that swim around us like fog, watching us always, making the animals afraid, waiting to re-enter our bodies in our dreams. The invisible ones march with us, send nightmares to the beds of our enemies. They can travel in the eyes of birds to see what is not here or now yet. This is why they will always fight more bravely than you, and can never be defeated.

Men of Rome, the time of Rome and the time of the Druids are both coming to an end. Our two worlds are both in peril from the rising forces that you have awoken in the northern peoples. We will hold the line for you as long as you need to withdraw. In bidding to govern them together, you have inadvertently shown to them the revelation that they can be governed at all. Your single-mindedness has taught them the potential of tyranny of any kind, the weakness of pluralism. Now twenty centuries of fanaticism will fall upon the earth before your Pax Romana returns. This is what I read as inscribed in the stone of time, nothing can erase it, and all that is left is how best to negotiate the transition, to preserve the old ways, to bury beneath skin and bone all that we would hold dear amid the rising flood of darkness that advances upon us.

And as the priest finished speaking, his voice trailing off: already he was moving backwards across the swamp, tentatively at first, then faster, impossibly fast perhaps. And as the spell on my men was released, some of them made to move after the demon, but quickly fell dangerously into the water, their armour weighing them down. It is conceivable that there were concealed stepping stones known only to the druid, but search as we could we were unable to find them and quite unable to give pursuit. Stranger still, in the course of his monologue, the two Damonii guards had disappeared somehow, in front of our eyes. They were simply no longer present. My men were in an odd condition by then. Though not lacking in physical bravery or strength, all of them shared the sensation that what they had just witnessed was not something susceptible to our science, neither by violence nor reason.

I sent word back to the Cadder Fort for support by an additional Cohort, and upon their arrival our number divided and marched both ways around the swamp, re-uniting at the other side to thence climb into the hills where we believed the enemy stronghold to be. Although prepared for engagement, we found not a living soul throughout all this duration, even when we at last chanced upon their sacred ground. This must have been what locally we had heard rumoured of as "The Warlock's Anvil": three massive stones, the foremost of which balanced atop the other two, in the centre of a large circular amphitheatre in the hillside. Nearby were stone circles and chambered burial mounds. This must have been their *Forum*, to transpose it to our civilised terms: a religious centre from which their whole society may be governed. But there was nothing there which we could sack or ruin, nor any attendant priest or guards to take prisoner. It was a cunning location. With a contradictory magic that reminded us of the white druid himself, this natural amphitheatre of grass afforded a panoramic view to the south of the entire Alclyd Valley, including our wall of Antoninus Pius, and yet was so contrived as to be fully sheltered from view from anywhere as far away as our current defensive positions, and for that matter from anywhere closer until one was actually upon the place.

This *Warlock's Anvil* was a perplexing thing. Although I saw many menhirs and obelisks while growing up in Gaul, all those were just small enough to imagine being erected by a team of slaves or suitably fanatical or intoxicated savages. But the stones that now confronted us would have required the hands of the Gods themselves to have been put in place, such was their size and positioning.

Although not a soul, as I have said, came before our eyes while present in that place or in any of the territory we had crossed, my men and I shared the sense particularly at *The Anvil* of being constantly watched by something. In fact, I am somewhat discomforted to have to relate, in confidence of course, that such was the strength of the illusion that when we came to withdraw, we felt compelled to do so in battle formation. That is to say: protecting our rear with a carapace of shields and spears, lest by some trickery we had not yet fathomed, the Damonii should spring into visibility behind us and catch us unawares.

Before we left, however, we examined the menhir, and found that it was deeply stained with blood, some of it fresh. Nearby were piled the discarded breastplates, helmets and shields of legionaries, resembling, if you will forgive the distaste of this likeness, nothing so much as the litter of oyster shells from a banquet. I assigned an Immune to take careful note of the Milite name and Cohort colours from each of the shields, while a Centurion climbed with the aid of his officers onto the top of the rock, wherefrom he returned in time a little shaken. He said he had seen entrails, whether animal or human he felt unable to attest, arranged and raked about in patterns as if some divinations of truth had recently been sought there.

Lastly, I paused at the side of the longest face of the menhir and examined its elaborate carvings. These were hunting scenes in the characteristic Picti or Damonii style, beasts pursued by painted warriors on little ponies. They were already very old, perhaps several centuries, judging by the moss and weathering. Towards the southernmost side, at the left of the composition, beyond the boars and the dolphins, I could just make out men on horseback, with breastplates and plumes. They were galloping southwards, pursued by spears…

*   *   *

I wake up on my back, on hard cold stone. I sit up and am immediately assailed by throbbing pain in my limbs and head. It is a bright midsummer's morning, the birds singing, straightforward enough, except for my unlikely situation: I have slept for several hours in the open air on top of an enormous boulder.

I climb unsteadily down, remembering as I do, broken fragments of the night before: countless cans of beer, and the unwise consumption of hallucinogenic mushrooms from the moors around here, mushrooms once cultivated, it is said, by the ancient druids… But what was that weird dream I was having? After the spinning colours and shapes and voices of the first few hours, by way of contrast, it had all seemed strangely logical, if a little sinister.

The huge boulder is balanced on two others, and sits amid a large natural amphitheatre, an ancient quarry perhaps, cleared to form a setting for these stones. I notice very faded carving on the side of the main stone, probably Pictish, and over this other layers of graffiti, from 18th and 19th century tourists, skilfully inscribed; then there at last; some faded spraypaint from our ephemeral age – which another season will erase entirely.

I walk to the front of the hollow and an astounding vista opens up before me: it is the whole Clyde Valley, indeed the entire thin waist of Scotland at this point: from Dumbarton to Grangemouth, with Greater Glasgow stretching out between. I feel for a moment as if my eyes are borrowed: how new and peculiar the distant towerblocks look, glittering like broken teeth in the new light, the encampment of housing estates, the ribbons of tarmacadam roads unwinding across the fields in the foreground. But I sense something is missing: it's like a scar, a memory of a scar across my eyes. I know there should be a green turf wall from right to left across all this, snaking up and down, punctuated by the timber palisades of forts, but all this is gone, or invisible now. Instead I see the cool waters of the Forth and Clyde Canal in places, emerging teasingly from the woods here and there like an exotic dancer, baring her leg.

I wonder where my friends got to. Doubtless they were not so drunk or stoned as me, and spent the night in their own beds. Time to descend to the village below to find them, the suburb where I have grown up. This will be the last summer then, the end of an era, before I start my studies at university, in that city in the distance.

Looking for the path down, I find an old air-raid bunker from World War Two, and the concrete platform for a gun emplacement, located, incredibly, in the middle of a partial stone circle.

For a second I can imagine it up here in 1941, the anti-aircraft gunners sending flak spitting up into the velvet night, the droning of bombers overhead, the sirens wailing down below. This vantage point would have afforded a good view of them as they flew in from the east, watching in fear as they dropped their bombs to the west on Clydebank, or occasionally on the city centre. The cloud-banks lighting up orange and pink like lightning flashes over the sea.

How surprising that I have never heard of this place before in all my seventeen years, though it is less than fifteen minutes walk from my home. It is like some sort of forgotten key, the lost centre of something. And this, more or less, is what I also say by way of verbal diversion, to the farmer who intercepts me warily on the way down, on the way off his land, a worryingly muscular chap with faded blue tattoos on his forearms. *Sorry mate, I was just investigating that intriguing ancient monument you've got there.*

And in return, before we part as he closes the gate behind me, he passes me a nugget of information: *...some say it was the sight of an ancient battle, or an altar for pagan sacrifice or witchcraft, but the name of this whole moor itself translates as* Rock of God, *whatever you want to make of that...*

I stroll down the road, still a country lane here at this very outer edge of the great rash of brick and steel, the rapacious metropolis that crouches on the horizon, poised to swallow my life.

I will make my way down into the village, I'm thinking, as the shadow of a huge metal bird sails in overhead, a Boeing 747 beginning its landing run down towards the distant airport. I watch its cruciform shadow progress across the flickering fields below.

I search my pockets for money, to at least see I was not entirely foolish last night, but instead I find a folded sheet of paper covered in feverish handwritten notes. I don't remember writing any of this, but as I begin to decipher it my attention is quickly absorbed, and I pause by the roadside for a minute, to read on...

Late sunlight on my face. I wake up in the wreck of a burned-out car...

~

9a: _Automan

Late sunlight on my face...

Late sunlight on my face. I wake up in the wreck of a burned-out car. In the middle of wide, low cornfields, on a dirt track. Vandals must have stolen this vehicle during the night and, evading the police, crunched and thumped it this last mile over rough terrain to meet its strange death. But what of me? I look down and see that I am blackened too, my ruined body fused to the car seat, my bones showing through here and there, just as the car's own skeleton has emerged through smouldered leather and plastic. My veins and sinews are gone, but in their place I see plastic wiring now overlaid, intertwining with my corpse. I ask my hand to move, and to my surprise it responds. It reaches from where I sit behind the wheel, its bone fingers scrabbling through the sea of black wreckage on the floor to retrieve the fragment of a wing mirror. I bring it back up slowly towards my own face. I see my blackened mask with yellow-smoked skull showing through, and for eyes the plastic iridescence of broken headlamps, a weak light hidden within.

I scream out loud, and my skull's grimace widens fearfully. Crows take off in alarm from the neighbouring cornfield. I try to move my legs to escape. The burnt-out wreck creaks and rocks. The glove compartment falls open; on the passenger side, and smoke and steam hisses out, together with sheets of yellowed paper, their edges charred.

The crows call and wheel overhead. I clutch with my free hand some of the billowing sheets: they are handwritten manuscript. I pull them closer to my broken face and make out a line:

The eyes opening. Again, again, the light breaks in and binds us to its demented dance...

~

Dundas feels his cold autumnal face break into an involuntary smile as Martha approaches, her feet crunching over the gravel of the cemetery paths. She is late and he has been standing, gazing out over the city below, his clouded breath mingling in his eyes with the smoke from the distant chimneys: hospitals and breweries, lamentation and intoxication. He almost moves to kiss her but she diverts him into a brief, glancing hug, muttering something implausible about how she might have been followed.

He sighs and they walk together, discreetly apart. Dundas tries to think of what to talk about, wanting to avoid Stark at first, but recoiling equally from discussion of their relationship. His mind keeps flicking towards his wife Marjorie, or jealous questions he wants to ask about Martha's nights out with her work colleagues, like an itch he daren't scratch. *They have these all over the world you know…*

Martha nods, *Necropoleis…*

That's the Latin plural is it? This is a

small one compared to some you know. Like Pere-Lachaise in Paris, or its equivalents in Buenos Aires or Cairo. I dare say down-and-outs live in those too. The council try to drive the winos out of here now and again, but they keep coming back. They've claimed it now, as their own little world.

Venice has a good one… -Martha says, -they have a whole separate island, San Michelle, that everyone can glimpse on the horizon every day of their lives, hovering there like a vulture, very symbolic. But in Glasgow we have them on this little hill, with its very own Bridge Of Sighs to connect it to the land of the living. He couldn't actually speak Latin, you know…

Stark?

Not as far as anyone knows, his fellow professors, his friends and correspondents. He would have known quite a lot of individual words and phrases just from reading the Classics, but to write an entire tract with correct grammar and syntax of the period he would have required help. Apparently it's too well done not to be the work of an acknowledged expert in the field.

Or could he have been secretly teaching himself, a correspondence course?

Possible, he was a man of surprises after all. But he would have been living as a tramp at the time remember, if your forensic timeline based on the paper and ink are correct. Imagine a tramp sitting here on a tombstone swigging his Buckfast and writing a mock Latin treatise, it's crazy isn't it?

What about the Greek and Italian then?

Equally strange. They are in fluent colloquial dialect in each case, with many current local idioms, as if they are the work of native speakers. But as far as we can tell, Stark had never formally studied the languages, nor spent more than a few weeks in either country. Considering the difficulty of the Greek alphabet, we have another mystery.

What about the weird grave-robbing stuff then? Those delightful photos I sent you? -Dundas grimaces and pauses, leaning on a crumbling obelisk.

Colin Visconti? Well nobody knows why his grave was defiled. Like you said he was a harmless guy in life, a bit lonely, presumably one of the reasons he killed himself. I interviewed the thug you told me about, Brett Neilly. He was in the Bar-L for aggravated assault – a right little charmer. He stuck to his story: it was just him and his mates – no one else involved. So how Stark could have known the details without being there is hard to fathom.

The corpse was tied to a wheel and rolled through the streets. Surely you could find some witnesses?

It was a cable drum, on fire. Surprisingly few witnesses. Most people probably didn't understand the significance of what they were seeing, and once it came to a halt your guys cordoned off the scene pretty quick.

Well we're getting nowhere then, -Dundas sighs, realising they have completed an orbit of the hill, and turning to descend towards the bridge.

I fared better with Finch, Martha says, getting a notebook out, and starting to follow him, -*He was having an affair…*

Oh dear… -Dundas says bitterly, his lip curling.

Martha catches up -*With a local woman, of dubious repute, shall we say. His wife found out and left him, an ugly scene, a major guilt trip, hence the starving himself to death and tearing his house to pieces. His parents were old and had died the previous year, all of which fits with Stark's weird letter about the drugs and the hair in the gutter. The other woman was called Nadia.*

Not bad, but how did Stark know this Finch guy?

I'm not sure he did, unless you can get me

more notes from the file on him, like what school he went to, previous addresses. Oh yes, and this Nadia had a brother in law who had been working in America in the World Trade Centre when the planes hit. He was in a middle floor in Tower Two, but he survived. Finch met him at least once and could have heard his story. The guy is called Woolf, Jewish American, and him and the sister had two children Finch would have met, a bit like the stuff in the Piranesi letter.

Interesting... Dundas nods his head, approaching the Cathedral Precinct. *I contacted Interpol about the nightclub singer Hamira Mediora and they wired me a photo. She's on a CIA Watch-List, apparently. She was probably resident in the UK for about 5 years as an illegal, but she never applied for citizenship. She's thought to have fled for Morocco last year after a visit from immigration, but she made some recordings, tapes only. She left just before she was due to sign a record deal, you might be able to track the sound engineer down...*

Dundas sees they are about to part ways and they almost shake hands, but then, as their eyes meet, Martha glances over her shoulder then shoves him back from the edge of the bridge and under the shelter of a tree. She leans her face up and they kiss. He smells the fragrance of her hair as he turns it over in his hands. She drops her bag onto the cushioning bed of damp autumn leaves and pushes him against an ancient sarcophagus covered with moss. Its face bears the faded inscription *ET IN ARCADIA EGO.*

~

10a: _Mortadore

The eyes opening. Again, again, the light breaks in and binds us to its demented dance before we can pause or choose. And without choice, everything is tyranny, reality entraps us. But how to catch it and hold it in your hand, and see it before it sees you? Blinded instantly by the familiar, we can only grapple like fools, crippled from that moment forward. I roll out of bed, a flowerbed as it happens, and there we are: this time I am standing in the middle of a pedestrian precinct, brushing soil and litter from my clothes. Some dazzled passers-by seem almost ready to applaud this debut, my emergence from cotoneaster bushes like stage curtains, before they hurry away in trepidation.

I move shakily across the street and look for a café to revive me. I find a seat where I can see the sky, and keep my eyes up there as the hot caffeine pours down my throat and re-connects me to my body. So many memories in that sky, fragments drifting like clouds, like the strangers that flicker by, grey and gossamer-like, my eyes not focused on them. My discussion is with the clouds.

And the clouds seem to say: -*Remember us, we are the guardians of your dreams, the scouts of your future, the memorials of your regrets. Remember how we first awoke you as you became aware, a child in your cot on summer evenings, laughing, smiling at the honey flavour of life's light. It was us your eyes first looked up to. Or later, on bored windy afternoons, you watched grey stormclouds racing in battle formation and prepared for the world's end. Or going on holiday, looking from car windows, you watched our white galleons drifting in the ocean of blue up ahead, dancing with distant peaks, like ice cubes in lemonade, we sang of summer and glamour.*

It's hard to believe that there was once enough time to look at clouds all day, but there was and I did, and now I stop and remember and wonder if my clouds, discarded childhood toys, old friends, have missed me. Do they blame me for it, are they spurned, twisted with envy of all the things I have wasted my attention on since?

Here they are, those wasteful things right in front of me now: people. I swig my coffee again and focus on the passing strangers hurrying this way and that. It's possible to love them, you know, or to hate them, or to think that you do, to become drawn in, to become like them, and then there is no escape. Then you are a cloud among clouds, part of bigger weather. Then you have no concept of the sky. Then it is easy to die, to fade away, your little white puff of life evaporating, like an unheard SOS, an unobserved smoke-signal, lost in the drudgery of the endless parade towards nothingness. How easy a thing it is then, to die.

But now one of them breaks off: a passing stranger rushes in, and throws leaflets onto every table, thrusts one into my hands, then departs. Surprised, I lift it to my eyes, and begin reading…

Have you heard Madame Mortadore sing? In a basement bar not far from here, she appears every night about nine and rips the air to ribbons with her voice. The bar is an underground vault. Perhaps it is the remnant of an old railway tunnel. It still shakes every quarter hour as the trains go by. The curve of the stone vault overhead seems to sigh and sweat with all the weight of the weariness and sorrow of this old city. It seems to shake and weep even before she takes the stage, and then her voice just picks it up and keeps going with it, carrying it and nursing it a little further, sailing down the river of night, before abandoning it again in the small and smoky hours when everyone is drunk or tired, every eye is closing and the band are packing up their instruments.

Have you heard Madame Mortadore sing? She's not from around here of course, as you'd guess from her name. And she sings mostly in some other language whose sentiments seem purer and more intense than anything we could express in ours. And even when she sings in English, it is never a song you have heard before in your life, and the way she says the words in her broken accent – it is as if your language is just being invented at that moment, or never used before in that way. It is like hearing a blessing or a curse, it leaves you both healed and wounded.

Have you heard Madame Mortadore sing? Sometimes she splits the air into rectangular segments: some light, some dark, in patterns like chromatic keys, and they fan out and spiral from her mouth. The room distorts, the walls implode, the windows melt and weep until their muted sunlight pours like twisted tears of gold: dribbling onto the floor and splashing as it lands on the tables. The customers cover their faces as the sparks of hot wax gnaw into their eyes, bringing them to tears.

Then the violins soothe the room again with a sweet reprise, sawing the air until it reassembles in horizontal segments of orange and lemon, that swing from side to side, like the bow on the strings, slowing and easing and healing, until the room and the scene return to sanity as you wipe your forehead or put your glass back on the table from where you were using it to shield your eyes.

Have you heard Madame Mortadore sing? Long after you have left her club and returned to the world above and are pacing the old pavements again: you find they are not the same pavements anymore. You feel they are haunted by some melody, perhaps the last one you heard her singing, and that it continues to vibrate and resonate, at a pitch too low to evaluate, moving through the concrete and steel of every building and its foundations, moving through your shoes and toes.

And no matter what you do for the rest of the evening or sometimes the day after it, it is as if Madame Mortadore is on your shoulder, or weeping inside your heart. You look at your lover or your friend or your children and suddenly their hair or their posture has the sadness and dignity of one of the doomed heroines of her songs. Your every action is like another verse you are writing for her, your life has the gravitas and drama of a ballad or an elegy. And although you know it must always end badly and sadly, you're damned if you won't just stick around a while to hear it all out, enjoying the beauty and inevitability of its pattern, the sweetness of despair.

She sings every night in her club, every single night without exception throughout the year. And mostly every song seems to be a new one, only occasionally is a familiar one repeated, and then never the one you expect. No one dares to call out for a favourite or an encore. Madame Mortadore is unreachable, her obscure language is like a glass screen. Her face is lined, her age and dress make her too old to be your lover but too young to be your mother, and too dignified to be anything in between. Her beauty is haunting because you wish that you could have known her 10 or 15 years ago in Lisbon or Lima, Krakow or Sebastopol or wherever it was you once overheard someone say that they thought she was from. She always dresses in black.

There is a rumour that she was widowed in a civil war. That her lover wrote some of the songs she still sings, that she is still broken-hearted without him, that she only goes on living because he made her promise to keep singing until the end of the world. Sometimes she is tired and she wants to stop. But her love, the memory of her lover's love for her, won't let her go. She keeps singing even though sometimes it is killing her.

Sometimes her voice makes the drinks on every table, in every hand, vibrate and froth up and erupt, pouring over like the foaming waves of melancholy oceans, the waves of the last beach she walked along on the last night with her lover. And the drinks taste of salt and sand, and everyone's faces drip with spray and fog. Then the lights all turn crimson as the setting sun in her song sinks into the water and turns red as the blood-stained shirt of her lover, which she brings to the ocean to wash the next day, her eyes blinded by tears, her hands wringing and wringing.

And this is the most dangerous part in one of her performances, when the guitars play flamenco and the snare drums take up a warlike beat. Because if anyone is wearing buttons or zips then the buttons start to clatter together like boots, like the marching phalanx of soldiers, and the zips start to rattle back and forth like ammunition belts. The buttons fire off across the room and glasses get smashed and men have been known to emerge from the premises with fragments of glass lodged into their bleeding vests and tunics and to run home to their wives like wailing babies only to discover that the fragments have magically turned into rose petals.

Have you heard Madame Mortadore sing? When she lets you go, the tinkling, twinkling triplets of her octaves lead you up the old worn stone stairs, returning you softly to the world above, the notes cascading the scale like your feet on each tread, until she releases you into some summer square with church bells ringing and birds diving and twittering. And every yellow and green leaf is like a note that plays, and your head is a forest of music. Your body is a sonorous serious old tree-trunk that resonates you and holds you to the ground. And your thoughts are the birds and the leaves and the wind and the music they all make together with their tongues and fingers and feathers, crafted and gilded and glittering as jewellery. And looking up at the sky again after all that, you know that the clouds can only applaud...

I finish my coffee and croissant, pay up and set out into the streets again, clutching the street-vendor's leaflet, intrigued and invigorated by the prospect of finding the cellar of Madame Mortadore. I look up at my clouds in their sky again and see them wince, preparing to weep again. *I know, I know,* -I say; *-Later, later.*

I searched for the next ten years, wandering the streets at night, listening intently in back alleys, asking questions and directions in every bar and club I could find. Sometimes I thought I was getting close, then I would come upon a notice on a doorway saying that Madame Mortadore had moved on, her band *The Clouds* would be playing at such a place and such a date but always, when I got there, the information was out of date or changed.

Sometimes on quiet summer nights, I imagine that I can hear the muted notes of some of her music, as if playing from a distant room or basement with the window open, and I stand perfectly still on a street corner listening and listening, but always the wind direction changes or traffic noise distracts me and the trail goes cold again.

Sometimes I wonder if I might have imagined the existence of Madame Mortadore, or if she might just be a character in some surrealist novel I have stumbled into, by an unknown author. But then again, maybe we are all characters in just such a novel, if only we could read it.

Sometimes I almost lose faith for a moment, but then I reach for the tattered flyer folded in my pocket, worn but still legible, and I turn it over and read the lyric printed there, an English translation of one of her songs, and I remember why I will always search for her, imagining her voice:-

I tried to cry out as you left, but my throat had gone dry as sand...

~

I tried to cry out as you left...

11a: _Anatomicasa

I tried to cry out as you left, but my throat had gone dry as sand. No tears came at all as I stayed facing the closed door afterwards, the frosting of its glass bending reality like a snowstorm of white light. Instead, the drains stopped working, and the water ran out. Coincidence? The house, so recently purchased, had doubtless not intended to be landed with me alone, had not bargained on this sudden change of plan. So it should have come as little surprise that it would immediately turn on me and lash out.

I might have enjoyed the tears, the little salt parcels of warmth. They might have melted this edifice: a face of ice that could only grow colder over coming days and months. Eventually I would become a glacier of numbness, a diagram of a human being, a grey abstraction, but for now there was the plumbing to attend to.

Perhaps it was the plumber himself who started the transformation. I expected him to be like all the others before: to crawl beneath the floor at some exorbitant hourly rate, and emerge a few minutes later with a broken pipe in his hand. But instead he ripped up several floorboards in every room, showed me a secret lake that had been building up there for years, then promptly left. He was too busy, he had to leave on another job. The whole visit had taken less than three minutes, even though he had somehow managed to leave several cigarette butts in every room. But my whole life had been changed. I felt both violated and strangely exhilarated, like I had received a visit from a surrealist priest, a kind of initiation. He told me to leave the floorboards up to let the basement drain away, and not to use the water. He never came back.

Hours, then days went by, as I sat on the floors, contemplating the ragged holes and the torn planks, the chilly darkness exposed beneath. I was drawn against my will to the raw edges of the broken wood, like open wounds that I was scratching, itching. Eventually, I picked up a hammer from where the plumber had left it, and, remembering his practised technique, began to lift a few more floorboards. I prised and ripped and pulled, soon enjoying the feeling of destruction, carrying with it – as it always does – a certain freedom from consequences, from the burden of reconstruction, or from the bother of thinking about it.

How could all that water have flowed beneath us unnoticed? Every bath or shower or washing cycle, everything we thought we were ridding ourselves of was merely building up, amassing into a secret ocean of darkness, unheard and unsmelt beneath us, beneath the multiple layers of domestic routine and laminate flooring. Everything we had thought was throw-away, ephemeral, was really just making out a long detailed charge-sheet, an indictment to be read out against us later. The music of running water, supposedly incidental, had been the song of our lives. Now I felt as if the plumber had been Saint Peter. I felt as if I had been judged, and then abandoned to purgatory.

So I bought floodlights and heaters and dehumidifiers. As the waters receded I climbed down onto the solum and began to tentatively explore it. Standing in the mud, I saw each room from a new perspective with the floorboards at chest height. I had discovered a new house beneath the house I thought I knew. I hurried home from work every night, not daring to tell anyone about my new frontier, my all-absorbing hobby.

The worst thing about it was the darkness and dampness and cold so I knew I had to conquer these things first or I could never move forward. My plumber had abandoned me as a kind of test, of that I felt sure, and I was determined not to fail in my trial. I lifted more floorboards, I got the solum dry and well-lit, and then one day I came home with a car boot full of paint cans. I suddenly knew with absolute certainty, that my dirty secret needed to be made part of the house now, to be integrated into normal domestic life – habilitated.

It took me about a week and a half, but I painted it all blood-red: the dried clay, the compacted soil, the engineering brick, the underside of the joists, everything. The topside of the floorboards and the rest of the house I left just as they were, but it was the underbelly I wanted to uncover, to make voluptuous and vibrant. I wired up permanent lighting and prised many of the remaining floorboards apart until a spectacular effect emerged: each room could be lit solely from below, by red light in striking shards and silhouettes emerging through the filigree floorboards.

I had the feeling that I was only just getting started, and began to worry that the neighbours might get wind of my adventures. I sewed all the curtains shut, not with thread but with broad leather straps, the effect was almost fantastical, oversized, as if looking at laced-up boots or the back of the corset of some Victorian governess.

What little water I had been able to use since the plumber left I had now diverted into a little pond under the floor towards the back of the house. It occurred to me that the whole network of copper water pipes throughout the house was now empty and redundant, a waste of something elaborate and secretly beautiful. I returned from work the next evening with a car boot full of bags of sand. Now I devised a way to turn the entire house into a kind of hourglass: if I topped the tank in the attic up in the morning then I could have an entire day of fine white sand slowly falling out of every tap and shower head throughout the building, and draining gracefully away down plugholes and drains. The sound was peaceful, mellifluous even, the visual spectacle pleasing, like a ruined ancient city after some bloodless apocalypse.

This inspired me to smash open some of the sanitary ware. With the sink cut through, it was then possible to observe the beauty of its cast shape, the perfection of its compound elliptical curves. The further sand released by this fissure onto the bathroom floor was like a strange dry fountain which I arranged to drain away slowly into a pipe under the floor.

Returning all this sand to the attic each morning was a logistical problem I solved by removing more floorboards and ceilings and fixing a block and tackle to the attic roof trusses that I could then see from where I stood on the ground floor. I raised enough excess sand by this method to also allow for some to pour slowly from above into each of the hall cupboards every day until their doors spilled open around tea-time, making a spectacular vista to welcome my return home each evening, like being lauded by an avenue of opening and welcoming arms.

I became curious as to what other networks might lie buried under the skin of my house, and what I could do to uncover them. Ever since we had first entered the house, I had noticed the intermittent tendency of some power points to fail, some lights to trip a fuse in the main board. Beginning with these, I followed the route of every wire I could find, chiselling out the plaster that had concealed its course all these years. Once exposed, these veins and arteries of coloured wires seemed too beautiful to hide again, so I sealed them back in with clear resin, rendered flush like clear rivers of glass, windows onto secret channels of fire, meandering, elongated.

I could see you weren't coming back by now, months had gone by after all, and I began to find our furniture and clothes an irritation. I began with the bed. I shuffled it into a vertical position and then screwed and bolted it onto the Living Room wall. Then I set it alight. I watched in awe, as if in slow motion: the spread of the greedy orange tongues, the blooming of black ash, the blowing of tatters peeling off like batwings. The smoke needed released quickly so I sledge-hammered open a ragged slot in the external wall, then another, in the opposite corner, to encourage a through-draught which quickly resembled a force-ten gale. In this space I experimented with further burnings of tables and chests of drawers, sometimes dowsing the flames half-way, marvelling at the picturesque transition from varnished veneer to charred carbon, the gruesome torsos and severed legs of furniture one could retrieve from the brink of oblivion.

I needed somewhere new to sleep, so I brought home a large quantity of rope, real thick white rope that might once have rigged a galleon. I felt as if I was leaving port on an exhilarating voyage. I knocked some more holes in the walls and floors. I stretched about thirty or forty spans of the rope in various long diagonals through the house from arbitrary points on the external walls, anywhere I could get a secure hold, by looping or tying into brickwork or joists. Gradually I found that all these disparate paths, no matter how fabulously chaotic to the eye, nonetheless naturally coalesced and criss-crossed about a central point that magically emerged. And there, after weeks of weaving, I found my cradle, as comfortable as a hammock slung on the palms of a south sea island, an intersection of balanced forces, where I could hover in space all night at the centre of the house. Now just a single vertical rope left hanging was sufficient as a ladder on which to make my ascent every evening into my spider's web.

I had always wanted to see the stars from my bed, and now what was there to stop me? Skylights and dormers seemed too prosaic. Instead I simply applied random violence, just as I had to the walls and floors, and quickly produced a ragged and dangerous-looking puncture a few metres across, through which the rain fell unopposed for a while, usefully topping up my limited water supply. Then I used the transparent resin again, and with the aid of timber shuttering, cast the whole opening closed in beautiful waterproof plastic, hard and clear as glass.

It was beautiful to lie, bouncing comfortably in open space, beneath the stars and moon, in such exquisite and perverse freedom. It inspired me. I took the television apart and re-wired its constituent parts without their polite plastic housing. The exposed cathode-ray-tube I then hung in space on a rope of its own and set swinging every night like a topical pendulum, spouting news as it went, throwing fabulous flickerings of light through the dimly-lit house. It moved nearer then further away from me, as the mood or the moment suggested, a distressed little beacon, skinned alive, its guts exposed.

Next I started coming home with the car piled high with another strange cargo: pieces of plastic replicas of human beings. Borrowed and begged from the back door of department stores, I gradually assembled an army of tailor's dummies that I placed, akin to the statues in the tomb of an ancient Chinese ruler, side by side like soldiers standing up to their chests in the blood-red basement void. Their expressionless faces made a formidable array, peeking out of holes in the floor of every room, dressed in the discarded clothes, the extensive wardrobe, of you and I.

Finally, I realised that my house was approaching a level of perfection in which I would no longer be willing to leave it. I carefully weakened an area of wall from the inside in preparation, then on one final Friday evening I drove the car straight off the end of the driveway and crashed through the walls into the study, where the floor joists creaked then gave out, the bonnet sliding straight down into the glowing crimson undercroft, the boot and spinning rear wheels left cocked angrily in the air like a dying wasp.

Unexpectedly, I had twisted or even broken an ankle, maybe cracked a rib, but as I climbed aloft again like a caterpillar into my forgiving cocoon of ropes, I realised that I didn't really need these things anymore. I had drip-feeds now, slung from the attic rafters: one of rainwater from the roof, another of baby-food from a gallon-tank in the loft. What more mobility would be necessary?

Perched in my new nexus, I could see at last that my house was an organism and that I could interface with it and with the elements that underpinned it: those of fire, wind, earth and water, and beyond these, commune also with the stars and the moon and the other mute guardians of God's imponderable universe. Sticking wires into each ear that led to TV and radio aerials on the roof, and an internet cable up my anus for good measure, I closed my eyes to the sweet bedtime music of humanity's incessant whisperings, the hourly news bulletins, its lullaby of endless suffering. I smiled and slept again, waiting for doomsday.

Somewhere far below me in the gloom, draped with cobwebs, I knew the vital organs had long since stopped working: the boiler and central heating choked with sand, the fridge-freezer entombed in its own ice, the gas fire and hob disconnected. The clocks had stopped, the body of the house was exquisitely dead, but I was the dormant micro-organism within it, the seed of destruction whose time to bloom had come.

*　　*　　*

What on earth have you done to this place?! -your voice exclaims, crossing the threshold with a pile of shopping in your arms. *-Are you ready to do some DIY this afternoon then?*

Oh sorry, deep in thought… -I say, gathering up all the A4 sheets of lined paper I have been scribbling on for the last hour in the Living Room, and letting slip in disarray onto the polished wooden floor around me. I should know better than to let the place get untidy.

What have you been writing about then? -You ask, smiling, as you open the fridge door, *-None of your weird stuff I hope?*

No, no, no, would I do that?!

Read it out to me then, you say, juggling with the apples and oranges.

Trapped, I pretend to read my handwritten notes, but make up something different as I go along:-

Summer evening at last. The centre of life. In our house that we have rebuilt together here, over many months and seasons…

~

12a: _Casamundi

Summer evening at last. The centre of life. In our house that we have rebuilt together here, over many months and seasons. We stand at the summer window in the room that looks out over the trees and gardens of suburbia, the shadows of leaves falling and playing over our faces at the glass, as the evening breeze sighs.

The hour glass, the looking glass, at the vantage point where all the paths of the world have led us home to. And the clocks tick somewhere, echoing, in another room, echoing with the sound of polished wood and summer evenings, every evening of every remembered clock in each remembered house that told the time to here.

The evening and the town are full of summer, it pours out with the birdsong and distant sound of children's voices, and the sighs of cars, the faint buzzing of bees and motorbikes. We see and hear everything through this screen, this looking glass, perched above the town, captains of our house tonight above the drifting sea of leaves.

Your face is beautiful, your eyes are blue glass, spinning the world around inside them as you smile, and your smile is the gap in the leaves, the opening in the clouds that lets the sun through. It breaks the world open like a cracking egg, pouring out the warm gold from within it. Your mouth opens slowly, with the inevitable motion of a breaking wave, and your words wash over my face like cool water, shocking, refreshing, impossibly slowly and deeply, shaking the walls:-

This is the singularity, we are at the centre point now, at the pivot. The numbered years and moments from your birth can be spun around this point and they will lead forward to your death, our death, in a car crash, in 18 years, nine months and 2 days...

But what are you saying...? -I start to recoil, but you place your hand on my lips, and your smile is a sun that is obliterating the room, removing all shadows. The flowing strands of your brown hair are falling over your eyes like leaves and branches and filtering the light. And your eyelashes sweep across my brow like a witches broom made of tiny insects. We kiss. And from this still point, you suck time backwards and turn the room upside down.

I open my eyes and you step backwards in the summer room and, stretching a leg behind, you rotate effortlessly with two steps until you are standing on the opposite wall. Now you are reaching out to me, looking upwards to meet my gaze, and when I take your hand it is as if some invisible sea swell, an eddy in the river of time, is catching me from below, and I am gently swung up and around to join you on the wall.

Now what was a wall is a floor, and the view from the window is of our village before it was a suburb. I see a scarified landscape of open mines from which they are building the great city to the south that will one day envelop us. Everywhere there is black smoke and ramshackle railway lines, spoil heaps and the sound of metal tools on stone, chipping and chiselling.

What's happening? -I ask.

It is 1854 and we are moving through dimensions, you see it's so easy really when you grasp what time actually is. Events form a landscape over which you can walk while standing still, just open your heart and the world will turn under you. We are falling through space and rotating around ourselves and the sun, and thus every moment is a unique place. We are the maps of this journey. You are a temporary conflagration of atoms, a quantum constellation, a fantastical spatter of paint by a celestial Jackson Pollock. When you say that you cannot alter the past, you are describing your own immortality. Your pattern through time cannot be altered, it is eternal, and you can revisit it endlessly, forwards, backwards, sideways.

Am I dead then? -I ask in horror, as you lead me onto the ceiling and the world rotates again.

Ha! -you laugh, *-wrong question! You are always dead and always alive, if you truly understand what I have just told you.*

Now the inside of our house has changed, and as we stroll upside down along the ceiling, it is as if we peer through a subtle fog at former and future inhabitants of the house below. Wallpapers change, strange children run about, old ladies die in bed, dogs bark, somebody slits their wrists in the bath. We look upwards at these scenes and the changing light from the world beyond reaches us in some diffuse underwater ambience, rotating in circular patterns, tunnelling us out. I feel as if I were Dante with his Virgil, traversing the underworld.

Then, out of the cold mud of the Somme, like figures of grey clay, the bodies of young men regain life and stand up and then march backwards by roads and by boats: to return home to here and to the nail that has sat here for a century, left half-hammered into a skirting-board inside our hall cupboard. One of them lifts a hammer and sucks the nail out magnetically and retreats with his fellows, taking the gable of our home with him. We watch it disassemble stone by stone, revealing the sky, as the scaffold deconstructs behind it. Drawn by the expanding light, we float down the staircase to the doorway as each step disappears in turn.

Out to the garden: towards the Yew Tree which seems slightly younger now. You look the same, but your eyes cloud with horror as a pair of boots sway into my chin. We step backwards and look up to see that a man wearing these boots is hanging from the tree with a rope about his neck. A crowd are gathered around about, but unable to see us: a priest, a magistrate, an unwashed crowd, hecklers shouting abuse, policemen in antiquated uniforms and shining boots, relatives snivelling, women's mournful singing somewhere, Irish accents. This is Dennis Doolan the railway labourer who allegedly killed his foreman and was executed for the crime, taking 20 minutes to die. A poor immigrant scapegoat for the indignant protestant crowd.

You lead me running, like we are children, around the outskirts of the onlookers under a grey bleak sky laden with rain, until the dull clouds fade and the Yew Tree, alone now in its meadow, grows magically younger in new sunlight as we advance upon it, enchanted. Daisies, Buttercups, Bluebells spin and flash around its base in the alternating patterns of seasons and years.

Turning around the trunk once more, this time we chance upon a well-dressed young man; Thomas Muir of Huntershill, home from his law studies in Edinburgh, his head hot under his new white wig or perhaps enflamed by the book he is reading: *The Rights of Man* by *Thomas Paine*, news of the French Revolution. Shaded by the Yew Tree as he sits on the grass in this corner of his wealthy father's estate, what dangerous seeds take root in his mind? In less than 2 years, this living pillar of the landed establishment will find himself suddenly proclaimed a hero of the working man and an enemy of the state and deported to Australia. Just now he unexpectedly reaches up and catches a bee in his hand, its drowsily angry rumblings starting to echo within the cathedral of his fingers. He holds it gently, amazed by his own absent-minded daring, suddenly afraid as to whether to release it suddenly or to dare to crush it.

We run on, getting younger as our tree does, for another circuit of its branches. Now the town around us is disappearing into farmland. Changing patchwork quilts of fields, the flickering of forests encroaching. Farmhouses, barns, horse and carts, dirt track roads heavily creased by hooves and rain. Our tree is nearly a sapling, wagging up and down between seasons, as if wavering over the business of life and how to negotiate the shading canopies of its competitors; all of whom will die before it.

Until the huge hand of William Wallace brushes it, the same hand that held, at Stirling Bridge, a broadsword to dazzle the effeminate generations of the future. Now, in a moment of absent-minded reflection, he is talking to a friend whom he wonders if he can still trust, his other hand under his cloak just touching the hilt of his dagger, the familiar texture of it rubbing his skin; a thousand dizzying rotations of twine. He wanders incognito, outlaw in his own country, and begins the climb up the long hill and over to the pastures beyond, where soon he will pause at the fated well and the farm where he will betrayed to the English soldiers.

Later, butchered alive, eyes closed in indescribable pain, he will focus his dying thoughts on the last pure thing he remembers: his strange memory of a sapling tree, its bark smooth as a woman's skin, its little leaves flickering like her hair in a breeze in the sunlight. He feels his own body breaking like branches, growing outwards, reaching beyond himself, thinking of the Yew that will outlive everything around it, patiently unnoticed, growing ever stronger. Imagining: what mighty longbow its wood might one day make, and where its last arrow might fall, far into the future.

But as the arrow strikes the earth, the tree of knowledge unmakes itself finally and we wake up from our daydream. Back in the house we climb down the wall onto the floor again: in another room with another window and a different view of the same suburb that was once a town. And now it's later, the sky beginning to redden like blood over the trees and all the drowsy little roofs in rows. The bird song is quieter and slower, and strange light and reflections play on our walls like turning oceans and emerald armies, the quiet machinations of leaves and shadows. The bees and the mysterious distant motorcyclists have all gone home, their droning fading away to nothing.

Now your face is beautiful and your eyes like dark pools where evening will grow until all the night overflows and pours out from them to soothe the world with silence as we walk the late streets together. Walking aimlessly, endlessly searching for something we've forgotten, sighing, debating, ruminating.

And nobody in any of the houses will know us, and none of them venture out, not daring to leave their televisions without the protection of their cars, their metallic insect-armour. Pale, frightened molluscs, retreated to the last chamber of their spiral shells, the sound of television static washing their ears like the memories of lost oceans. We will walk by, and it will be as if we are the only people left in the whole town, and the passing cars just empty machines running on rails. As if we are dead or in a dream. Adrift in our own constellation, marvelling at the night sky, the painted stars.

But our thoughts are suddenly interrupted. Here in the last room the ceiling collapses and the Apollo Moon Lander crashes through and lands on the floor on the carpet between us, shaking the whole building. Grey dust of plaster or moon rock swirls in slow motion through the room, and we are choking but unable to move. Our hands freeze to the armchairs, mouths forming words we cannot hear, as if in a vacuum. Then as the dust swirls, a metal hatch is thrown open, a ladder let down, and, one after the other: two astronauts lumber down backwards, awkwardly, bouncing off the floor as if it is rubber.

And the last thing I see is the American flag being planted in the sofa in the background, the television filled with grey flickering static behind it, and a huge white helmet looming up closer to examine my immobilised face, the dark glass orb of the visor filled with blue water; swishing with fishes.

*   *   *

I think I recognise some of that, you see... -Donna is saying, as I finish reading. Mussolini continues to scuttle around the darkened room, exploring under the white dustsheets that conceal every chair and table like Edwardian ghosts. -*The walks in summer, around the neighbourhood, while we talked about life, that sounds like us, don't you remember?*

I shake my head blankly, downcast, looking warily at all the handwritten sheets; which now surround me in threatening piles, as if closing in.

She places her hand on my cheek and catches an unexpected tear there, which she brings back up to my eyes like an accusation, her own eyes watering now too. *If you don't remember then why are you crying?*

I don't know, I say, and we clasp hands together, rest our foreheads against each other's shoulders, and wait like that for a long time. I can hear the puttering of the candles in the room, the occasional car passing outside. Time passes, then I hear Mussolini's breathing, his paws scraping on the floor, his snout nudging at my ankle.

Read this one now, -Donna says at last, -*it's one of the strangest, as if you are wandering the city with amnesia, and meet some girl who thinks she knows you. I wondered for a while who she might be, but well... none of this makes sense does it?*

I take the manuscript, its handwriting is old and faded now, and begin reading:-

When I walk out into this city, the sky swallows me. Always at dusk and in autumn...

~

13: _Ultrameta

When I walk out into this city, the sky swallows me. Always at dusk and in autumn, I wake up when everyone else has finished their day's tribulations. I begin again, like the butterfly from its cocoon, reborn briefly, to choose another name, another death. The sky is blue turning black, as if bruised, and the clouds tinged with colour seem to rush towards me, or to wherever I fix my eyes on the hemisphere above me, as if to mop my brow. Each day destroys me in the end, uses me up, because I open myself to it so utterly.

The clothes don't matter. They don't even smell of me, in so far as I even remember that much about who I am supposed to be. Ideally, they are somebody else's, borrowed or stolen, and if they just hang there on me, maybe not even entirely well-fitting, so much the better. I walk, let's say, in a suit I don't even recognise, and it feels strange and loose against my skin. That's comforting because it means I don't know it and it doesn't know me – that's fresh because then anything can happen. I'm wiped clean every time, memory and identity gone, a mystery and a stranger to myself and to all the other strangers that I pass. This is freedom.

I choose any direction then walk under the darkening sky, collar turned up, in this city I call *Ultrameta* because nothing stands still here. I begin to look for clues: the grain of sand in the oyster's shell, the smallest fragment can start me off on this evening's journey to invent an identity. A traffic light changes to green, a falling leaf in a park seems to turn in mid-flight and point to a street where a light suddenly goes on or off in some intriguing way that makes me want to make my life go there. Then I just go. Having no baggage that I can remember, I can take these choices lightly. No job, wife, children, parents, passport, driving licence, bankcard, no anchor, so I drift forever.

Tonight I walk into a coffee bar, of the suitably anonymous variety, where specimens of the evening's flotsam like me can sit perched at the counter on stools, crows on telephone wires. The electric light is slightly too harsh and there are mirrors in unexpected places, giving me glimpses of myself and who I might be and whoever might be watching me. These are my real clues of course: until somebody speaks to me, I am nobody – I have no personality. But a few words are all I need, and a look in the eyes and pretty soon I can tell them what they want to hear and construct myself to suit.

A girl with brown eyes comes in and starts talking to me; her hair is long and straight. I can see her back reflected in that mirror there. Suddenly she is talking urgently into my face, telling me that she thinks she knows me. I look so much like the husband of a friend she was talking to last week, and she can't understand why I don't recognise her. I can see her mouth, but the sound somehow doesn't reach me. My eyes roll until I am watching closely the surface of my coffee sitting on the glass counter top, from the corner of my eye. I'm seeing it closer and larger until it fills my whole field of vision. There are waves crashing across it with crests of foam and a vortex is turning there like a typhoon. I grab her mouth, lean closer and look into her eyes. Then I see everything that's there all in an instant: her entire life from start to finish, what will happen next and how it will end.

It's all so quiet again: she's stopped talking. I move my head to one side to see past hers, to get a glimpse of myself in the mirror. I see that there are ears, see my hair and chin, but in the centre there's only a hole with cogs turning inside: ancient, blackened cogs, some fast, some slow, but all of them unstoppable. I grab her shoulders and I spin her around on her seat to see this reflection but as she turns my face appears over the cogs, sliding from left to right just as her eyes pass over it. And I'm complete again for now, I have an identity.

I lean down and kiss her left cheek, then look at our reflection again. I pay for us, and we leave and walk out into the labyrinth. The city is white in the moonlight now, like bones. We walk, the jagged shards jut up against the sky. The whole city is a skeleton and we're walking through its rib cage. My companion is taking my hand, leading me now to the top of a hill where we wait for traffic lights to change as a flow of ghostly white cars whistle through, shimmering with speed. The lights change, then there is a noise of tarmac and stone cracking. Several buildings start sliding past in front of us, dust and debris billowing out from under their ragged bases like torn skirts. An entire city block, like stage scenery on the move, is changing location to seven blocks downhill – a more desirable area. The group huddle together like a little herd of elephants, all their disparate roofs and towers and steeples and flags sticking up like the heraldry of a bold nocturnal crusade. In some of the passing windows, I can see perfectly normal domestic scenes: clothes being ironed, dinner served for a family of four. The dust settles and the traffic lights change again. We cross the road before some buses advance upon us.

She's leading me somewhere. Towards the moon, where it hovers low over the ocean. Walking downhill again, I notice the tall buildings thinning out, as we approach a more derelict area. Old buildings must have been demolished recently or collapsed: whole blocks have been cleared away and now only pavements are left, with solitary lampposts hanging over us, some of them flickering in a state of poor repair.

She seems to have calmed down now, as we walk, whoever she is. She punches my arm, playfully perhaps, and says: *So, do you remember me now? Or are you not who I say you are? And why have you changed your appearance?*

I don't know who I am, I answer her truthfully, *nor you either. Does it matter? What or whom am I supposed to be? What kind of man is the one I look like? Should I apologise for him? I don't mind apologising for him, since I have none of his pride, presuming he has any. Defending him... will be more difficult on the other hand, without some more knowledge.*

Madman, she says, turning her eyes on me with a mock-deranged expression, *I can't figure you out. You're either a madman or somebody somehow addicted to melodrama... to romance at any cost. Or then again... maybe you ARE somebody else?*

I feel like I AM somebody else, this time I think... on balance.

This time?

Yes... I feel as if there have been many times, is that not the case?

I don't know... she says, looking down at her feet, her voice dropping, *...not this bad...*

At last we come to a solitary house, surreal because everything around it has been removed. A grand little townhouse with an overgrown garden and rusting Victorian gates, very elaborate, I run my hands around its fantastical twists and volutes. A tram rattles by behind us and shakes the ground like an earthquake as we walk across the moonlit garden; and I notice the surface of a bright pond rippling: silver against the black hues of the ivy twisting everywhere across the ground.

Inside, she leads me in semi-darkness up a broad staircase into an upper room with a bare wooden floor, its planks creak under our feet. Its walls and the ornate cornice and skirtings appear to have all been painted black, but over this I can dimly make out various white lines: astronomical diagrams and geometry theorems, like some intellectual graffiti. *I would have liked you to meet my father,* she says shyly, her eyes on the floor, and gestures to where he stands alone at the window, looking out over the view: of the great bone-hard city on the hill, the derelict plain here beneath it, and the dark ocean off to the right. The window is large, full-height like patio doors, but very old and subdivided into many panes by peeling mullions and astragals. The rough sackcloth curtains are fawn and laden with dust. Stepping closer, I see now that her father is actually a white plaster bust, a heroic Edwardian torso, with a chequered waistcoat buttoned around him, perched on the chipped plastic legs of a tailor's dummy. But his head turns somehow, and his deathly-white features flex a little and he speaks in a weary, hushed tone: *Ahh you've come again I see, I expected as much, will she remember anything this time?*

But Father, I say, *I've never seen her before in my life, although conceivably in my dreams, if I'm not dreaming now. And anyway, how do you know me?*

Fool, he replies. *Nobody knows you. Except maybe the inanimate like me and innocent children like her, before you close her eyes forever. Why must you torment us by coming here? Isn't it enough that the city fathers see fit to demolish our district stone by stone year after year in preparation for the next stage of their great plan: constructing new glass palaces for the heartless ones, those faultless maestros of youth and savagery?*

Then I feel a hand on my left arm, and I see that his daughter has come to rescue me. I look at her soft living face and smile, then return my eyes to her father who is now just a lifeless statue again, grey and inert, but with a single droplet of moisture on his cheek which I reach out and catch with my finger. I turn and hold it out to her, but just then a cloud of the turbulent night sky clears and the beams of moonlight intensify, falling across the large empty floor of the living room behind us. As we watch, the floor changes into a silvery ocean, criss-crossed by tiny waves. Enchanted, we link hands and walk slowly across it towards the black rectangle of the open door to the hall, the moonlit water lapping over our toes.

She takes me up a further staircase of creaking timber; narrower this time, into a large attic with several skylights propped open to the night air. The room has been a library it seems, and I see shelves around the room but notice that most of the books are now heaped in a large pile in the middle of the floor. She grows very quiet and walks in front of me, reverently, kneels at the base of the pile and begins picking up one book after the other to examine.

I walk slowly closer to her from behind. She picks up each ancient book, wipes its cover clear of dust, reads the title, opening the first few pages, skimming gradually through the rest then sighs bitterly and discards the book onto the pile. Then she picks up the next one, on and on, *ad infinitum.* The process becomes frantic, her hands darting in agitation. I kneel down next to her and see that her eyes are filled with tears. I put both my hands over hers and close them over the book she holds. Her body stills and calms at last; its unexplained disturbance fading away. I pick up a few of the books myself, fill my arms with a bundle and take them over to one of the open skylights. She stands up and follows me. Our eyes meet, agreeing a sort of plan. Standing either side of the window, we take each book one by one, then whole piles at a time, and hurl them up into the starry night sky above us. Most just open up into the air, white pages fluttering like feathers, then fall off to the left, caught by the wind and bounce away, thumping off the roof slates as they fall to the ground below. But our eyes light up and we laugh together exultantly at this: that every tenth book or so hovers longer, flutters its white pages, then lifts off and flaps away into the night, flying towards the ocean and freedom. We laugh and shout as we continue, freeing and condemning books at random for over an hour, until the attic is empty.

At last we are left without a single book, just staring at each other, the old sadness returning. The night wind blows across our faces in the silence, the same wind, with its smells of dust and ruination and of the city beyond with its taste of stale waste and fuel. And then time breathes in.

With the same reverent, yet destructive gestures we applied to the books, we gradually remove each item of the other's clothing until we both stand naked in the white moonlight from the skylight, our feet bare on the rough wood of the attic floor. She closes her eyes and I place my right hand on her left breast. She becomes whiter and whiter as I press my hand harder and harder against her skin. Slowly, surprisingly, my hand moves through and into her chest, without any blood flowing. She is quite still, her eyes closed, as I find and then slowly withdraw: a living, sleeping bird from her chest cavity. I hold the bird in both hands – a dove or a wood-pigeon, stained with a little blood. Her chest is open. The bird springs to life, and like the books before it, I set it free into the starlit sky over our heads, as the wind gasps like a hungry giant.

I dress and carry her naked in my arms down the staircase to the garden, and she opens her eyes again a little, her face still very pale, saying *won't you stay tonight? Why are you going to leave?*

I carry her out into the overgrown front garden, saying *Because I have to die again, to choose a death, it doesn't matter which, but chose it before it chooses me. Tomorrow, nobody can recognise or remember me. There are always little changes, or I can take steps to make sure that there will be, put my face in the fire until I find a new face, and then everything will be different again...*

As I bend down next to the pond, she sits up a little and glances at her chest ... *the wound...* she says, ... *open again... will it ever heal?* I run my fingertips over the tiny red edges of the slit between her breasts, sealing it like an envelope, then lean to kiss her. Then I lower her body down into the cold still water. She floats there just below the surface. I place my hand over her eyelids and close them, gather up the autumn leaves strewn around among the ivy, wet them each in the pond and wrap them around her body until she is entirely encased in dead leaves, in shades of red, gold, brown, and green. A dusting of moonlit frost now partially covers every frond and stem of ivy in a kind of skin. Perhaps the pond will freeze before daybreak.

I leave her there to catch a bus back into the heart of the city. I think I see a dim light emanating from the upper window where her father had spoken to me, but it might just be a trick of the moonlight.

The bus is late and empty, like a magical carriage for me, its only passenger. I don't like the driver's black moustache.

He watches me, his only passenger on the back seat, in his mirror. Without the usual ballast of humankind the vehicle lurches and bumps violently. The driver seems to check my image in his mirror after each jolt as if he is trying to impress or torment me. His moustache makes it difficult to say whether he is laughing. Tired of this, I risk even more jolting by standing up and going upstairs. When we reach the terminus, I come back down, but the driver has been replaced. *What happened to the other driver?* -I ask of the younger, clean-shaven man. *Him?* -he grunts, and points to the back of a uniformed man walking away, but he doesn't look the same either. I turn to step out, but he grunts again and says: *Hey, he left this for you... He said you left it here last night.* He hands me some folded papers. Confused, I accept them, and walk hesitantly, reading:

These are the notebooks of Ultrameta: the city of the soul...

I turn a page over:-

Something happened about a year ago I never told you about. How could I tell you? It affects not just us, but the fabric of the entire universe. My wife and I were in a car crash, or rather we weren't. I know what I saw. Suddenly we were going to die, but I was very calm. There were three cars, the one overtaking us was going to hit the oncoming one; it could not be stopped, the trajectories were mathematical, all three cars were marked for destruction. I watched it happening, time slowed down, just like it does on those occasions. Why does it slow down? Well, let me tell you what it does next, most people don't live to find out...

Slowing down in mild fascination, I find I have just bumped into an old down-and-out, leaning against a wall of the bus station. I pull myself together and walk more briskly towards a café. But stopping at a junction, I can't help reading some more:-

Maybe we are never meant to know certain things because, if we ever came to understand their implications, we would go instantly mad. In the normal system of the world, we appear to live and die to order like helpless little sheep, on the unknown whims of the unknown shepherd. But alone among all the things we observe in this world, there is only one that never actually makes any sense: death itself. It is counter-intuitive. We know deep down that consciousness is inextinguishable. This is not a wish, but an unshakeable intuition. What if death were just an optical illusion?

I find a suitable all-night café, push open the glass doors, enter and pull up a lonely perch. The barman pops up from below the counter, a dishcloth in his hand, a toothless gap in his smile. I order a coffee and ask to borrow a pen. I test my handwriting on a napkin and compare it to the notes on these strange crumpled papers. They match up. I continue reading:-

At the point of death, or of supposed death, time actually slows down then changes course in order to alter events. Nobody can experience death, so death is avoided, an alternative history is pulled out of the ether and dropped onto our plates. An infinite number of realities can be generated in order to divert death. When the cars crashed, they didn't crash: I saw them bend, I saw them pass through each other. I thought for a while that I might have imagined it, but days later, the universe began throwing me a few clues: a sunset sky looked obviously fake; every cloud identical, I would overhear total strangers saying my thoughts out loud on the train. Then I knew that I was dead, that we all are, and trapped in a game...

Leaning back in my seat, I feel I'm running out of time again. It must be about four in the morning. I drink my coffee and smoke a cigarette, take a last look at this day's face in a fragment of public mirror. I scarcely feel that I have got to know myself or the world, but maybe next time will be better. But I like what little I can see of the traces she's left on me, changes in my face. The eyes are tired as ever, the body ticking over, buoyed up by its little electric shocks of contact, its rejuvenating acts of congress. This time I am too tired for electrocution, and there are few cars around for me to contrive a collision with. I pay up, catch a lift to the 14th floor of a towerblock, break the lock to the plant room, and stroll out onto the rooftop, scarcely pausing to admire the view. Same old city, though the blur of the lights at speed makes an interesting variation. Going down, I remember looking up at all the old books with their fluttering pages, and wonder if one of these times I might fly.

*   *   *

When I swallow this city, the sky walks into me. Always in autumn at dusk, somehow, when the day has finished everyone else. Again I begin, a cocoon losing its butterfly, dying briefly – another death calling out my name. The sky is black turning blue, as if tainted, and the swishing cloth of coloured clouds turns my brow to that hemisphere above, wiping my eyes. Each day uses its end to my destruction – it opens me up so utterly...

Inescapable city: your streets run to meet me, envelop me like a mother I have lost, or persistently forgotten. Familiar, unfamiliar. Every time, the fresh crop of faces, poison flowers turning to the sun, crowds of eyes welling with worries. They pass me by, known to nobody. Yet I am haunted by fragments, broken imprints of voices and features. I remember a girl, last night perhaps: was there a name? I was running my fingers along the smooth surface of her face, searching for clues, traces of my identity. Now, I think she may be dead.

Nothing. I remember only other, more distant fragments. Being a child once somewhere, sitting on a floor confronted by a mass of jigsaw pieces, my heart sinking at the prospect of ever re-assembling them into a picture. Later, as an adult, I might have solved that puzzle in half a minute, laughing. But this is all that I feel now: that child's bewilderment, a blank sheet drifting closer to the mysterious centre of life, vanishing into a snowstorm of atoms, seeking new form.

*   *   *

Disquieting, isn't it? -Donna asks, leaning over me with a mug of some steaming liquid, -*and this is how you like your coffee by the way, I still remember, milk and no sugars, I've heated it up on the fire...*

She sits down again on the floor with me and we face each other cross-legged, as she fishes absent-mindedly through the pile of writing. The flickering candles surround us in a hallowed atmosphere, Mussolini laps happily at a saucer of milk by the fire.

Donna shivers suddenly, holding her mug of tea, rubbing her shoulders, the yellow glow of thirteen flames dancing together in her eyes as they widen to meet mine as she talks: -*It was as if you were out there without me, without even the memory of me, or of us, and wandering lost, maybe even harming people somehow...*

*Am I... -*I stammer uncertainly, -*was I capable of that?*

She shakes her head, *-I didn't think so, but read this next one. Of everything you sent this seems like the only one in which maybe you are remembering us, it even seems addressed to me at times, it gave me hope...*

I look into her brown eyes and die a little at the thought of the inexplicable hurt that I, or some stranger who has become me, once did in my name. I bow my head, half in sorrow, half in shame, and begin reading:-

The music stops, the blood boils down to nothing, to clear water, to air...

~

12b: _Thanatavista

...of atoms, seeking new form...

The music stops, the blood boils down to nothing, to clear water, to air. At last we move beyond the noise of flesh and I can see things as they are, breathing in the vacuum, hearing what the silence says.

Stripped of hunger, of lust, of heat and cold, I see you naked of everything, even of skin and bone. I meet you in the half-light, in the cool hush of the abandoned places, the boarded-up rooms of the old house. How musty it is, the dust floating in the air, the damp walls talking to each other about us, exchanging memories, making secret symphonies of our traces, our smells. Decay is a cosmic undertaking, a grand project. This is how the divine lavishes its sadness and love upon us at last, after so many years watching from afar, unrequited. It is how nature consumes its own children, a beautiful obscenity, sacred and profane.

You are a pattern of wallpaper in a locked bedroom now. I am the white net curtains, fading and rotting, eaten by dust. But through the shutters and the glass, the summer morning light still pierces my heart on occasion, and I inflect and refract this warmth, and send its beam to play upon the far wall: where your printed pattern of leaves then curls and dances again in memory, the old gramophone records play, the floorboards creak under the dance steps of our vanished feet.

I am a rusting iron spike in the overgrown garden, lost among the grasses. I was once gleaming metal, was once the frame of a swing that I sat in as a child, kicking the earth away with my feet, straining my face forward and upward with each foray into the sky, into the imagined future. On quiet afternoons, I closed my eyes as I swung, longing to fly, the inside of my eyelids red under the sunlight, strange patterns on them like folded wings.

You are the still surface of the lily pond now choked with moss and weed, where sunlight plays and glimmers, blinking between the swaying reeds. The flicker and glow of the light is your smile, your laughing face. More than the sum of its parts, beyond mere biology: your face was an amphitheatre where the divine came to play, to make miracles happen, summoned by my words, my prayers.

I am the carpet now old and worn, rolled in a corner: which once spread luxuriantly across the wide lounge. Soon the new people will manhandle me down the stairs, take me to the garden and burn me, make smoke of our memories. But once: my weave held your little wet feet as you emerged from the shower. Once: I cradled us as we sat together in front of the open fire on winter evenings. My pattern was like the long straight furrows of endless tawny-coloured fields. Our eyes played along those furrows as we sat and talked, lying on the floor on Sunday mornings, debating the meaning of life, but never unlocking it.

You are the old severed wires, redundant electrics, bypassed by the new people. Secret tangles left buried in walls, under floors. Connections that can no longer mean anything, carry no current, eternal puzzles. But to us, in our time, they brought us light and heat, meals we cooked together, glimmers in your eyes as we sat at the table, warmth in your hands. The pathways of our lives are thus re-routed, closed over now, become mazes, labyrinths, prisons from which we may never escape.

I am the dark green ivy that eats into the blonde stonework of the house, climbing skyward incredibly slowly, patiently, a ladder for ants; a landscape on which centuries of their histories are enacted. My feet have spread across the patio, I climb and drape myself like a paternal blanket over the shoulders and waists of the statues of nymphs, protecting their modesty. Their sightless eyes bear tears of moss now. I stuff their ears and mouths with my news of the fall of civilisation, the sleep of reason. The pipes are choked and rusted now, no water runs.

You are the sunset in the garden, the shimmering of water vapour rising from the earth as the summer sun glows red and orange, sinking as if wounded, into the tangle of nettles and long grass. You are the wide pale sky of blue along the flat horizon, yellow at its base like the curling edges of a fading book that nobody will ever read again. I see your figure appear in the haze, and wild red roses climb and twist inside you, lifting their lazy heads, their thorns harmless now to their only admirers: the tiny pilots, the clouds of insects, birds light as feathers.

I am the old chest of drawers in the hallway that we bought in a junkshop and sanded down together, then the days of varnishing, sleeping freezing cold with the windows open in October, so as not to choke from the fumes of the varnish. The grain emerged slowly under our hands, the warm colour of bare wood like living flesh revealed. We brought life back to the inanimate, and now in return I live here in the drawers and the ornate legs. Perhaps you are the handles that you polished so meticulously, the steel wool running around all the elaborate twists and turns and flourishes, rubbing until your fingers were red and sore.

Will the new people ever rest? Or must they press on until they have obliterated every trace of us? They can never succeed. We wore down that doorstep that they now traverse daily without thinking. They are one with us. Strangers, and yet strangely intimate. When all the paint we brushed on is gone, papered over or chipped off, there is still the sound of our brushes patiently tip-tapping through the corridors of time, our sighs, our laughter. Though they make a pyre of our belongings in the garden and burn it, still you and I will meet and mingle in the sweet smoke that mounts the sky, serenaded by autumn crows.

We watch the new people sometimes. We are there in their mirrors, flowing at the corners, turning backwards in the steam of their baths. We are in their floorboards, creaking, bearing the weight of their future on the strength of our past. We carry them as they walk about on their little errands and chores. We bear what they do to us, we endure it because we understand everything they do. They think they are so new, so unique, an experiment that might not work, people so good that they cannot possibly die. But it has all happened before, and the pattern is as good and as familiar to the touch as the grain in the leg of a chest of drawers, sanded or varnished or painted, seen or unseen, the pattern is the same, the pattern is unchanging.

The minds of the new ones are closed, we cannot enter there. But their children's laughter is like waterfalls or beating wings. For a few years, before the world claims them back, we can play in their daydreams, this is our refuge. When they play alone, we talk to them, guard over them, show them pictures in their heads, open up doors to other worlds. We will always have children now, you and I, because we live where they go to dream.

Maybe there are some things of ours in the attic, and when the new people find them they will sift cruelly through them, discarding what is not valuable or antique. Perhaps an old photo shows your smile, as alien to them as our outmoded fashions, our antiquated clothes. Our drawings and paintings will all vanish into the flames. They will think we were cute and quaint, how sad that we were not immortal like them. But we whisper in their window frames, in their attic timbers as they creak in the wind at night: *we were like you, and you will be like us...*

I cannot remember the moment of my death, our death. It scarcely matters here. It is as if all of life were just an incubation, the sleep of a caterpillar in its pupa, preparing to be freed and released into this flood of golden light and knowledge. Imagine a view from the highest point in the world, from which all can be seen, without eyelids to blink, nor head to turn.

I remember instead the words of my father once, when I was alive; a child on a distant beach, holding his hand, overwhelmed by the beauty of a summer's day by the sea. The beaches were not yet polluted then, the world was still young, man had not defiled nature. Sunlight in my curly blonde hair, my little head was struggling to express what I felt to him, the emotion that arose inside me at the sight of the golden fields on the coast, the breaking waves on the rocks and sand, the grandeur of it all.

I know son, I know... -he said, -*sometimes your inside just gets too big for your outside.* Then perhaps I guessed for the first time what I know now: that the body falls away like the skin of an orange, peeling as the hot sun rises in the sky of our hearts. Fear nothing. We are found, we are all found, and nothing is lost.

*   *   *

I'm not sure why you felt comforted by that… -I say, stroking Mussolini's ears back, putting the manuscript down on the floor, *-doesn't this one seem to imply that I was dead, that I thought we both were?*

Perhaps, -Donna says, *-but then how could a dead man write, and send letters? What mattered was the sentiment, the memory preserved.*

I see your point, but what about this one here? -I pick a folded letter up and straighten it out, *-It's talking about "your disappearance" here, rather than mine, what's that about?*

Read it, she says. *It's written as a woman, no kidding. It's kind of like you were trying to imagine what it was like to be me after losing you, how infuriating is that? Except as usual, everything's mixed up and distorted. We, I mean you… I mean I… have a child in this story, although he never seems to say much… the whole thing's kind of creepy actually…you tell me what it means, it's your handwriting…*

"Suburbia is a good place to hide, to dream, to disappear without a trace…"

~

11b: _Telemura

...all found, and nothing is lost.

Case File 296-07: Margaret Francis Alloway. Photos of body covered in grey paint; close-ups of her closed eyelids and mouth. Cause of death: malnutrition, dehydration & poisoning by ingestion of trichloroethylene. Subject was former Teacher of Classical Studies, mental health deteriorated after miscarriage and violent split with male partner current whereabouts unknown. History of self-harm and hallucination, suspected schizophrenia. Abode found in state of aggravated disrepair, one room flooded, other defaced with saws and chisels. Later diary entries show increasing state of delusion and isolation. References to mystery child taken as manifestation of condition as previously outlined. Final entry appended hereto as de facto suicide note:-

Suburbia is a good place to hide, to dream, to disappear without a trace. The city was changing too much, was changing faster every year, every day. Sometimes even the way home would be blocked or diverted, a street's course or its name somehow altered. A train station would be inexplicably closed or a bus route changed without warning. Is it just a symptom of getting older to increasingly lose track of these things? Or is our world and every other world disintegrating by the day, tending towards chaos?

Your disappearance was the last straw. The city just swallowed you one day, and suddenly my son had no father, and I had no husband, and then we had no choice but to retreat here, behind the privet and the rhododendrons, behind the sound of the lawn mowers and the washing machines, behind the poker-faces of the white rendered bungalows that stare each other down in an endless tarmacadam stand-off, violence indefinitely postponed in the hostile silence of distrust.

It wasn't long before the changes followed us, even into this very house, but at least here we can keep track of them, make meticulous records to try to keep the whole thing under control. My memory isn't so good now, and sometimes I sleep for days, but at least little Charlie keeps me straight, bringing me coffee every morning to wake me up, presenting me with yesterday's diary on a silver tray, to remind me of what I wrote before, so that I can reflect on our latest situation.

It's just as well we both sleep so soundly, although in my case I must confess the effect would not be achieved without medication and fortification. Charlie sleeps in the room with me, in a little cot by the radiator, and every night before we sleep I tape up the gaps around the door and over the vents on the windows. Nine times out of ten the night probably passes without incident, but I have heard and even seen the spiders too many times to underestimate them, and when they decide to move *en masse*, it is easily enough to terrify me, never mind Charlie.

When we first came here I was not so cautious. I even lifted the floorboards of an occasion, and stuck my head down into their kingdom and poked around bravely with a torch and a stick. In the daytime of course, they are usually quite inactive; but the extent of their draping cobwebs, the vast arrays of their white trailing curtains blowing slightly in the subfloor breeze should have alerted me to their unusual numbers and organisation. They must have some kind of central intelligence, some kind of plan or a motive to account for their nocturnal manoeuvres, but I have yet to divine it. All we do here for now is hold the line, try to keep life bearable while we manage the frequent changes that are thrust upon us.

The first unusual detail I noticed when we entered the house were the pots of paint: ten or twenty of them piled high, not in the attic or the garage as you might expect, but in the middle of the living room. It immediately seemed like some kind of cryptic warning from the previous owner, and sure enough on the top-most pot there was a little handwritten note in red ink: *do not throw these away, but keep them close at hand, you will be needing them.* I couldn't think what to make of it at the time, but the instructions were so specific that fortunately I heeded them.

That same day I remember finding a spider in the bath and scooping it up into a glass with a coffee mat and taking it to the window to put it out. Charlie squealed with delight and horror as the creature beat itself repeatedly and frantically against the glass, but then something must have distracted me, perhaps a neighbour came to greet us at the door, but at any rate, by the time we remembered and returned to lift the glass the next day, the creature was quite dead, cruelly suffocated by my

169

neglect. I told myself I had not meant to kill it, but still I felt a pang of guilt.

The next thing we noticed were the noises in the middle of the night. At first it would be the little scraping sounds: gradually building in intensity. Only later would I recognise this sound as the armies of spiders marching about under the floor and in the walls, deconstructing and relocating sections of partitions by carrying a million tiny pieces on their backs. This was not a loud sound, but soon another one followed, and it was quite specific in its meaning: horses' hooves clattering on the timber floorboards.

At first my astonishment was so intense that I forgot to be frightened, and simply ran to the room next door and pulled the door open, throwing on the light: immediately there was silence. It was an empty room with no activity within, my confusion was acute. This phenomenon was repeated at perhaps hourly intervals throughout the night for the following month. You can imagine the effect on our sleep, although Charlie, showing the resilience that children so excel at, soon adapted and accepted the noise as normal and slept through it.

By daylight I repeatedly examined the room, but was unable to find any explanation, any abnormality. Added to this, the sounds had gradually increased in their depth and intensity. By now the sound was of a room filled with perhaps five or six horses, all galloping in a circle, some of them even neighing and whinnying, as if distressed or pursued by something.

At first I thought the room was not changing, that these nocturnal recitals were not leaving any traces. But then after a week or so I saw that black blotches were appearing on the walls. Gradually, each day, they darkened and coalesced. I thought they might be mould or damp. I tried to scrub them off the wallpaper and failing; decided to strip the wallpaper off instead. But the same pattern persisted on the bare plaster wall underneath, and kept on growing unabated. I began to see that it was somehow animal-like in its appearance, like leopard or zebra skin.

I bought paint from a DIY store, pure white matt at first, and brushed it over the whole room, but the blotches reappeared overnight. I tried a darker shade: peach and then even dark blue, but nothing succeeded in hiding the markings. Then in despair I found myself staring into space in the hallway one day, when I noticed an open cupboard doorway and remembered the strange paint pots that I had stored there after finding them on my first day. I took one out, and sat on the stairs to read the label, while Charlie played with his toy cars around my ankles...

T E L E M U R A : the paint of the ancients

(brought to you by Brentworth Industries Ltd)

Many recipes and formulae have been lost to history. The burning of the Library of Alexandria in 641 AD destroyed much of the priceless knowledge of the ancient world: the secrets of Greek Fire, Pilemma Weaving, Damascus Steel, The Philosophers Stone. Homer spoke also of a paint colour mixed by the enchantress Kirkaei in her cave at Aiaia, that could turn warriors into the colours of rocks or waves, granting them invisibility at will. Plato said that the inventor Daedalus rediscovered the formula and used it to paint his mechanical guardians, the automatons, to waterproof their structure and deflect the harmful rays of the sun. It is unclear whether Telemura was an impervious coating or a colour with strange optical qualities like iridescence or phosphorescence, or perhaps it was all of these things.

*Dante preferred Horace's take on it: that Telemura was
"...the colour of all colours, where grey meets blue and
fawn, where the purple of twilight melts into the neutral
mist of morning, the end and beginning of all colours,
both no colour and every colour, zenith and nadir of the
spectrum of light, the pupil of the eye of Zeus himself
wherein all light vanishes and all emerges..." Alchemists
and philosophers across the centuries have tried in vain
to rediscover Telemura's formula: Aristotle, Albertus
Magnus, Paracelsus, Isaac Newton, the Count de Saint
Germain, each mixing and remixing pigments, scouring
the earth for rare minerals to add to the brew, to take them
over the elusive threshold of light and find the colour of
colours. Stir well before use. Load brush liberally, and
apply in one even coat. Touch dry in 4 hours, re-coatable
overnight. Always use in a well-ventilated space.*

I laughed for the first time in a while, but a little nervously.
The claims were ridiculous, but with the genius of modern
marketing: were not really claims, only sly implications.

I looked again at the disobedient wall of the room, the
re-emerging leopard spots, and realised that I had nothing to lose.
I opened a pot and stirred it and began applying it to the walls.

Initially I thought it was just white paint, as I worked
near the light from the windows. It was certainly pale, but then
as I worked in my own shadow I saw that it was grey, a fawn

grey. I took it onto the wall next to the door and began to see brown and mauve, a purple overtone. But then as I worked towards the next corner, the whole wall and the rest of the room began to reflect each other, and I became convinced there was a pink in it somewhere that was turning lilac then pale grey blue at the corners. Was there a word for such a shade? Teal, taupe, mushroom? There seemed to be no definitive hue to it and so no naming possible, perhaps the colour was so finely balanced that the tiniest change in light from the window or in the eye of the beholder could tip it into a different area of the spectrum. I did not understand it, but it made me feel strangely calmed. As I stepped back, I saw that as it slowly dried it was still changing colour, it was almost alive. So it was no colour and every colour. It was *Telemura*.

That night the horses did not return, the clattering hooves fell silent. I began to sleep soundly again, but not for long. Perhaps the spiders saw that they had been defeated by the mysterious paint, and resolved to make a show of force to send me a message. I was soon surprised by what they were capable of. Their nocturnal scraping began to grow in intensity over a week until one night they reached a deafening crescendo in which the whole house shook and we could hear walls breaking open and timbers snapping. Charlie and I lay awake all night in terror, with blankets piled around the bottom of the door where occasionally we would see some of their million industrious legs appear for a second before returning to the fold.

In the morning, we emerged tentatively to discover that the whole of the study had been cut away and altered and re-aligned. Upon opening the door, one immediately saw that the timber floorboards fell away at about thirty degrees, and all the walls and ceilings had been shifted with them. Somehow, the spiders had immaculately sealed and finished their own work: the rugs and the chairs and tables were all glued fast to the tilting floor, the books still rested snugly on their shelves, the lightflex had been solidified and stiffened until it held like a metal rod at an angle. It was amazing, and although we were horrified at first, over coming days our secret admiration for their skill grew, so that soon we even occasionally used the room, by sliding down the floor and resting in a corner and reading a book or two in the light from the tilted window. Charlie was more agile than me and more confident and trusting: I preferred to keep a length of rope around my waist tethered to the stair banister in the hall outside, in case I should want to get out in a hurry.

I thought then that the spiders might have made their point and would choose to leave us alone, but I underestimated the extent of their ambition, could not conceive of the vast canvas on which they were expressing themselves, nor what they were saying. We were allowed silence for only a few weeks before another flurry of activity began. We took comfort from each other and the impression that they did not want to harm us, just continue with their experiments on our environment.

This time I did not immediately notice what they had done. It was a room we hardly used after all, a spare bedroom. I went to open the door and found it locked, which surprised me, but when I went to retrieve the key from the hall cupboard I found it missing. Then I noticed one curious difference in the bedroom door from how I remembered it. There in the middle, at the same height as the door handle, was a perfectly cut circular hole, about the size of a fist. My fingers touched its smoothly sanded edges with fascination: within its centre there was only the blackness of the room beyond. I fetched a torch but could see little through the hole. Then something occurred to me. The diameter of the hole and its location seemed strangely specific, as if meant to signify something. Taking a deep breath, I rolled up my sleeve and began, tentatively at first, to reach my right hand and arm inside it. Then something clicked: the key to be precise, which I found was inside the lock, on the far side of the door. Carefully I turned it and the door opened. Inside, I found not a room behind it, but another almost identical door only a few feet away, as if the whole room were now just the size of a cupboard.

This door too was locked and at first I had no idea how to unlock it, but for some reason I suddenly took the notion to try the same key again. This I did, except that first of all I found that the only way to remove this key from the previous door was to close it and lock it. Then the next stage of the enigma dawned on me. I had to trap myself in the cupboard, reach my hand out through the hole and turn the key shut on the outside, then take the key back through, turn around and use it on the next door. I did so and the next door opened at once, revealing this time another cupboard with two more doors in different directions, each of which could only be unlocked by the same key, which again could only be used by first locking the one behind me. All doors, needless to say, had exactly the same central circular aperture through which my slender arm could just reach and turn and so enclose myself then move forward.

And so I progressed through several of these chambers until suddenly I became terrified. It occurred to me it could only be a kind of trap, that I was a lab rat performing some weird test, that I had been lured by my own curiosity, the idea being to entomb me in this labyrinth of doors, separating me from Charlie. I panicked, I screamed, I fumbled with the key, I thought the lock would not open anymore, I beat on the doors in tears. Gradually I calmed down, and guided by Charlie's voice outside and, trying to stay strong for him, I made my way back to the outside.

I swore I would not go into that room again. But after only a few days my curiosity overtook me. What could be behind all those doors? What could the spiders be trying to hide there? Charlie and I cooked up a plan, and, using a ball of string for guidance like the old Greek hero in the myth, I set out boldly to make my way through the labyrinth of doors.

We went up into the attic and I paced out the room's dimensions on the floor. I drew various diagonals and halved them until I knew I had the room's centre. Using a knife and an old saw, I slowly cut my way down through the floor, between the floor joists, and down through the ceiling into the chamber below. Of course, when I shone a torch down, I saw that it was just another small room like all the others, with three identical doors leading off at different angles. But this time, and making Charlie promise not to follow me but to wait behind and sing so I could hear him, I lowered myself down from above, into the room below, and drew the string out behind me as I tried every door and explored in different directions.

Locking and unlocking door after door, I found nothing in the chambers around the centre of the room, and began to make my way towards the hallway instead. But this in itself was not easy. After many doors, I finally came upon a room with a length of string travelling across its floor from one side to the other. I was horrified and puzzled, I knew it should not be there, but gradually I faced up to the fact that it must be my own string and that I was hopelessly disorientated. But here was a dilemma: shouldn't I be able to grab this string and use it as a shortcut home? I was now one hour into this sortie, and just to retrace my steps would take the same time again. But how could I know which way to go? One way along the string was probably a shortcut back to the hole in the ceiling, but the other, if I chose wrongly, would only lead me back to where I was already. Worst of all, the string seemed jammed tight in whichever direction I tugged it, so that if I tried to pull it too roughly in the wrong direction I would risk breaking it and losing my lifeline back to the outside.

Although I had told Charlie to keep singing outside, it had really been to comfort him not me. Since I could already no longer hear him through all the plaster and timbers, the prospects of him finding me and cutting another hole for me to escape through seemed remote. What if the batteries in my torch ran out? Defeated again, I returned monotonously to my original point of entry, and eventually, exhausted, hoisted myself back up into the attic.

I slept for several days after that before being woken by the next experiment. The spiders were on the move again in the dead of night and this time we could hear metal breaking and water flowing. In the morning Charlie and I found that the door to our living room was locked and that nothing could shift it. Looking in from the garden revealed nothing except that the spiders had closed all the shutters and fastened all the sash locks.

It concerned me greatly that they would move upon a piece of territory so important to us, one used on a daily basis. We shifted our fridges and freezers through to the bedroom as a precaution: all ten of them, in which we had been stockpiling food so as to avoid the terrors of the changing world outside. The noise of refrigeration while we slept was now considerable, but it is amazing what you can adapt to, and how comforting any noise can be when you at least understand its origin.

After the sweat of moving the fridges, I gave myself a cold shower and, while standing in the bath, I noticed a single spider on the edge of the overflow. I meant to go get a glass and ferry it out, but I was tired and hot. I thought it would survive above the water until I was finished, but for once I overestimated the creature. The spinning current caught it, the smooth enamel was too much for it to resist and it was swept down the plughole before I could react to it. It seemed a small thing, a single life extinguished out of millions, but I knew in my heart that I would pay for it.

That night the noise reached a crescendo, and after the sound of pipes breaking we heard the rushing and pouring of water for hours on end. Next day, puzzled by the lack of any physical change within sight, I set about gaining entry to the living room at all costs, and began prising at the hinges with a chisel, taking off all the facings and loosening every screw I could find. By late afternoon, I lifted the door out in my hands and lowered it carefully to the hall floor and looked up, astonished.

I told Charlie to stay well back at the bedroom door as I approached in trepidation. I raised my hands and ran them in nervous wonderment over a vertical surface of glass, perhaps six inches thick. Behind this, our whole living room was exactly as we had left it except for one critical detail: it was now completely flooded with water from floor to ceiling.

The cushions floated and travelled about the room on underwater currents, the curtains and the house plants waved and twitched as our now liberated goldfish swam about the whole room in majesty, their meagre little tank now open to their new, extended world. Portraits and landscapes on the walls hung at angles, drowned and stifled. Soaked books occasionally took to the air and winged across the room like disorientated birds. Drifts of bubbles would sometimes rise up from air pockets in the sofa or folds in the rugs.

Once I trusted that the glass would not break, I just stood there for hours watching, my hands on Charlie's shoulders, our eyes filled with tears but our hearts amazed at the spectacle. Now our world was in retreat and I wondered what boundary of it would be struck at next, and it wasn't long before my question was answered.

One morning, after another flurry of midnight activity, I arose to find that a rectangle of black tar had appeared on one wall in the kitchen. I kept Charlie out of the place and tried to ignore it at first, but gradually it grew in intensity each day until I saw that it was an opening: the size of a wide door. The thing was black and wet and yet apparently harmless, or odourless at least. There was something about it that seemed to both fascinate and appal me. I got a red velvet curtain and brass pole and fixed them over the top so that I could keep it out of sight for most of the day.

Still I would find myself drawn to it at least once a day, when Charlie was safely out of the way, and I would pull the curtain back and sit on a chair and stare at the thing: gazing into its dripping, shining surface, wondering at its purpose. Sometimes I thought I heard sounds from within it: sounds of the sea perhaps, of seagulls, of sea breezes, or playing children.

I leaned closer to it than ever before yesterday, and closed my eyes, reaching my hand out to touch it. Forgetting myself, I leaned too far forward, but instead of my face making contact with wet black tar, it passed effortlessly through some kind of portal. I found myself on a summer beach and was suddenly filled with an inexplicable happiness. I felt as if I was inhabiting some once-cherished memory, but one that I had forgotten until now. The beach was wide but strangely dark, as if made of volcanic sand. The sky was similarly dark as if brooding before a sudden thunderstorm. It was as if everything was being seen through dark glass, a pool of oil.

But the wind was in my hair, and I was happy, and I saw footprints in the sand in front of me and I knew then that they were yours, that I had found you again, that we were about to be re-united. You would be young as I remember you, we would both be young, if I just turned around and followed these footprints back up the beach to wherever you were hiding. But then I heard the cry of a seagull getting louder, until it turned into Charlie's voice calling me, and I pulled my head up and out with a guilty jolt. I was back in the kitchen staring at my own reflection in the wet black mirror, except that now I thought I saw a beach and a sea there as a background to my own image.

I felt the black tar in my hair, and gasped in horror, closed the curtains over and rushed to wash my hair clean before Charlie found me.

*   *   *

What have I done? I should have kept the kitchen door locked, the velvet curtain more tightly drawn. Today my beloved little Charlie has vanished through the forbidden door. I found one of his little shoes on the floor by the opening, with a shred of seaweed and pool of sand and water. I should have kept my diary entries hidden: despite my warnings never to read my notebooks his curiosity must have overtaken him. My teaching and his swift learning have worked too well. Were he ignorant and illiterate he would still be innocent, he would not have come to this. The spiders have tricked us, have stolen my last treasure from me. I can only pray and hope as to the true purpose of these events which I do not understand. Perhaps through the doorway he has found you, where I only found your footprints. Perhaps you and he are at last re-united and now only I am in torment, longing to join you.

I have torn down the curtain now and dashed myself a thousand times against the doorway but it will not open for me again. Instead I find I am coated in blotches of the black oil from the wall's surface. Now in front of the bathroom mirror, I weep and dab at the oil stains, trying to remove them.

Suddenly I recognise the patterns of the black stains, like leopard spots or zebra stripes, and understand the difficulty of removing them. Instead I strip naked and cut my hair, then shave it down to the scalp, shave my armpits, and, sitting on the bathroom floor: shave finally my pubis and the tiny hairs on my legs and arms, all the time weeping. I don't understand what I'm doing, unless perhaps it is to be as smooth and pure as when I first entered this world, so that I will be ready to leave it again.

There are four cans of Telemura left. I balance their cold metal against my shivering flesh and gathering them up, take them all with me to the Room of Horses. With a fresh brush from the cupboard I wet the walls again until they acquire the glimmering pallor of twilight beaches. Now I begin to hear the sound of hooves again, quiet at first, then building in intensity. At first the noise seems to come from the walls themselves as I paint them, but then they seem to be building inside my head... were they always there? Were the white horses only ever inside my head? Could I have imagined them? Didn't Charlie say he heard them also?

I dip the brush deep into the pot and begin to apply the paint over my own body. Immediately I feel warmer, the film of paint protecting me, taking away my goosebumps and shivers. I paint more and more, myself, the floor, the windows, the window glass, frantically, ecstatically. Gradually I feel calmer, my weeping is subsiding. The sound of horses' hooves is growing stronger and louder inside my head, except that now they are more like drumbeats, strangely enticing, they fill me with an illicit excitement, like a prelude to an execution.

I notice a few spiders at the threshold to the room, but they are unable to move further, their limbs dissolving with a tiny hiss as soon as they touch the glittering paint. I take comfort in the paint, even as I mourn and long for my lost son, my lost lover: you. I run my fingers through the thick wet brush. I paint out my ears, my navel, my vagina, my anus, warm paint seeping into my body, the overpowering fumes choking me, stinging my throat and nose and eyes. I lift the last pot and pour the remaining paint down my throat in long gulps, gagging. I fall to my knees.

I see at last that my body and the room are the same mystical shade of grey: mushroom and coffee cream and yet pale blue sky of winter dawn, lilac of delicate flowers in forest clearings, subtly alive and flickering, yet magnificently grey and mute, declined and sexless, beyond taint or corruption, healed. I paint out my mouth and eyes and vanish into the fumes, into the floor and walls and ceiling, into the pale summer beach of sleep. The drumbeats, the horses hooves, stop at last, dead. Sweet silence reigns again. Suburbia is such a good place to hide, to dream, to disappear without a trace.

*   *   *

Well? -Donna asks, laughing, -*I take it you didn't go for a sex change while you were away did you? I take it you're not a woman now?*

How would I know?

Now she really laughs, falling backwards onto the floor, so that Mussolini climbs up onto her face, licking her ears.

These for a start! -she says, sitting up again, clutching her breasts, -*You'd have a pair of these wouldn't you? And nothing down the front of your pants... C'mon, you're not really telling me you have forgotten the difference between men and women are you?*

I shake my head. *No, I don't think so...* Then I consider this some more, and say; -*but indulge me...*

Indulge you? -she asks, fixing me with her stare, head leaned forward, her long hair crossing her face like a pendulum, before she sweeps it back again behind her ears. A long silence falls and grows within the room, even Mussolini holds his peace, until the sound of the candles burning can be heard again.

Alright then, -she says, standing up, *come closer to the fire.*

I do this, as she takes her shirt off and turns to put a hand on my shoulder. I flinch and she looks into my face, saying: -*What's wrong?*

I... I... I don't think I'm used to anybody touching me, it feels... intrusive, dangerous.

That's odd, -Donna says, looking off into the darkness to her right while some thoughts in her head come back into focus. -*That's what's it says in the next letter... the one you haven't read yet.*

There is just one left? -I ask, *then you must let me read it now. What does it say about touch?*

Donna thinks, looking down at the floor, as she kneels in front of me. *It's you as a woman again I think, except this time you're like a nymphomaniac or something, but everyone you touch, every man, sees the truth of his life and is destroyed by it, even as he makes love to you...* -Her voice trails off dreamily, until she returns her eyes to me with a start.

Where is it then? Let me read it.

She looks around on the floor, searching randomly amid the piles of paper and finally holds it up. I reach my hand up towards it, but she pulls it away behind her back and puts her face into mine whispering: *No, you can't have it until you touch me, until you destroy yourself with truth... until we've found out whether you're a man or a woman...*

She puts her lips on mine and breathes into my mouth, then rummages her lips around a bit, then explains to me that I am supposed to keep my eyes shut during the lip-rummaging for some reason, as if there is an etiquette about these things.

She removes her clothes, and I see that all her skin is smooth and hairless like a child's, and that everything about her design is more curved than mine. Her body is so much better proportioned too; she has good genetic advertising, one might say. She gradually removes my clothes, then insists that I satisfy this hungry little fox she has between her legs. It feels furry to the touch, like a rodent or a quivering honey bee. My suspicions are confirmed when Mussolini gets put out of the room, obviously to stop the two of them fighting. I can see the thing is swelling up now, as if it knows I'm here, as if it has a mind of its own and is determined to eat me.

The touch of her arms and legs makes me warmer anyway, so I am happy to get closer, but then she suddenly grabs me down below and sticks me right into this fox thing. It is like I am stabbing her and she is dying and I want to apologise at first, but in between gasps of pain she's telling me to keep on doing this distasteful thing to her. It occurs to me that this all seems to involve the body parts we use for urination and defecation, but I sense that such hygienic concerns would fall on deaf ears during these precise seconds. Who knows what I'm putting where but I go along with it all anyway, until this strange hollowness grows inside me and turns into a kind of vertigo, a light-headedness. But now she is really in agony apparently and I feel as if I am assisting a euthanasia. Then my vertigo turns into pain too and a kind of tunnel opens up inside me for a second, then closes over again. It is as if I have died momentarily then been re-born, but that is probably an overstatement; the impression is very fleeting, possibly illusory.

Now Donna is soaked in sweat and sort of sobbing and panting at the same time for some reason, as if she has just been chased by a tiger and got away by the skin of her teeth. She hisses into my ear: -*Male... I'm certain of it... Definitely male.*

I lean over her, and she still clings to me, ankles against my ribs, as I reach for the last handwritten letter, and our hands and fingers meet and entwine and diverge, arms reaching together across the floor, fighting, pushing the letter away, then only just catching it and bringing it back, up to my face. I unfold it behind her head on the floor and flatten its pages down and start reading.

Donna looks up at me oddly, her breath coming back.

What is it? -I ask.

Oh nothing... -she says, -*don't mind me.*

I kissed your President only last week. And I must confess, out of sheer mischief and despite the risks...

~

10b: _Himeropa

...to disappear without a trace.

"If any man in ignorance draws too close and catches the singing of the Sirens, he will never return home to see the joy of his wife and little children at his homecoming; for the high clear voice of the fair-faced Himeropa will bewitch him..."

-Homer.

"Supposing truth to be a woman... what then?"

-Nietzsche.

I kissed your President only last week. And I must confess, out of sheer mischief and despite the risks: I lingered there a little too long and sent my tongue into his cheek. He scarcely knows who I am, I suspect. Just some bohemian singer in a local nightclub, whose reputation has been spreading recently. We looked in each other's eyes for just a second afterwards, before the bodyguards and the weight of history swept him away downstream. But I believe I saw something there: that seed of recognition, of weakness, of fear.

I'm not from around here of course. Everyone can tell, as if my name, my skin tone, my accent: are all just slightly tinged with a drop of some alien colour, but the trace is too faint now to identify precisely. I have been called everything in my time: dago, wog, spik, chink. *We don't see many of your sort here,* -the kinder ones say. But I enjoy this *otherness:* it is a habit I have acquired; it is why I came here.

There are various stories going about. That I was widowed in a war, that my family were slaves, that I was raped by my father, stowed away in an oil tanker for 6 months, worked as a prostitute in Lisbon. I suppose all are true or lies by varying degrees, depending on your attitude to metaphors, your love of a good story. The drunken fools in the nightclub where I sing – they catch fragments of my life from my songs or from my exchanges with the other musicians, and they weave these into entire fantasies of who they want me to be. I do little to discourage them, not so much from mischief as from sheer inertia.

I just let all these misunderstandings fall around me, I think of them as tributes. I enjoy the confusion, and the anonymity they afford me. I wear them like silk scarves, gossamer, smoke or fog. But even the most sordid of these stories are perhaps more grand and noble than what actually befell me.

I had a husband and two children in the port of Neraz where I grew up, on the shores of the Mediterranean. We were poor but moderately happy. Like most people in the town we had little knowledge of any other life so did not poison ourselves with envy. Neraz is an ancient town, its centre unchanged since Roman times, whose labyrinthine streets seem to grow out of the steep grey hillside like a colony of barnacles. Being a busy port, it has probably harboured most of the world's diseases in its history, but one day I caught a virus there like no other before and my life was changed thereafter.

As I lay in a fever, my whole life, every memory, began to replay at random. I suddenly saw that life was not a straight line I stood at the end of, but a circle within which I stood at the centre. From this viewpoint I could travel to any part of life at will – time was an illusion. Gradually, as though hidden in the shadows, I saw my future memories emerging also. Like timid birds from unseen shores, they came to land on my wrist one by one, if I could just lie still and quiet for long enough, if I made my mind ready for them, as light as a bed of feathers.

I saw that I would leave and travel to a distant city where nobody would know me and I would live under an invented name. I saw that, like the birds, I must polish and hone my voice each morning at daybreak until it was sharp enough to pierce the heart, bright enough to lift the sun out of the ocean. I saw the faces of the people I would meet who would help me, I heard the words I would use. Then I travelled backwards, back to my earliest memories of playing alone in the gardens by the fountains, and with the sand and the pebbles down by the shore. I saw there what I had forgotten: that when we are youngest we are not alone, but a presence lives in our head and whispers to us and watches over us. Why do we forget? I met this presence again and saw that it had watched me always, content to have withdrawn and observed me from afar as my mind grew and left its care. I knew then that this presence will return at death to enfold us in its arms, but I saw also it was neither good nor evil, but both savage and merciful by turns. I saw that it did not judge our behaviour like some churlish vengeful God of the church or the mosque. Rather it encompassed and accepted responsibility for us as its creation. We were its expression in everything we did. There was no guilt necessary.

I saw many things that to this day I cannot put into words that anyone will understand, except before birth or after death. I saw the patterns of wood grain on wardrobe doors blow into the turbulence of stormclouds and waves: I heard their music, the mathematics of creation itself, constantly modulating and changing form inside me. I felt how a flower can become a shoe or a knife just by brushing its hair sideways, re-aligning its atoms like a shoal of silver fish. I remembered how, as a baby, I had tasted the intense feelings of colours, how each shade we see is trying to share with us its story. I saw that there are talking faces everywhere in stones and leaves: changing expressions, whispering to us as we pass by oblivious. I felt the laughing sigh of the wind encircle the earth and choose me as its bride.

As my memories spun around me, I saw the darkest ones last, the forbidden ones my mind had bent and hidden to protect me. I saw that my father had done something unspeakable to me when I was less than four years old. I recalled the smells and the jolts in the present tense, like every memory in my fever: it played like a movie clip, so I relived every horror, but amplified with the burden of hindsight. I awoke in a cold sweat of disgust, my hands writhing over my own body. I felt as if my life were a sacred jar I had been forbidden to touch, but breaking this rule in secret I had scattered the pieces over the floor. Now I was trying to sweep up all these fragments and hide them before my parents returned. My hands swept over my feverish body, but as I awoke fully I realised that this guilt was not mine to bear, that others had shattered that jar and so they must pay for the injury.

As my fever subsided and I sat up in bed, I realised that my mind had been permanently altered. I saw clearly that my sister was laughing at me because she thought I was exaggerating my illness to avoid housework, to feel sorry for myself. I saw that my husband only loved me if I wasn't ill, if I wasn't inconvenient to him. I saw clearly that this was not just mine, but everybody's problem: that what we thought of as profound love was merely a tissue of convenience, and if our lives change or diverge then this construct will quickly give way and disintegrate. I saw how no one really knows or loves another person, just holds onto them for a while as they dream, eyes closed, our hands searching blindly over each other's faces, painting imaginary features over white canvases of flesh. I saw that no matter how deeply you try with how many partners, you will still die alone without ever having been truly known or understood for a second. This knowledge almost overwhelmed me with sadness for a moment and then a strange exhilaration came over me, as if the truth, no matter how cold and shocking, was like fresh air, life-giving.

I stood up shakily and went over to the window. I opened the shutters and saw as if for the very first time: the vast blue ocean that filled the high horizon. It glittered like a jewel, it roared like a lion, it smiled and bared its white teeth, its million white horses. Then I knew that it must carry me to a whole new life and all the tumbledown houses and alleyways of my youth were just arbitrary scenery I could sweep away with a flick of the wrist. I knew that my face, my body and soul were all the possessions I required, and with these and the cunning of my words I could turn myself into anything I wanted to be, could bend every foolish man to my will for a while. I felt electricity begin to pour through my veins, giving me the grace and stealth of a tigress.

I could feel already the wrench of leaving my children without saying goodbye, my two baby boys. My only solace was that my fever had shown me their futures: I had already seen that they would survive without me, and although they would be strangers to me, so were all children strangers to their parents. The sacred aura around them is not our love or our ownership but the reverse: they are on loan from a higher power, who protects them until they forget him. I saw that although to harm these immaculate little strangers is the worst of transgressions against nature, to assume them as your property is equal folly.

I found them playing on the stairs and I sat with them for a moment, running my fingers through the locks of their golden hair as they concentrated on a jigsaw they were trying to solve. Too absorbed to pay me much attention, I just sang them a little melody under my breath. Then distracting them for a second, I stole a single piece of the puzzle from under their noses and hid it in the folds of my dress. Later, on board ship, I would while away the hours working a tiny hole through its centre with my hair clip, through which I could thread a leather thong. I wear it to this day around my neck as an amulet. It is a worn and faded fragment now, but still recognisable as part of a picture of a sailor on a boat.

I looked into the eyes of my poor weak husband for the last time and told him I would be back in ten minutes. Then I went to my father's house by the back streets and let myself in during his siesta. I remember the rugs hanging in the shady hallway brushing my cheek as I passed, like pleading children, their bright colours screaming for attention. Without waking him, I entered my father's room, slit his throat like a pig's, then washed myself in the yard outside, the blood whispering over the cobbles, vanishing down the drain. I felt no emotion then and never have since. I hid out in the tar barrels at the dockside until nightfall and then stowed away aboard *The Mariella* as it sailed at dawn the next day for Malta.

There were other boats. In Piraeus I fluttered my eyelashes at the captain of a fishing boat, and he gave me free passage to Naples. He thought he'd consummate our little bargain on my first night on board, but I consoled him in other ways until the final night before we reached port. Then I let him kiss me, but even as he clambered on top of me on his damp little bunk, I felt the life drain out of him prematurely. He sat up and covered his eyes in horror, weeping like a baby as his ardour subsided. He said he had just seen himself through my eyes, as a blubbering unshaven seal in a string vest and that every movement he made was as if he were penetrating himself with a harpoon. I tried to embrace and comfort him, but even as I kissed his ear he shivered and grew colder again, saying that this time he had seen what his crew really thought of him, that his first mate was plotting against him, and the pilot had informed on him to the harbour authorities. *It is in their eyes,* he kept muttering, *it has always been there, but now I can suddenly read it*... I calmed him down as best I could, but a terrible brawl ensued on the quayside the next morning during which I slipped away unnoticed.

Next I fell in with a nightclub owner in Rome and, while in our four months together I learned a lot about the music and entertainment business, all he learned was that he was not the real father of his first child, his wife no longer loved him and his accountant had been embezzling from him. I however, developed no small affection for this man who was as kind as a grandfather, but felt compelled to finally leave him before his life's disintegration progressed beyond any hope of redemption.

Now I knew for sure I was some kind of carrier of an unknown virus, and half in despair, half in curiosity: after months of drinking and loose living I found myself among the harlots of Marseille. There I set about making myself enough money to get back on the straight and narrow. Men's sordid appetites presented no new mysteries to me, and I hoped, since kissing is banned in such places and protection is encouraged, that I might discover for myself some new *modus operandi:* a way for me to continue functioning as a physical woman without causing psychological damage. But it was not to be. Coincidence or not, in only my third month there I overheard the *Madame* whispering about how the takings had fallen recently and many loyal customers had been having personality crises or inexplicably failing to return. It was too much, and I panicked and packed my bags that night.

I was in Paris after this, where, confused and lonely, busking and hanging around outside rehearsal studios, I ran into the famous Brazilian singer Prasabao. I caught his eye one night as he shuffled out of his limousine in the pouring rain. He brushed his aide aside and took his umbrella in his own hand for a change so that he could come over and listen to the strange deranged girl who was singing under a streetlight, her hair dripping wet, accompanied only by a double bass and a snare drum. He said I seemed possessed by the *Duende*, as Latin people call it, which has all the metaphysical dimensions of the Germanic *Angst* or *Stimmung* for instance, but with a note of madness and a love of death which only the Mediterranean peoples can express.

He wanted me to sing backing on his new album. He told me I had the voice of a fallen angel, that I had shattered all the mirrors in the glass palace of his fame, his prison. He was full of this kind of romantic nonsense, as you might guess from listening to his records. Of course he had a thousand girls throwing themselves at his feet every time he stepped out in public. Of course, he told me they meant nothing compared to me. I was the *real deal,* he said, and how right he was, except I wonder if the terms of the deal turned out as he imagined.

I got Prasabao to teach me guitar, piano, how to write songs, how to speak Portuguese, Spanish, English and German. But as he dissected each of his songs in order to explain them to me, something terrible began to happen. The more I questioned and the more he explained, the more we both realised the underlying patterns that were common to all his songs. Sitting on his knee at the piano, I would smile as I recognised a system or a technique, a run of chords, an inverted melody. I would smile because I thought he would be pleased that I was mastering his art. But slowly I saw that these observations were as revelatory to him as they were to me. As months went by, I learned much and began to write music myself with growing confidence. But by the same degree, I saw that I was robbing Prasabao of his spontaneity, that I was creating in him a new self-doubt.

For the first time, his brimming self-confidence that had carried him forward all his life began to recede. Even his legendary confidence with women began to leave him. Our analysis of his lyrics exposed them daily as *schmaltz*, templates of sentimental confection designed to push all the right buttons in teenage girls and unfulfilled housewives. He saw at last that, rather than bringing hope or happiness to the world, his songs were lies that made the perfectly good lives of decent people seem shabby and inadequate to them in comparison to his sugary fantasies. Compounded by his own limousine lifestyle, he saw that he had become a fountain of bitterness and disappointment in the world, a magnet of envy.

Seeing his own words of love exposed in this way gradually robbed him of the ability to say anything romantic again, in songs or in private. The great seducer was rendered powerless to woo. As he slid into the depression and alcoholism that was to be so well charted in the media that year, I moved into the shadows of his life, frightened by his growing paranoia, his accusations that I was sleeping with his friends. These fears became so insistent at times that I even wondered if they weren't voyeuristic fantasies, requests he could only express openly by cloaking them with mock indignation.

Towards the end, I would often awaken to find he had been just looking at me naked for hours, or running a chaste hand across my skin, like an artist's. But when I moved towards him his eyes would fill up with tears as he found himself inadequate.

Even months after I left him and we were continents apart, he still insisted I was his muse, that I belonged to him. Rather, I felt by then he had belonged to me, but in the same manner as a worn-out pair of old boots: something that repeated use has made very comfortable and easy on the eyes but which to wear again would be perilous, would only risk destroying them.

I wept when I read about his suicide, but I cannot say I found it unexpected. I cried for him, but perhaps I also wept for my own discovery that there were no idols in this world worth worshiping, or rather: that to try to truly get to know them is always to unravel them, to destroy the very thing you seek.

Since then I have travelled through many countries and cities on my way here, gradually developing my singing and enlisting the musicians of my band. As they and my few other friends will tell you, it is only those who keep me at arm's length who seem to survive my acquaintance. If you have some commitment or prejudice like marriage or impotence, then buy me a drink; your foundation might be safe. But if you are like most men, then that little quiver in your heart or in your trousers is never far away, and if you once yield to it then you will think that you can have me, and well you might, except that the rest of your life thereafter may prove a burden heavier than you have strength to bear.

Perhaps my music is too strong a ferment to risk taking undiluted or in all but the smallest of occasional sips. Maybe this is why the band and I like to change the venue, and even my name every so often. I have seen too many fresh-faced young clerks or well-dressed middle-aged fathers reduced to the pale sweating likeness of opium addicts, that desperate expression, the grimace of skulls. It begins with them turning up every night, then pushing to the front of the audience, asking for my autograph, buying me a drink. It ends with them stalking me, trying to follow me home. It ends with the abandoned wife, the neglected job, a forgotten life, the descent into debauchery. If they're lucky, after this short-circuit there may be re-birth, a new start from the hard-won *Nadir* of self-knowledge. But most end up as vagrants. You find this unlikely, my friend? Then you underestimate the value of those shackles of habit about your wrists: you fight them, but a lot of the time they are all that keep you up. Let me take this example: just try speaking the truth for one whole day to everyone around you, and by the end of it I promise you will be sitting in the gutter too.

So just imagine the trouble if your President fell for me, enchanted by my singing, if he called me up! I know, it sounds like a crazy fantasy doesn't it? But I saw that fleeting look on his face, and he seemed strangely haunted at his next Press Conference, his eyes watering. I think he will remember that kiss.

As for myself, I have learned to be at peace with my own company and my many memories; which flock around me of an evening like gentle doves. I live alone in my loft overlooking the riverfront of this city of yours, where I can watch the sun rise and set and the boats drift back and forward on their way to and from the boundless sea, now out of sight, over the horizon. I have a few canaries in cages, who sing to me now and again, and I reward them with a flight about the house, as much freedom as their little hearts can bear. I have tasted every flavour of life, and now solitariness presents no shadowy horrors. I no longer need any man to tell me my name and my purpose. Nature has spoken to me and I have understood. The amulet around my neck reminds me of the price I have paid to live in truth, the missing jigsaw piece, the memory of my beloved children. For each person the price is different, for most the sacrifice is too great.

So this is why I sing, and why the wise among you should be content just to listen without wondering too much as to the personality behind it. Just pick the rumour you like best, and stick with it. I have learned to enchant and soothe other people with my voice just enough to be bearable, whereas actual physical contact would risk too much damage. What does it matter who sings or even writes a song anyway? I am only the carrier, remember, and you are the hosts.

~

Snow is falling when Martha finds Dundas inside the ruins of Fraser Finch's house in Helmlea Gardens. *Careful,* he says, closing the steel door behind her, *-I should really have brought us two hard hats, health and safety and all that...*

Martha shakes her arm free of his protective clutch. An ugly gesture he thinks, and not a good omen.

In the cleared central area of the building, they are able to see up to both the front and rear elevations, each now propped with safety scaffolding.

Where did he die? -Martha asks.

Dundas smiles grimly. *-Sort of everywhere, Martha. The roof was still on back then, and his body lay undiscovered for three months, so he dissolved really from about that point there at the half-landing of the stair.*

Dissolved? -Martha contorts her face.

A mixture of battery acid and garden fertiliser, the forensics said. He had inadvertently managed to lace himself with some kind of electrolytic mixture that, after death, enabled the bacteria in his gut to re-metabolise his body proteins into nutrition for Serpula Lacrymans...

Martha raises a quizzical eyebrow.

That's Dry Rot, more commonly known as. A fungus that eats buildings. Sheets of networks of feathery roots, grey and yellow, then fruiting bodies, mushrooms. All it needs is a little moisture and off it goes for years, can grow right through stone, brick, plaster, and wood of course.

Martha leans to look at the blackened pool of moss and fungus surrounded by white threads growing from the end of the broken staircase, its second flight just running out into space.

Don't get too close, Martha, the fruiting bodies can blow spores into your lungs...

You're kidding me? -Martha exclaims, -*that's like something out of "Aliens"...*

No... seriously. Dry Rot can infest and ingest an entire house given enough time. It's amazing stuff really. I can show you photos sometime.

Is that what those are? -Martha asks, pointing at the folder under Dundas' arm.

Dundas looks downs and remembers: *–These? These are the photos of Finch's remains. Want a look?*

Laying them out on an old trestle, Martha reaches her hand out to touch them, as if in disbelief.

Apparently, we each contain about a thousand trillion bacteria, that's ten times the number of actual human cells. They outnumber us. Over 500 different species inside every one of us, obedient little buggers mostly until the day you die; then the party starts and they set about converting you into something different. As Finch's body decayed, the fungus grew, fruited then spread out. It partially redistributed him as a mycelium network…

Then some of this guy is still here? –Martha almost gags.

Genetically speaking, possibly. There may be some of his DNA in the moss and fungus, although we did hose the place down and fumigate at the time. I mean, it was four years ago, Martha, and we're talking about a process at the molecular level… you're not going to find a finger or anything.

The wind changes and a few snowflakes land on the plastic covers of the photos and Dundas starts to fold them away. When he's finished he finds Martha over at the rear façade, looking out through the blackened walls towards the snow-covered back garden.

So he's part of this building now, this guy… Martha says, almost dreamily.

Dundas half laughs, snorts. *Sort of, Martha, I suppose. But he's just dead like anyone else.* He leans against the stonework and looks sideways at Martha who gazes out into the garden, eyes miles away. Finally she speaks:-

I've always loved snow. It reminds me of when I was a child. What is it that it does to the world? Wraps it up like a Christmas present or something? It makes everything look so new and pure, and yet deathly cold. The garden you played in every day, the world you thought you knew, was just taken away overnight and replaced with a new one… like a revelation.

And yet it's so transient… Dundas says.

What? -Martha seems to wake up, looking at him.

Revelations, moments of insight are always fleeting, don't you think? Like the snow always melts too soon, unless you're old and afraid of it of course…

Were you ever a child, Walter?

He smiles and shakes his head, *-Oh I doubt it, don't you?*

Back in the car, Martha suddenly remembers something, fishes around in her handbag and produces a cassette. *Do you mind?* -she asks, and Dundas shakes his head silently, turning onto the main road.

Three minutes later, as snow falls over the windscreen, Dundas turns off the wipers and turns the car into a lay-by, and to Martha's surprise turns the engine off. Not saying a word, he just continues to stare over the steering wheel, transfixed by the music he is hearing.

It's Hamira Mediora... -Martha says. *-I managed to get a copy of her demo tape sent up to me.*

My God... Dundas mutters. *That's like nothing I've ever heard before in my life.* The hairs stand up on the back of his neck. The voice is deep then high, guttural then soft, moving between mysterious Arabic half-tones and a lilting operatic sadness.

The next one is in English, -Martha says. The snowflakes falling on the window gradually make the car's interior dark. When Martha moves over to kiss him, she can taste the tears on his cheek for the first time, his body suddenly shivering in the cold.

~

9b: _Homunculi

...What does it matter who sings or even writes a song anyway? I am only the carrier, remember, and you are the hosts...

My nerveless fingers slip, the charred sheets of paper fall away one by one, and sail on the chill breeze into the autumn cornfields, peeling away like dead skin, the memories of my time among the living. So now I must be dead, or rather I have woken up, while the rest of you sleep on.

But my condition has certain advantages: now inanimate objects obey me. I tell my left arm to move and electrical wiring from the car wreckage around me springs into action. Like little hissing snakes in primary colours, these attach themselves and intertwine around my ruined body, filling in the gaps.

Gradually, like some new reptile separating from its shell, I am born again, a compound man of bone and plastic, wire and rusted metal, extricating itself from a burned-out car. My headlamp eye blinks in the late sunlight. My right foot snaps and I replace it with what was once a wheel, now a buckled rusted disk. Like this, progressing a little unevenly, I trundle and stumble away from my blackened technological eggshell – towards civilisation.

The farm track leads back towards a small hamlet: I watch it growing as I approach. My breathing is heavy, but broken now, blended with a kind of electrical wheeze of actuators and hydraulic fluid. I can see down through my own face, now patched with the small antiquated glass chambers of thermal diode valves sparking red and orange, obsolete technology. The printed circuit-boards have been saved for my chest and skull where they continue to interact inquisitively with a restless network of wires, seeking to optimise my performance, requisitioning all available hardware.

I reach the garden of the first house at the edge of the fields. I leave a little trail of oil and blood across the pristine lawn. I press my face close to the patio doors, the picture window: my unimaginable reflection looming towards me for a second. Inside, a woman paints a canvas on an easel, her back turned. I place my fingers on the door frame and send a current around it until I feel the lock and disarm the electrode. Then the door springs open.

The woman drops her paintbrush and spins around, smudging her hands against her smock: -*Who's there?! What do you want?!*

I step into the room, and I see her reaching for a piece of wood against the wall, but she seems unable to find it. I move to the left but she keeps looking ahead, addressing me as if I have not moved.

Are you blind? -I ask her from the side and she turns again, my voice breaking like a wave of static on a de-tuned radio.

What is it you want? Money? I have only loose change in the house! -her voice is trembling.

Nothing... -I say finally, *or the truth perhaps... but relax, I will be gone in a few moments.*

She steps backward, and, feeling for a chair behind her, half falls into a sofa.

Y-Y-Your voice... -she stutters, -*something's wrong, isn't it? Are you hurt?*

Damaged maybe... but aren't we all?

She puts her hand to her head, brushing the hair from her sightless eyes which dart from side to side across the room intermittently, like a silent metronome. *Yes... I suppose you could look at it like that.*

Do you wish you could see me? -I ask.

She stiffens, her hand tensing on the sofa arm, -*Are you trying to read my thoughts? Who are you, please? And what do you mean by barging into my home like this?*

I don't know who or what I am, but maybe you can tell me. What happened here last night, out in the fields? Did you hear anything?

I was here painting, -she says, standing up, gesturing towards the canvas. -*All I heard were the usual noises, the Saturday night demons, joyriders – they're not even teenagers you know. They're children or they should be were they not the brutalised and debased offspring of a damned generation. Juveniles, so even the police can't touch them. Like us, they must just stand by and marvel at these little gargoyles in hoods and tracksuits who dismantle nightly our civilisation, our faces lit by their flames...*

And if you're blind, -I say, wheeling across the room, my metal scraping slightly on her polished wooden floor, *-then what on earth are you painting, and how can you see it?*

Now we stand almost side by side in front of her easel. She raises her hand towards it, as if her fingers can feel it without touch, as if it gives off light or heat.

But it's just a scene of a perfect field, -I say, turning around. *-It's the view from that window, a view you can never see. How can you paint it?*

I saw it once, and I remember it always. It lives on in my heart and my imagination. Beethoven was deaf, wasn't he?

Now I notice for the first time that classical music has been playing quietly somewhere in the house. *And what if I told you that it had been torched?* -I ask *-That the demons had devoured it in the night and replaced it with smoking black wasteland?*

They haven't, not yet at least, and when they do I will still have the painting. The perfect field will live on inside the world of my canvas, the way I remember it, glowing gold under an autumn sunset. An evening like the last one I ever saw, on the night of the car accident when I lost my sight and my lover and nearly my own life. So long ago now. But there are different ways of seeing you know, and many realities...

I turn, *-and that's how it is now you know, a sunset over the glowing fields.*

I know, she says, and thrusts her palette knife straight into my side.

I clutch her hand, and instead of withdrawing the knife I push it slowly, further and further in, as she begins to struggle.

With my other arm I hold her neck, and push her arm up to the elbow until the palette knife emerges on the other side of me, burning flesh and electric hissing. *There, -*I say, *-are you happy with that now? How does it feel, right up to the hilt?*

*But what are you!? -*she gasps, *-my God, how can you be alive?!* Her other arm searches over my torn frame. Her touch recoils in the way that seeing eyes would brim with horror.

I withdraw her arm, and push her back onto the sofa with a hiss of steam and the crack of electrics, lest they try to assimilate her into me.

What am I? I suppose I'm the future. If you think things are bad now, just wait until the demons grow up. You'd be glad you were blind then. Tell me, what are the opposite of cherubs called? Goblins? Homunculi?

Don't hurt me... I'm sorry... I can answer one of your questions, she says, her head in her hands, starting to weep in fear and confusion. *There was an explosion last night. I know that sound – it's a petrol tank igniting, and I smelt it in the air. They must have blown up a stolen car, the children, out there in the fields.*

And where do they live?

She lifts a shaking hand towards a corner of the room behind her, *-Over there, over the hill, in the towerblocks on the estate, the concrete wilderness that they have tattooed with their spay-painted logos; strange insignias like the hieroglyphs of a new language only they can understand. Every morning, their signs are found further afield, on the walls and gates of good people. It isn't safe to go out after dark, their howls and barks fill every night with terror. And night is falling now. Let me call you an ambulance... I'm so sorry I tried to hurt you. I was frightened... everyone's so frightened these days... what's your name? Your voice reminds me of someone I think...*

Her words trail off as I stumble out into the evening air, the wide sky overhead starting to catch fire as the sun departs. Behind me, left in the room alone, she continues to confront and negotiate with empty space for some time. A pool of oil and wires left behind at the patio doors continue to hiss and writhe after my departure, before slithering their way towards her Hi-fi system and injecting themselves into the back of it. The Beethoven transmutes into Stockhausen.

The other side of the hamlet is bound by a roadway, a blurred river of lights and sound. I approach its precision, my half-mechanical body quivering in excitement, as if gaining strength from this technological Ganges. It makes my knees bend. I kneel and pray before its exquisite dangers, its sleek impenetrability. I dig my metal fingers deep into the edge of its tarmac. I push my face forward until passing cars miss it by a millimetre. I smell their petrol, the heat of their tyres on the road.

Beyond this, on the other side, I see a hill of scrubland rising up – a no man's land – and beyond this, a daylight moon now beckons behind the bone-white towerblocks, the implacable teeth of the estate – the home of the homunculi.

And just as I ponder how to cross this river, I see some dark hooded figures on an overpass dropping stones and concrete slabs. A car window smashes and the vehicle careers out of control. A crushing impact. Wicked laughter peels from above. The car, now embedded in a wall, bursts into flames, the dimmed occupants gesticulating helplessly before vanishing into the miasma of heat. Their brief screams are like the screeching of car brakes but less effective: they stop nothing.

Confusion is mounting, cars slowing, sirens sounding in the distance. I cross the road in the gathering dusk, unnoticed.

Darkness has fallen, as my creaking frame and buckled wheel carry me into the home of the homunculi. I am quickly surrounded by the concrete teeth of towerblocks, a broken crown of some concrete utopian vision long discredited. I am dwarfed among its ruins, a miserable white grub traversing a bleached carcass.

At street level, this is a landscape of ruptured tarmac and untended grass, burnt-out wrecks of cars and ruined garages, boarded-up shops. Buildings that might once have been locked-up at night and held activity and commerce, then progressed to "dangerous structure keep out", are now finally open again as the playthings, the wendy-houses of the demons, the un-children who have known no childhood, who will find no adulthood, who have no future. Their avid eyes gleam from the shadows of the ruins that I pass.

The first stones whistle past my ears as my arrival begins to draw their interest. I hear their language, their shouted cries; perpetual punctuation of fucking this and fucking that, strutting peacocks of brutality, constantly competing on some abstract scale of cruelty and crudity. Every building I see now in the moonlight is tattooed to saturation point with their graffiti, their nick-names, their logos, their taunts, their boasts. Fuk Yeez awl. Mentol Teem. Yung Fleet. Nightly gang-war is their recreation of choice.

Finally, my way ahead is blocked by a gathering of ten or twenty of them: all small and hooded, as if stunted by generations of malnutrition, offspring of single-mothers perpetually drunk, beaten and smoked as kippers throughout their pregnancies. *Hey Mister, ar yoo Polis?* -they crow. Their little hands begin to reach for me. *Hey! He's wired! This cunt's goat fuckin wires under hiz jaiket, he's fuckin polis man!*

They touch the wires, and sparks and flashes leap out, one of them is electrocuted and sent reeling backwards by about ten feet, another one is held in contact a little longer then slumps on his side, smoke emerging from his hair, the rubber of his training shoes melting. Still another is rapidly entangled around the throat by a swarm of wires that emerge, snakelike from my arm. I hold him up like a ventriloquist's dummy until he's spilled out his last expletives and expired. Still rolling forward, now the crowd is gathering around me, but backing out into a wider circle, tentative, afraid.

Eventually the little gargoyles think of a trick, and master it. Like some bizarre game of hockey or shove-ha'penny; they use scaffold poles and planks to hold me at a distance and shuffle me towards the den of their leader. They are nothing if not resourceful.

The King of the Homunculi is covered in tattoos from head to toe. He looks me up and down and asks: *Whit ur ye man? Who sent ye? Ur ye sum polis contraption, man, a parkin meeter wi wheels? Ah mean, whit's the fuckin sketch man?*

I don't know what I am. I woke up like this, wondering what I am, and so I set out on this journey, asking those I met, looking for clues, trying to travel back to the centre of the mystery of all this, to find my creator and confront him with all that he gave me: my broken body and mind, these warped and flawed creations.

Whit, ye think we made ye, ya maddy? Ah'm no a fuckin spark man, ah'm no a mad professor. Ah've never clapped eyes oan ye before, an let's face it, ah'd no forgit in a hurry if ah hud.

Didn't you burn that car I woke up in? Down at the fields beyond the village?

We torch a loat a cars every night mate, but not wi cunts in them generally. Torch them so the polis dinnae git prints an shit oaf them.

He sighs and takes a long look at me, then his mood seems to suddenly change: *-Here mate, let me show ye sumthin...*

The King of the Homunculi drops his façade and beckons me to follow him to the inner sanctum of his den, followed by two of his praetorian guard of neds with chibs.

Ahh noaked this crackin big plasma thi ither night mate. Look at it, it's a fuckin belter, int it no? Thing is, ah cannae get it tae wurk like, and here seein' as you bein' a machine-human hybrid and all, mibbe ye can rig sumthin' up wi' it eh? Ah mean c'moan Scrappy Man, let's see ye dae yir tricks, make it zing. Let's see ye dae it, spoil me, I want it all because I'm worth it...

He leans closer to examine the plasma screen, keeping on babbling all the time, until with one impressive flurry of movement lasting less than a few seconds I take the coaxial cable, Ethernet cable, scart lead, universal serial bus lead, and parallel interface cable, and shove them all, firmly and respectively, into his throat, ears, nose, and anus.

The guards are fairly straightforward to electrocute with a flick of 240 volt mains power supply, while the King's cries I subdue by force-feeding him his own mobile phone, which, conveniently downsized through repeated and unnecessary redesign by the manufacturer, is thus able to pass, though not without some difficulty and tissue damage, down his throat and into his stomach where its irritating ring tones are at last quietened.

So now the plasma screen flicks into life in the semi-darkness, and the homunculi arriving on the scene are stunned into silence at the superlative picture quality experience on offer:

On the screen, a Roman legion marches into the glass and steel ruins of a partially-flooded city of the 21st century. They are confronted by aggressive gangs of heavily tattooed Caucasians: the designs on their skin are the fantastical tendrils of Celtic and Pictish art; like the Book of Kells, but also intertwined with the unmistakeable visual swagger of street art, sprayed stylised graffiti…

Powercut. Everything goes black.

*   *   *

Huv ye enny last wurds fur uz, Scrappy-Man? -sneers the brand new King of the Homunculi, no more than an hour into his tenureship. His gargoyle features lean closer, uplit eerily in the deranged light from his flaming torch. One of his cohorts starts a ceremonial drumbeat on an empty gallon-can of vegetable oil from the local chippy.

Yes, I have. I have no right to have ever existed. I am a freak, a fabulous anomaly in a grey world, something easier to ignore than to understand. Burn me now, and let my butterfly life and death be like a siren wailing through the streets of this sleepwalking city. Let me dazzle the commuters, the traffic-jammers, as I pass them by, the miserable rich, time-starved, contentment-starved, who hurry in their metal shells past the outskirts of housing estates that resemble war zones, where demoralised robots move jerkily around among the graffiti, as if malfunctioning, sustained on Buckfast, Termazapan and dole cheques, servicing the Bookies Shop like bees in flowers. Our world is both monstrous and beautiful, and yet we are mostly blind to it, blinkered, hurrying on, tuned into radio, TV, infotainment, the anaesthetising soup of non-thought. It keeps us on the level, smoothes out the peaks and troughs, man. We are all junkies. So burn me now. Fix me.

And with that, the homunculi bind my wrists to the spokes of a timber cable drum two metres in diameter, and set me burning and rolling through the darkening streets of this city. The town is built on a tilting plain towards the sea and now I roll the whole length of it, spinning fabulously in the crucified pose of Da Vinci's Renaissance Man. If I had a stomach, I might be sick. Now every street I have ever walked in my long and many lives gyrates and coalesces into one symphony of speed. May every man, woman or animal who has ever had anything to do with me now pause and look towards their street's end to see the momentary blaze of this magnificent passing. I am red and orange with fire and anger, I am white with speed, I am cold blue with melancholy. What a show.

My flesh burns in the turning wind, my bones go black, my scream cuts into the night air. I do not wait for traffic lights, I move faster every minute. Until at last my scream is laughter. I feel nothing anymore except exhilaration. The blood red sky fades into extinguishing blue as I am spat out at last from my treadmill town, too bitter a pill to swallow, this life lets go of me. I spin off the end of the last street and sink into the forgiving ocean which receives me with a sound like a long sweet sigh.

~

8b: _Bedrock

...*like a long sweet sigh*

...I spin off the end of the last street and sink into the forgiving ocean which receives me with a sound like a long sweet sigh.

I finish reading, fold up these curious notes and return them to my pocket, stepping down from the farm gate I have been sitting on, to resume my walk home.

How did it ever get so late in the day? Now I must come down from this hill; leave this view behind and descend into the town of my birth, my childhood, to find myself again. My head hurts, my limbs ache, but something else is wrong. The pavements seem suddenly older, more worn, fissured with moss. Passing cars seem faster, more frequent, smoother, colder, more silver, deflecting light, no knowable faces within. My footsteps echo through streets used only by machines – no dog walkers or playing children.

The gardens of my friends are unexpectedly overgrown, as if their parents have moved house or become suddenly senile. But wasn't I here only last night? I knock on a door, but it seems abandoned, windows boarded over. I shiver in the shadow of a porch, look about, move back onto the street, late sunlight burning my eyes.

I hear a sound from across the road. There is someone knocking on the frosted glass of their door, waving from inside, fumbling with keys in the lock, impatient to gain my attention. I move closer, a woman's voice, muffled by the door, is saying: *Raymond! ...Raymond... what are you doing here!? I can't seem to get the door open... Raymond!*

The house is overgrown with ivy, ivy on the paths, ivy up the walls, even encroaching on the window glass and door frames. Puzzled and yet strangely entranced, I walk down the garden path towards this door, the shape behind it growing ever more animated and agitated, until my hand reaches out to touch the frosted surface of the glass.

The door springs open, and the woman falls out, almost into my arms, her long black hair enveloping my face in a warm rainstorm. Her tumbling motion terminates with her holding me face to face, her hand on my shoulder. I have never seen her before in my life. She smiles broadly and kisses me on the lips. I am shocked and stumble backwards. Although attractive, she must be twice my age, wrinkles around her eyes, a few grey hairs starting to show on her head.

What's wrong Raymond? You look like you saw a ghost...

How... how do you know my name? -I stammer, embarrassed, stepping backwards.

Her brow furrows, her dark eyes quizzical, then she laughs: -*Ahh... one of your gags again eh? Don't mess about, Ray, and come in out of the street before anyone sees you. Here I'll put the kettle on...*

Taking advantage of my increasing confusion, she slaps me on the back and ushers me into the house and locks the door before I can object. Her face is close to mine again and I flinch involuntarily. *You're all clammy, Ray, like you've been sleeping rough or something, what the hell have you been up to? Out on the ran-dan again?*

She leads me, numb like a sleepwalker, and sits me in the living room, then returns with a mug of coffee for me and kisses me on the brow, nearly making me spill it. *I'm running a hot bath. I think you could do with it, what?!* -She pauses, looking down.

Please don't do that... -I say quietly, eyes falling to the floor

Oh, a bit delicate are we, eh? Say, what were you up to last night? Drink? Drugs?

Before somebody sees...

She is moving about the house while I talk, walking in and out of the room, tidying up. On the windowsill I notice a vase of black roses dropping the first of its petals to the floor, the sound like a tiny thunderclap from a drowned world.

What?

I run my hands through my hair, trying to think straight:-*You just said a minute ago, "Come inside before somebody sees"... why would you say that? And look, I'm sorry, but how do you know my name?*

Ray...woahh there... you're getting weird now. You come here every other night these days, usually after dark

though, right enough, so the neighbours don't talk and your wife doesn't find out?

Wife!? -I say, standing up.

Yes, and no there's no need for a standing ovation. In fact usually the mere mention of her has the opposite effect on your capabilities.

My what...?

She comes back into the room, and we face each other again. She reaches into my inside pockets and searches until she withdraws a small polythene package of powder. *Give it a rest Ray, either this gear has seriously messed with your head this time, or this is one of your weird fantasies or role-playing games, in which case it isn't working since it isn't very funny and it's certainly not turning me on.*

Look, I'm sorry -I say: -*I don't know what's going on but this feels all wrong right now. I don't know who you are, as far as I know I have never met you before, but you are acting like you've known me intimately. It's like I'm in some weird dream or nightmare but I can't wake up. I've never been here before in my life, this house, its colours, its smells, this is completely alien to me. I feel sick, I think I need to go outside, I'm sorry...*

Oh you poor thing! -she says, then clasps me to her chest. *You need to sleep this off. You can hide out here for a while from Maria, but first the hot bath.*

...From who?!

Forgotten the dragon's name at last now, eh? Well.... That IS progress...

And who are you?

Nadine, of course, Mister Memory. Nadine, and pleased to meet you... again.

I sink into the hot bath my head still spinning from last night's forgotten excesses, too tired and shell-shocked to resist this stranger's inexplicable hospitality. My head falls back, my eyes close, time passes.

*   *   *

I wake up suddenly to find myself shivering uncontrollably. The whole surface of the bath is ice, frozen solid, only my neck protruding. I can see my limbs jittering in the slush down below, unable to break through. I am crying out, but my breath is just a hissing white fog rasping through the air in front of me, spraying frost outwards.

A grey raincloud starts to form inside the bathroom in the air above, darkening until a black vortex at its centre releases a snaking arm downwards, the tail of a tornado reaching down to scrape at the ice's surface. Looking closer at the turbulent changing surface of the cloud, I see that it is a woman's long black hair, twisting, treacherous, voluptuous.

The vortex breaks through the surface of the ice, and I feel warmth flooding in as I shudder violently. The black snake of hair is moving downwards and upwards, twisting around me as my body jolts rapidly from extreme cold to hot. The hot quickly becomes unbearable.

I open my eyes and find I am in front of an open fire now, on the living room floor, writhing to free myself from a sheet of long wet black hair that has been clinging around me. Nadine's hands are on me, pinning me down, her face breathing next to mine, telling me to calm down as I panic to break free. I am sneezing and coughing up liquid ice as I shudder violently. Some of this fluid lands on the flames, dousing them a little, some more lands on Nadine's bare arm and she bows her head over it, running her tongue and lips over it, gulping it down.

I am unclear as to whether she has been encasing me in this living cocoon or assisting me in escaping it. Each strand of her hair almost seems to have its own life, like the snakes on Medusa's head.

I break free, and swing my arm too hard as I do so, sending her reeling backwards across the room. I prop myself up on my arms, naked, the fire behind me hot on my back, an empty black cocoon of hair lying on the polished timber floor between us, bearing the clear imprint of my whole body, crouched, foetus-like. Nadine, starting to cry, emits a low animal whine as her hands writhe, drawing back from her face to reveal her now entirely bald head.

I try to stand, shakily, to make my way towards her, but she wails, covering her face, gesturing defensively, scrabbling for the door handle, leaving the room. *Come back, come back, I just need to understand...* -I call out but I fall over, my foot dragged down by a loose strand of hair that is now writhing, malevolently reinvigorated, working its way up my inside leg. I fight at it, tear, bite through strands until my gums and fingers bleed, finally escaping the room.

In the hallway, I try each door in turn to find only an empty room behind it, until I try the bathroom. When I prise the door open with a cracking sound: a complete vertical wall of ice is revealed behind it. As if poured into a mould, it bears the imprint of every grain of the panels and handle of the door itself.

I feel I can discern some movement behind the ice. Rubbing my hands across the frosted white surface I gradually clear a smoother transparent panel to which I press my eye. Distorted, as if seen through the bottom of a hundred beer glasses, I think I can make out Nadine, seated there, semi-conscious, head thrown back in a trance, as a stream of black hair pours out of her, into the pipes, onto the floor. Turning around, I see that the living room door I have just shut tight is already fringed around its edges by hissing black hair, leaking out from under the threshold.

Outside it is winter now, the season inexplicably changed, snow on the ground, my disorientation complete. I step back from the gutter at the bottom of the garden, as I hear gurgling from within: snakes of black hair beginning to emerge, searching for me. I notice my footprints behind me already in the snow, think of the network of drains beneath every street, every house in the town, the difficulty of escape.

The sun is going down, night will fall soon, the world freezing up in cold storage. Even in snow, these streets are inescapably familiar. I seem to know vaguely where my feet are taking me. After a few blocks I turn into an avenue that feels like home.

I arrive at what looks like my parents' house, but already something is wrong. Several of the old trees have been felled and cleared away; the hedge, dripping with snow, is wildly unkempt. I go around to the back door, old habits being hard to break, and my heart lifts at the faint familiar glow within. My hand turns on the handle and it emits a dry creak I have heard since childhood. I can hear it anywhere. I have heard it inside my head in many times and places throughout the world. I have played it to myself like a lullaby. The day this handle is oiled is the day I will die, my identity crumbled into dust on the wind.

The kitchen floor is covered in dirt, drifts of sand, the walls and furniture stained and decayed. I stop in my tracks, then two old white-haired creatures emerge from the shadows and shuffle towards me, arms outstretched. I barely recognise them, and yet some part of me cannot refute the likeness. Here are my parents, or some grotesque semblance of them, covered in wrinkles, hair and teeth fallen out, a foot shorter in height – pitiful dwarves. Their clothes are stained and crumpled. They seem scarcely able to walk or speak, supporting themselves on tables that they pass, dribbling mucous from their mouths as words fall out so ill-formed as to be useless to my ears.

What... what happened? -I say, tears welling up in my eyes. *What's happened to you both?* The little grey dwarves reach me and cling pathetically at my legs, like the inhabitants of Lilliput.

Ray...mond... -they mouth, and hug me like they have waited a long time for me in some cold grey place in which my name was their only light and heat.

They sit me down at a table covered in dust and stains, pour me sour milk in a cracked stained mug, offer me stale bread curled at the edges. Their eyes expand and contract as I talk, like children or drunks, as if my elixir of news and youth is too rich a brew for their fragile systems.

How's... Maria...? -they say.

Who?

Oh don't be funny dear..., your wife... your good... lady... ?

Now it is my turn to stare blankly, and then I see it: that we are a trio now, of equally bewildered souls in a world grown alien around us.

You... don't... remember? Oh don't be silly..., you're too... young... to be losing your memory... like us... Have you banged your head, ...dear? -They laugh together now like little elves, their senses of humour grown childlike, their attention span shrunk to minutes.

They show me the room where I grew up, its dimensions now reduced to the cramped and absurd. I recognise pictures on the wall that I gazed at as my consciousness first evolved, on long afternoons of boredom waiting for adulthood to begin. I feel suddenly dizzy with the memory of the quantity of waiting and wishing that life entails. And all for what? To see those you love and admire shrunk to senile hamsters?

What happened Dad? -I shake him. *I left here yesterday and you were tall and strong. You were even frightening sometimes. You had sailed the world and fought with Germans, you carried me on your shoulders, you chased me with a bucket of water on Elie beach. You were stern and resolute, a giant whose feet I played at – whose head, way up there in the clouds, saw the future, saw the sense of things, knew the answers. Where has that man gone? What happened while I was away? I was gone only a moment, or perhaps a day – did I fall asleep and the whole world pass me by?*

I'm... still... here, son... he says, with difficulty, each syllable an effort, but a childlike smile on his face, tears in his eyes. *You were here yesterday... you just said you were going... out to meet some... friends...*

Yes, Dad, and I suppose I did, except that everything else happened too, didn't it?

Not... not... a... disappointment... I hope?

No, no, anything but. The world was like you said it was, but better. I just wish I could show it all to you now, how much better it was, how you didn't need to be so sad all the time while I was growing up.

His eyes glaze. He lights a cigar, now almost as big as himself and fills the room with mustard gas, and sighs reflectively, as if he can breathe easier now.

Been a fair... innings son. Time to make... way for the... next crop... of idiots.

Now Raymond... -my mother shuffles back into the room dragging her way through the drifts of sand, supporting herself off door handles and dado rails. A cupboard door she nudges falls open and more sand pours out across the faded carpets. *-Will you... stay... the night?*

No, no, thanks, I can't.

Come out for... Christmas?

When is Christmas?

Both their little brows furrow again in that look of abject vacancy.

Can't remember dear... Dad, can you... remember?

Who? What?

Christmas... When it is...

No... search me... never liked it anyway.

I hear a sound from the kitchen behind them and I go through to see black hair starting to emerge from the taps, the plughole, the overflow.

Mum, listen... I have to go...

Oh no... dear... don't... -she says, her eyes watering again.

I need to leave you alone now and take my trouble with me, but tell me what you remember. What happened to you?

But nothing happened dear..., life happens, it always does... whether you're paying attention or not... We're all abandoned to our fates...

But to you I mean. You were beautiful, you were young, dreaming, aloof sometimes. You cried to yourself in secret, you ran away when you couldn't cope with us, and we wondered if you'd come back, but you always came back after a long walk, God knows where. There was resistance inside you, hidden outposts, places nobody could reach, but now it's like you're surrendered, it's like you're a chuckling child on a Disney ride wondering what the next tunnel will hold. Where did that woman go? I never knew that woman, and now I never can.

I'm still... here, silly... -she says and presses me to her chest, but I know that she isn't, except that she lives in me. That woman is walking now, wearing floral print dresses and Eau de Cologne, walking through the chambers of time and consciousness. And soon that walking will have finished carrying her all the long and lonely unknowable way from her to me.

Before I leave I ask her for her address book. After much ferreting around and laughter and forgetfulness, the thing emerges, page after page of her big baby writing – at least that hasn't changed.

What are you looking for, dear?

Nothing... I lie, memorising my own address, my home with "Maria", whoever she is.

Mum, do you think I am happy with Maria?

Why...of course... dear... There isn't anything wrong is there?

No, no, I just wanted your perspective. Do I love her, do you think?

You never talk like this normally, dear, but since you ask... I'd say she means more to you than anything else in the world.

I kiss them goodbye and hurry out into the moonlit street, resolved to find my way back to Maria. But the black hair is out in the gutters now, eating all the snow. And as I approach her neighbourhood it seems to intensify: festoons of the stuff, sizzling, crackling like seaweed exposed at low tide; the hair is climbing up lampposts, forming bridges across the street.

Like the Prince fighting through the woods to uncover his Sleeping Beauty, I try to do battle with the hair, but as it tightens around my ankle and throat I am beaten back, retreating, giving up, always the coward where women are concerned, in awe of their supernatural power. I turn home, but with only a vague sense of where home might be now.

Slumped in the clothes of defeat, I catch the late train back towards the centre of our sprawling city. The full moon rides high above suburbia as I bid it farewell, the darkened gardens keeping their secrets, their hedges eating up the last traces of my life. I grew up thinking these silver rails were the way into excitement and fear, all that was yet to come, my life not yet started. They pointed like darts, to the centre of the bull's-eye. Now they are old and rusted, the sidings overgrown in the flickering pale floodlights as we pass. Whatever happened to me, my personality, vanished down this route, was sucked into the voracious city centre, the ashes of my identity scattered over the streets of strangers, on the floors of cars and buses, pubs and lounges and bedrooms, the humdrum apparatus of boredom.

I remember the summer evening I left school; I thought it was only a month ago, but now it feels like an age. I walked home across the fields, gazing up at the growing sunset, wondering, marvelling at the thought of all that I would do, the unimaginable achievements, the girls I would kiss. My body floated with potential energy, my feet scarcely touched the earth – I had won my freedom. I was so young and at one with the late summer sounds around me, twittering birds, lowing cattle, the drone of distant suburban cars. Everything seemed to make sense. I felt myself lifting up towards those clouds, that future, like a magnificent offering, a laurel wreath for the Gods to wear.

But perhaps the Gods are cruel. I turn now and see my face in the dark reflection of the train carriage window, as we begin the long rattling descent through the metal tunnels towards the city's cold mechanistic heart. My face is lined with a millions laughs and frowns now, my eyes darkened with the permanent stormclouds of consequence – I am a map of the world. But did I say cold? These old tunnels and vaults and bridges are still stamped with the craftsmanship and love of our Victorian grandfathers. Their city still echoes with their melancholy statues, their mossy quays that launched riveted steel hopes towards murky colonies, their arching carousels of bridges that clothed the sky like ladies corsets.

The train rattles deeper and deeper, the glimpses of the world above less frequent. I see flashes of light reflecting off pools of water on the tracks below, seeping upwards from subterranean chambers. How well has this old heart been maintained? Are the brick-vaulted ventricles too choked with moss to go on palpitating? Isn't there always a time of reckoning up ahead, when the systole and diastole falter, the lungs collapse, the rails run out?

I am reminded of a childhood fear on this journey, that the train would go too deep and fall out into the sea. Now it does indeed take a different turning: could they have altered the route in the time I've been away? How long have I really been away?

The doors open, and as so often of late, at night, I seem to have been the only passenger, not even a driver to be seen as I saunter out, not onto a platform, but the soft sand of a beach over which the sun is somehow rising again, a silver light blowing in from the waves, ruffling my hair, reminding me I am alive. The beach is wide, the tide far out, I have a long way to travel to the water's edge. I forget what age I am, what age anyone is. I carry my parents inside me as surely as I carry my children, born or unborn. And my lover waits where the sun melts into the glittering ocean, whoever or whatever, she may be.

~

7b: _Paternoster

...or whatever she may be...

I have seen the old photos. My father had a fine face *(façade)* once, a good *(bone)* structure, captivating pair of big eyes *(windows)*, and a strong dignified looking mouth *(shopfront)*.

Like every son, I thought he would go on forever. But it's not just about maintenance, is it? If we look closely at what maintenance really consists of in even a wealthy face *(façade)* over a few decades then we probably see that every atom has been replaced in the end: that what we think of as repair is really just complete piecemeal replacement. So in many cases, like my father's, it is decay that sets in and wins the day in the end.

Firstly his hair *(roof)* went and, not having the money for some grand remedy, we merely furnished him with a hat. It did the job in a way, but still the rain crept in and drop by drop began eroding the integrity of everything behind his face *(façade)*.

Then a vein *(downpipe)* collapsed, closely followed by a few more, and blood *(rainwater)* began to spread unchecked across his cheeks *(walls)*. Of course his eyes *(windows)* had also been gradually accumulating dust and deteriorating generally over the years. It was only a matter of time before an accident *(vandals)* befell him. A stone from the street put out one of his eyes *(windows)*, leaving unsightly shards until we covered it with a patch *(hoarding)*.

Somehow we imagined the structure would remain safe, but life and decay are merciless. The constant weathering, increasingly unchecked, weakened some of the muscle *(structure)* until sags and cracks and partial collapses began to appear all over his face *(façade)*.

His mouth *(shopfront)* had long since fallen largely out of use and, after the stroke *(break-in)*, it had to be abandoned and boarded-up altogether. During the stroke *(break-in)*, a fire was lit in the upper floor and much of the contents *(memories)* and B-listed interiors *(thoughts)* of my father's mind *(house)* were destroyed.

It was strange, and sadly haunting, to unlock the steel door at the foot of the stairs, with all its warnings of collapse and danger, and climb with my brothers, our hard-hats on, up into the ruins of the stair-well and walk through the blackened shells of all the parlours and salons where we, his sons, had been brought up. Looking upward through all the charred bones of exposed floor joists, we could see the pale blue sky with its grey spindrift clouds trailing southwards like rain-heavy bombers.

We remembered my father's stories of his wartime service in the navy, felt the enormity of the great thoughts that had once filled these rooms like music and stalked these corridors like diligent housemaids. We felt the youth and strength of our own bodies, and, with a leap of imagination, knew that our father had once felt this way also, that these rooms had been bright and new, polished floorboards and gleaming crockery, echoing with laughter and talk of plans and futures.

We stood there with our overalls and torches among the soiled oil paintings and eviscerated sofas floating in rainwater and, as I looked up at the distant aeroplanes passing overhead, somehow one of them peeled off and spiralled down towards us like an ailing mechanical bee. A spitfire in its original markings came crashing through the remnants of the roof and sliced angrily through several dozen floor joists until it came to a precarious rest: nose down, tail up, held within the mind *(house)* like an impaled butterfly from some archaic natural-history collection. We were shaken but happily unscathed, and once the fuselage fire subsided even the pilot got out and walked off laughing. Then below us we saw ghostly throngs of people in period costume come swimming in out of the street, moving this way and that, conversing feverishly, buying newspapers and groceries before hurrying off suddenly at the sound of air-raid sirens.

All that unsettled us more than a little, and after making the mind *(house)* as secure as its ruinous state could permit, we exited with the resolve not to return unless strictly necessary, lest a repeat of these uncanny events should occur.

But the City Council just can't leave things alone, can they? Last week they slapped an order on us and took custody of our father from us – the effrontery of it! Teams of men with truckloads of steel and concrete mixers arrived and began working, cordoning off the whole block, closing the street to traffic.

Today I see they have demolished everything behind my father's face *(façade)* and left it propped up with a steel skeleton. Everything they found inside his mind *(house)* they have skipped or sold to the scrapyard or antique shops. They tell us his noble old face *(façade)* will just hang there until they find some young healthy *(wealthy)* candidate to build a new mind *(house)* behind it and look out through his eyes *(windows)*.

I have my doubts about such a grotesque proposal. Already there are trees and grasses and mosses taking root in the bare ground behind his façade *(face)* and I suspect and hope that mother *(nature)* will take her natural course and dismantle and consume my father, long before any young whippersnapper arrives with half the gumption necessary to fill the old man's shoes. His stones *(bones)* were part of her cliffs and mountains once after all, and we should all do well to remember that everything is borrowed in this life, until its owner returns to put us straight about it.

~

It's unhealthy, Martha… -Dundas sighs, standing at the window and parting the blinds so that sharp moonlight falls across him and the wall behind. *It's like a fetish… a perversion… Is this the kind of people we've become?*

So what… -Martha mutters, staring blankly into space from the end of the bed, her knees tucked up under her chin.

Outside the quiet streets are still dark, but a few birds are starting to sing. Dundas remembers it will be Spring soon, and morning even sooner. *You've not been the same since you met him, Martha, or met what you thought was him or what he had become. Are you sure you still can't remember anything about that entire day?*

She shakes her head, eyes staring ahead; listless pools of blackness.

The copy-taker said it was your voice that phoned in, so unless Stark's a ventriloquist or impressionist then it must have been you talking, albeit in a hysterical or hypnotic state. It's as if you thought he was Jesus,

Martha. Is that what you think, that Stark's a messiah?

Martha speaks, her mouth slovenly, her expression heavy as if pained by some invisible weight:- *Silly question, Walter. What is a messiah anyway? The word means different things to different people. To a Christian, a son of God, a spiritual saviour; but to a Jew, just a man, a visionary leader descended from King David. I think he was, or is, a man with an idea, or who stumbled upon an idea, quite literally fell over it and tumbled right out of the world... or out of our version of it.*

And what was that idea? -Dundas asks, his voice suddenly distant and strange as he stares up at the moon.

Martha looks up and blinks, and for a moment in the stripes of moonlight imagines that Dundas has turned into Stark, staring right back at her. She shakes herself and Dundas returns, staring sideways. *The idea is that humanity is an Atemporal Group Consciousness. It's not that far-fetched. Ants and termites must have something similar going on. Perhaps the surprising thing is just that we aren't all aware of it yet. Maybe there is some kind of seal in our brains waiting to be broken, a safety mechanism, a psychic hymen. Humanity has done enough damage as individuals. Do you realise we each re-run our whole evolutionary journey in the womb* as a kind of reboot sequence? A foetus has webbed fingers and toes, even a tail until the tenth week then it's deconstructed and re-absorbed for the task in hand. Maybe we should look more closely and find clues to our future evolution there too. Physics and maths are not half as certain as we are about our relationship to time, it could just be a by-product of cell decay, shortening of telomeres, some onboard biological clock to help us navigate life. Sub-atomic particles can travel backwards in time, you know. Strange but true. They alter their behaviour depending on whether a human being observes them or not... perhaps that's a clue... that life is no accident in the universe, that consciousness is somehow at the heart of why the universe exists at all and what it is striving towards. Imagine an apple exploding into a thousand pieces that each fall and rot away to nothingness, then imagine a film of that scene played backwards in slow motion...

You're saying our relationship to time and to our own bodies is not fixed? That's crazy talk, Martha... the road to the asylum. You're losing it...

She stands up and goes to the toilet, and after several minutes Dundas wonders for the first time if she might become suicidal. To his surprise he finds the bathroom door unlocked and ventures in.

He is alarmed to see that Martha is covering an entire wall with an intimidating and chaotic display of Stark-paraphernalia. Photos of Margaret Alloway's body covered in grey paint; close-ups of her closed eyelids and mouth. An O.S Map covered in intersecting pencil lines and circles around sites of local ancient monuments. A second century map of the Roman Empire. Police diagrams of the intersecting ropes in Fraser Finch's house. Photos of the body of Valerie Henderson partially frozen in a garden pond covered with autumn leaves, close-ups of her nose and mouth emerging from the white surface of the ice. Photos of chalk geometry theorems drawn over black-painted walls in Valerie Henderson's house. Colour photocopies of oil paintings: Icarus And Daedalus by Frederic Leighton, The Fall Of Icarus by Pieter Breughel, Odysseus And The Sirens by John William Waterhouse, Hector And Andromache by Georgio de Chirico. Various Piranesi etchings from his *Carceri* series. A translation from Arabic of the lyrics of one of Hamira Mediora's songs, which he moves closer to and reads:-

> "*Snow is the blanket that God would throw over us, if he only existed, if only he cared for us. Falling, caressing, protecting our innocence, slowly and smoothly removing our differences; his hand on this sheet now reclaiming his progeny, less like a shroud*

than *swaddling for christening.*
Colours   depart,   tones   and
shadow   predominate,   turning
the   ordinary   to   revelatory;
showing the dream underlying his
masterpiece,   magical,   patient,
and gently victorious; a dance
in   a   paperweight,   a   memory
manifest, under the stars and
the   streetlights   innumerate;
sparkling   of   frost   like   a
children's   kaleidoscope,   the
blossoms of flakes passing under a
microscope, ceaselessly falling
and taking our eyes with it,
backwards and downwards away from
self-consciousness;   guarding
our   memories,   distracting   our
enemies, preserving our longing
in ice for eternity; drowning all
sound in a death that is beautiful,
drifting, enchanting, and sweetly
mysterious; laughable, playful,
infinitely serious. Snow is the
blanket that God would throw over
us, if he only existed… if only
he cared for us."

It's an odd subject for a person of middle-
eastern origin to choose for a song, don't you
think? -Martha asks, adding more handwritten
notes over the maps.

Why? -asks Dundas, backing away.

Well, snow only holds nostalgia for a European, magic for an African on first seeing it maybe, but never nostalgia. Surely sand or rain would fulfil that role in their culture?

Jesus, Martha. Dundas catches sight of his own angered expression in the mirror and winces. *You think Himeropa, I mean Hamira Mediora, is Stark, don't you? Have you any idea how insane that is?*

Why? Men can have an extra sex chromosome: the 47 XXY Karotype gives rise to Klinefelter's syndrome. It means high estrogen, excess breast tissue, sterility and potential imbalances in Dopamine levels in the brain, making you susceptible to depressions, psychosis and shizophrenia...

In plain English... you mean he would be a transsexual or a hermaphrodite? And you don't think his wife would have noticed?!

It's not that simple. Several species of fish can change sex during the course of their lives as a survival strategy. In fact, some of our chemical pollutants in rivers have started causing havoc by making them change sex.

Ridiculous Martha... and what about Visconti and Finch and Margaret Alloway? Are you about to say he became them too? We have birth certificates for some of these people, records of their childhoods !

Perhaps he met them and took them over... by hypnosis, possession, like a poltergeist...

Even more ridiculous.

Then how could he have known all those details of their deaths? Details you say never entered the public domain, even at the coroner's inquests. Like the network of ropes in Finch's house, the underwater room in Margaret Alloway's?

Perhaps he had a mole at Police Headquarters. One of my staff in his pocket.

Any candidates?

Dundas shrugs and backs away toward the door. *-None that would have had the knowledge of all the cases. That would have taken active research, someone working late at night for instance at my office, but then I would have seen them - I practically live there myself.*

Well then?

Unless I'm Stark... And now Dundas laughs, rubbing his face and turning back towards her, eyes widening: *-Or you are?*

With difficulty Dundas gets Martha away from the bathroom wall and back into the bedroom and sits her down. *Martha, this isn't healthy... you're killing yourself.... it has to stop. Alexander Stark just disappeared, lost his memory then wrote some crazy letters about things. OK, let's say he was clairvoyant or something, let's accept that. Maybe he had a brain like a de-tuned radio and picked up things, you know... all the thoughts of all the other suicidal whackos that were on the same wavelength at the time... that's pretty interesting and strange, granted, but it doesn't make him a messiah.*

Not yet anyway? -She interjects, -*until he rises from the dead.*

Dundas returns to the window, and sees a warm glow of light forming on the horizon, knows the sun will soon be lifting. *Perish the thought...* he sighs, *Look at all the trouble it caused last time.*

You don't believe, because your mind is closed, Walter. You're a plodding pedestrian, a train trapped on its rails. You won't entertain anything that's not been proved and tested on the Scottish Primary School Curriculum for at least three hundred years...

Dundas absorbs the insult, expecting it now like a bucket of water over the face. Indeed, he goes to the sink and washes his face while he considers his reply.

He looks at Martha over his shoulder in the mirror and notices the little asymmetries of her face which his familiarity usually blinds him to. *Maybe it's a good idea to keep your mind closed, Martha. If you leave it open there's no telling who or what might get in...*

She yells back: *So you think I'm losing my mind, you're saying you think I'm a crackpot now, and let's take note here: that's AFTER you've shagged me!?*

Yup, he says, nodding his head and rubbing it with a towel as she puts on her dress and shoes. His attempt to complete the sentence is interrupted by her slapping him hard across the face, but after a pause he still manages to shout after her as she slams the door on her way out; *I'm saying you need professional help now...*

He turns back to the mirror to his own perplexed face, then follows round to something that has caught his eye: on the bathroom wall Martha has pinned a handwritten letter from Stark. A new one perhaps, one he has never read. He is disturbed to think that she may have been withholding evidence, but even more disturbed as he reads it and begins to vaguely feel that it relates to him:-

"The Inhabited Man sits in his Winter overcoat on the evening train as it waits at the station. He counts the minutes before the train will leave, and gazes absentmindedly at the silver rails of the line adjacent, and it occurs to him that the rails are like the veins and arteries in his own body. He feels suddenly huge and empty, like this Victorian hulk of a station roof that arches over everything like a sickly sky.

The Inhabited Man opens his overcoat, and its heavy material rolls away like a crumbling façade. Beneath it we see he is segmented, subdivided into open boxes, a monocoque structure, eggcrate, latticework, just a scaffold on which to hang a sober human facade. But what a mess beneath. A cloud of chalk dust blows away from his coat and he worries for a second that the other passengers might see, might get wind of the disordered wonders he hides inside himself.

He slips a hand into his own interior and here is the house he grew up in, just above the section that holds the house where he was born, just to the left of the doll's house replica of his first flat as a student. But these aren't models, these are real and these are each him. In each of the miniature houses, amazed parents and friends back away in horror from the massive hand that intrudes into their world, passing seamlessly through their walls, appearing out of empty space.

The Inhabited Man pulls out his hand and looks up and wonders if all the other passengers are inhabited like him. Behind their poker-faces do they each hide such multitudes?- These hundred-thousand random stages and scenes in which the dramas of their lives played out, and still play out, trapped and frozen in time like flies in amber, snow in a paperweight? Falling, falling, the hapless protagonist of these inner plays is always tripping, joker, clown, stooge, butt of all the world's jokes, the curtain falling as he grabs its velvet surface and it tears in two with a comical rip. A lonely drum beat and a cymbal crash wash in the wake of the wave of laughter, immeasurably cruel.

He bares his left arm a little and sees the veins, the

pulse, the inescapable rails of the to and fro that must go on there, the routines that cannot be sidestepped or denied. His blood is a bored commuter between the lungs and heart. The destination boards outside purr and whir and the minutes click down towards the inevitable. He opens his overcoat again and reaches into the warmly lit interior of his suburban bungalow where his wife waits by the fire, singing to herself and reading a magazine. She does not look up to see his huge hand pass by in the darkness outside the window, does not notice its fingers intrude and turn the clock hands back on the mantelpiece behind her.

Through the wall, a naked girl, younger and more beautiful, lies on a bed half-asleep, satisfied and drowsy, mumbling to herself, not noticing that the blanket that is pulled over her now is not held by her lover, but by the enormous fingers of his hands, fingers whose touch and fragrance she knows but which at this scale could only fill her with cold terror.

The hand withdraws, and follows through instinctively to present his ticket to the inspector, the Inhabited Man calling his distant eyes back to this moment as the train is about to leave. But she seems alarmed, and repeats her request for a ticket until he looks down and sees that what he is offering out in his hand is not a ticket but a tiny velvet curtain. He briefly faints at the sight of this and his head slumps to his chest and there he sees that the woman in the warm living room can now look into the other room where the naked girl is waking and sitting up and walking towards her. On the open boundary between their two rooms, at the junction of disparate carpet, paint and wallpaper, the two women stand and face each other, reach out hands to meet as if to the surface of a mirror. He tries to cry out, and wakes himself up.

The Inhabited Man stands up in horror, knocking the Ticket Inspector aside, and lunges down the aisle then out onto the platform, stumbling, wavers, runs again, and throws himself under the 6.20 from Edinburgh.

The women inside him turn slowly, held in motion like marionette figures, dancers in a paperweight playing out an icy scene, trundling as if on rails towards the border of the next room and the black curtains automatically parting there to reveal a coffin laid out on a table. There the silence knots itself up like a handkerchief, like bitter curdles in the milk of time."

Towards the end of the letter and as he finishes it: Dundas put his hand to his throat and shakes, then slumps, partially collapsing against the bathroom wall. The letter falls from his hand like a broken arrow shaft that has left its poisoned tip embedded in its victim's side. Dundas sits on the bathroom floor for several minutes, breathing heavily until his palpitations subside.

~

6b: Scarabolis

...to put us straight about it.

Giovanni Battista Piranesi - 1720-78, Italian etcher, archaeologist and architect: became famous for his hugely exaggerated and poeticised etchings of the ancient ruins of Rome, and his imaginary Interiors and Prisons, heavily influencing the neo-classical movement in Architecture, the gothic in literature and the Surrealists.

I was awoken, not by the singing of birds but by the sound of giant beetles passing beneath the window. The citizens of Scarabolis have tamed these threatening creatures, and take rides inside them, clinging to their gleaming armour. Every household has at least one, and a giant kennel where it can be restrained for the night. They feed them a foul-smelling brown elixir that they ferment over centuries in strange underground orchards. They make the beetles run along black ribbons that criss-cross their fields like woven threads. This ribbon material has a surprising texture, rough and yet almost soft like cushions, and they constantly dig parts of it up at random and bury treasure beneath it. I wondered if the ribbons were sacred to them, they bestow them with such significance. Perhaps therefore these diggings are to enable citizens to bury offerings to their Gods like votive prayers or rosaries.

My hosts ushered me to their bathroom, indicating that this was their ritual each morning; to be blown about by cannons of hot water spewing angrily from pipes hidden insidiously beneath their walls. What alarmed me more, however, was the vast array of potions and distillations that the lady of the house had accumulated and stacked the bathroom high with on innumerable shelves. The bottles were in a myriad of different shapes and colours, each labelled brightly in a dazzling diversity of designs obtained from countless mystics and apothecaries scattered throughout their empire. Hypoexigesal Moisture-Rising Epidural-Enriching Nourishment Beauty Balm, with extract of Anthrax and Wasps Milk. Yellowcake UF6 and Aloevera Bunker Buster. Seratonile Bath Bombs with Hepatytis B Weapons-grade Plutomial Bath Salts. I became scared, in that locked room, that some of these volatile ingredients might combine and burn a hole in the universe.

For breakfast, they sat me down, not around a family table to discuss their dreams or their children's futures, but in front of their favourite window, one whose ever-changing view held the constant attention of the whole family. I was horrified. Violating our privacy immediately, a smiling man and woman, complete strangers both of them, sat right outside the window and looked in at us and told us terrible things. I wanted to cover my ears, and I turned to my hosts expecting to see that they were in tears, or preparing to pack their bags and escape to the hills. But no, they were quite calm, and assured me that this was what happened every morning and that they were used to it. The smiling people in the window said that their empire was ending, their enemies were invading, that Scarabolis would be flooded soon, that the orchards and fields were all dying, that everyone would choke to death on the fumes from the accumulating excrement of the giant beetles. Are these people not reputable Seers? -I asked, are you not afraid that these curses will come to pass? Not at all they said, there is still time left before the end. I was impressed, I must say, by their stoicism. Their love of their Gods must have made them very devout and ready to meet them.

I should explain that the Scarabolins are not like us. The mother of the house resembled an ordinary Italian woman it is true, notwithstanding her outlandish local garb, but the father had the head of a dog. How long ago this scandalous mutation had occurred among their race was not known, but now it was quite common for citizens to be half-canine, and not frowned upon in any way. Their two children were half-caste as you might expect: though pink-fleshed as their mother, their heads tapered seamlessly into wolf-like jaws and dripping tongues. They barked and snapped at each other as they rolled on the carpet fighting. Their mother fed them crows and sparrows on plates, which she fetched from an aviary in the hallway, discreetly ringing their necks as she returned to the parlour.

My hosts insisted that I see how they live and work, that I should come with them to meet their Lords and Magistrates in the centre of their great city. I was honoured, but afraid when I realised that this would mean I had to ride with them on their beetle. The thing was passive until I approached, and then it began to growl and shake. I was sure this was because I was a stranger and that it didn't like my smell. Frankly I was petrified, and secretly clutching the crucifix beneath my tunic and praying for protection from our saviour who seemed no less a stranger than I to these lands, so little had I heard his hallowed name. But the beetle seemed to calm, however, once I was sat down between the two wolf-children and, at the crack of a whip from the father of the house, it roared obediently to life and scuttled down the road.

Now this was bewildering. Other beetles were scuttling everywhere, and fighting with each other, locking horns, ripping off claws and antennae. Once again, my remarkable hosts were strangely at peace however, assuring me that their beetle was a prize fighter and would see off all the lesser breeds. It was all like some huge race, like a *Circus Maximus*, and uniformed stewards appeared from time to time with burning torches that they used to scald the beetles' legs and keep them in check. How could everyone endure such drama and peril every day? As if all this wasn't enough however, my hosts said they wanted to play me some music at the same time. I laughed incredulously, wondering where an entire band of minstrels could be concealed under the folds of the armour of a running beetle. But then some hideous rhythms began to pulse from out of the body of the creature itself, shaking us to the bones. I flinched, but my hosts seemed to enjoy it. It was nothing but a panicking drumbeat, charged and urgent like some buried memory of being born, over which a dying violin or trumpet would occasionally be allowed to fall like a forlorn flag of hope. The only vocalisations were in strange accents and an incomprehensible sub-language. This chanting, my hosts explained, was by a race of black slaves that the Scarabolins kept. They lived in poverty in walled ghettoes, trading lethal chemicals with each other, and were farmed like yeast by the white people who creamed off the best of what they produced for them – music and drugs.

As we approached the centre of Scarabolis, I became astounded by the size and height of their buildings, and overwhelmed by the urge to make drawings and etchings of them to show to my countrymen upon my return home. Palaces and warehouses and cathedrals stretched into the sky. They did not have windows, they WERE windows. Everything was glass. Glass was like a skin, and stone was reserved for tenuous skeletons that hid beneath this surface. In other words, these buildings were alive, made like living things, blasphemously copying nature itself. Alive also literally, in that through the glass skins as I gazed up, I saw citizens scuttling everywhere like ants, all of them moving frenetically as if engaged in some common enterprise whose nature I would never discover.

Thus in a state of shock, almost, I was helped down from the beetle's back by the little paws of the laughing wolf-children, and their parents led me towards a vast glass cathedral that towered above us in the blue summer sky. Before we reached the entrance, I had time to turn and see the streets around us, and notice to my astonishment that all of these were also teaming with citizens, all running around and around as fast as they could, as if running from something or from each other. It seemed like a game whose rules I had not yet been told.

Words cannot describe the scale or grandeur of their glass cathedral. Which God it was dedicated to, I was not able to ascertain, as if perhaps he was a secret God whose name was forbidden to be spoken lest this invoke his anger. First of all I was to witness the daily work of the father of the household: he took off his clothes and we saw that he was a bipedal greyhound, a lean and awe-inspiring physical specimen. Wearing only a bright identifying bib, his team colours, perhaps, he jogged out into a vast arena in the basement of the cathedral, and we took our place among the spectators to see what happened next. The ritual was feverish and mystifying. He and many other greyhound-men of competing teams ran in circles howling and barking, while other team members chalked up numbers on huge fiery blackboards which hung from the vaulted ceiling overhead. All the time, streams of paper fell from the ceiling endlessly, like confetti for an invisible wedding. I picked up a few and tried to read them, but they were like poems composed entirely of numbers, as if mathematics were the chosen music of this civilisation. Perhaps it was all a simple race that the spectators were betting on, but I never saw any winners nor any conclusion to the sport. In this respect, it was more like the activity of those pagan priests who strive each day to offer up the prayers without which they believe the sun will not be able to traverse the sky.

Then the mother of the household signalled to me that we were to leave the arena, and to ascend into the vast upper storeys of the cathedral where she would show me what her daily duties entailed. I became agitated as she ushered me into a large bucket of glass and metal. But then, when some of the stewards starting hoisting the bucket skywards with us in it, I fell to the floor and wept in fear, sinking my teeth and fingernails into the carpet. But my hostess caressed my head as if consoling a distressed pet, and urged me to open my eyes. After no little encouragement, this I did for a moment and saw that the bucket with us in it was now hundreds of feet in the air and sailing ever higher by the second. Seasick in the extreme, when we finally came to rest, I crawled out on all fours, expecting to be laughed at. But instead, here I found another huge throng of people, all quite engaged and absorbed in their own obscure mental activities, who paced to and fro, shouting to each other and crowding around windows that showed only views of numbers, this strange mathematical poetry again.

Then I was brought to the centrepiece of this floor. Here, under the tilting faces of the glass cathedral spire, were set up an array of large telescopes pointed down at the distant crowds below. Now the view from here was certainly beyond description. I could see the whole of the city of Scarabolis, its many other tall glass palaces and churches, its labyrinth of streets, and beyond this distant fields and sea. But through the telescopes, as they showed me how to use them, I was able to observe the individual faces of any of the million strangers running and hurrying around the streets below. I could see their very expression, a bead of sweat upon a brow. But now events took an unexpectedly sinister turn. My hostess ushered me back towards the perimeter of the room so we could observe what happened next.

The telescopes were not just for this viewing function alone: but on the hour, a clock would sound a chime overhead, and an ice pellet, hard as a stone and as large as a fist, would drop from a hole in the ceiling and land on a silver dish at the centre of all the devices and spin there at random awhile before losing energy and falling down into the neck of one of the telescopes. Then by some fiendish mechanism, with no living hand involved, the telescope would fire the ice pellet with terrible force and speed towards the distant moving crowds below. Silence reigned after the shocking event and eagerly my hostess led me forward to look down the telescope through which the projectile had just fired. To my horror, I saw there an innocent citizen lying dead upon the pavement, blood and melted ice now trickling from a wound at his heart. Nobody stopped to attend him, all his fellows too panicked and hurried to risk slowing for a second. And then, before I could protest this injustice, I heard a great beating of wings above us. And there above the glass lantern, as if lifting off from a ledge or perch, a fiendish black Harpie flapped into life, with two masked Scarabolins clinging to its talons. The gruesome scavenger swung down across our view then down towards the streets below, from where it retrieved the limp body of the unfortunate victim of the ice pellet.

I was asked to follow my guide to the next floor up, a kind of gallery to which the dead man's body would be brought up to by the flapping Harpie. I climbed the stairs and here I saw what the ice pellets were made of: a great circular pool of human tears was gathered here night and day under the glass spire, topped up by cups and thimbles carried by the harpies and their henchmen, gathered from every weeping child or despairing destitute they could find throughout the city. And now the doors above our head opened, and the body of the so recently-killed man was lowered in and hung from a silver rail on which I now noticed there were perhaps 10 to 20 similar victims, in varying degrees of transfiguration, as if the rarefied air at this altitude were curing their flesh like fish or hams. But now, as I looked closer, something astounding happened: the figure at the end of the rail, one presumably days old, began to stir, and was brought down from his hook by two masked attendants using long poles like fishing rods to manoeuvre him to the ground carefully. I was invited to look closer as they threw water over him to revive him. His face was now dirty and unshaven, his clothes soiled and torn. The attendants placed bottles of strange burning liquid in his coat pockets, and then the Harpies carried him off, down towards some distant pavement where they set him down to sit against a wall and babble incessantly. I watched through a telescope how the running crowds ignored him, except that occasionally metal coins were thrown at his feet.

I told my hostess that I did not understand what I had seen, and that I felt strangely sad, as we descended together to some of the lower floors of the Cathedral. She smiled kindly and gently laughed, and explained that these were their ancient customs here, that strangers were often perturbed or mystified, but that Scarabolins accepted that the ice pellets would hit a certain number of their flock each day, that therefore their loved ones might be taken from them at random and transformed into the half-dead ghosts who haunt their gutters and back alleys. Moreover, they enjoyed the risk, she said, and placed bets upon each other, on the possible outcomes of each day's firing of the telescopes. Without this, she said, their lives would be unbearably dull.

I stood there deep in thought for a while, surrounded again by the moving throng of priests and actuaries all chattering and flitting between their number-windows. It occurred to me that they looked more often into these windows than they did out of the glass all around them to see the view of their vast city. But even at the very second I had this thought, I noticed something strange in the distance, at the same height as us, but moving oddly. I presumed at first, that like so much else I had seen in Scarabolis since I arrived, this must be something normal to them to which I just lacked the necessary explanation. But as the threat loomed larger, my involuntary agitation overtook me, and I leant over to tap the shoulder of the functionary nearest to me and pointed towards the view of the city beyond, using my basic command of their language to say clumsily "Look... big bird... coming..."

To my surprise, he stood up and screamed, and the whole floor began to copy him moments later, like a breath of wind breaking over a bank of dune grasses. Soon everyone was running and sweeping me along with them. I lost sight of my hostess and her children, and before I entered that impossibly long well of stairs that would return us to the ground: I saw over my shoulder the vast white bird with its beak open, screeching towards us, twisting it neck to bite into the spire of that sacred place of worship.

When the bird bit, he plunged our stairs into terrible darkness and wrapped us in the stench and heat of the flames of hell itself. Climbing down through all that, surrounded by sweating prisoners, was as difficult and frightening as any of the nightmare scenes in my famous *Prisons Of The Imagination* etchings. More than once I remembered those dark fantasies as I climbed downwards, wondering if I would survive, or if this was God's punishment for me: to make my own devilish drawings come alive and entomb me in them.

Outside, I watched in horror, in sympathy with all the other citizens of Scarabolis, as more giant gulls came to devour their sacred temple, and beat it to the ground with their spiteful wings and beaks. When the awful dust clouds finally cleared, I stumbled forward, wiping my eyes, and sat at the edge of the ruins, dejected. Jagged shards of their spoiled masterpiece reached upwards to the disbelieving sky like anguished fingers.

I was reminded of my beloved *Roma*, but I did not have the heart to draw it. For a moment I had the sense that some cosmic sorcery was at work, that history was repeating itself, or that time was flowing backwards and I had no idea whatsoever where it might finally come to rest.

~

TRAFFICLIGHT MESSIAH

Exclusive *Stop Press* The following copy has just been phoned in by Herald Reporter Martha Lucy who has been pursuing the mysterious "Man from Nowhere" who eye-witnesses claim survived unscathed a 20-storey fall from the St. Andrews Tower at midday yesterday.*

It's all true. After the fall and the astonished crowd, our man made himself scarce. One minute, people were screaming and trying to help what they thought was some horribly wounded casualty, the next moment they were conducting a man hunt: if the charge was "leaving the scene of the crime" then this time it was the corpse who had got up and walked. The police arrived at the incident to find there was no incident, just an empty circle of disbelieving and bewildered onlookers each *on-looking* at nothing.

He moved fast, ducked through plenty of back-alleys, but long after he thought he was in the clear, he still hadn't lost me. I finally caught up with him in Bills Bar, a shady little jazz dive in the Financial District. He looked startled for a moment that I had found him. He had changed his clothes in the toilets and cleaned himself up, and now it was plain to see that he really was unharmed, not even a graze or a limp. He was an average looking guy, late thirties, tall, moderately handsome, normal until you met his eyes: because there you found something else; a hungry doorway to another world. To meet those eyes was fatal. They swallowed you with a sadness and weariness that drew you in, then imprisoned you with their laughing resignation.

He drank up pretty soon when I hit him with all my questions: who he was, how he could have survived that fall. He laughed and said I probably wouldn't understand his answers, but then he made me an offer: to follow him and live the answers for myself, to put myself in his charge for the rest of the day and listen to his teachings. The guy sounded like he thought he was some kind of messiah. I suspected from the outset that what I was about to sign up for might involve some personal danger, but I had no idea that I might be signing my life away.

Really, before I had even thought about it I was in his car, or rather a car he stole in broad daylight leaving its driver in a trance by the roadside. I saw then, too late, that this guy was a hypnotist into the bargain. He locked me in and drove off like a lunatic, and then I was getting scared. But he laughed again and promised me I would get out alive and unharmed if I just did one thing: read his manuscript aloud to him while we drove. So I did. And it was strange stuff indeed.

I can't begin to sum it all up, or to go into the details. Suffice to say, it was all handwritten, presumably by him, but all in slightly different hands as if years apart or in various states of altered consciousness, under the influence of mind-bending drugs or something. The gist was, this guy was convinced that he could not die and that each time he tried to he would just be shuffled sideways into another life and wake up with no memory of what had happened. This had been going on for years, it seems, until somehow one day he spotted a clue that let him in on this secret, and then his whole life changed. He began employing dozens of people to follow him secretly, to keep copies of his notes and then pass them on to the next version of himself. He was constructing a message of who he was, of what he was, that other people would carry into the future for him. He knew he could not do it himself. He knew that one day he might disappear completely, and then nobody would be able to find him, but that then the manuscript would be finished and here's the real point: he didn't just reckon this was happening to him; he reckoned it was happening to everyone. Therefore he believed that this manuscript would be the key to everything one day, and anyone reading it would be changed forever.

I know, it's major-league lunacy, trapped in a car with a prize whacko. I should have thrown myself out at the next set of lights. But then I remembered that this guy had just accidentally proven he was something special to several hundred bystanders, and that if I could just find out how, then I might have the story of the century.

When I finished reading, he asked me what I thought. I said I thought he was insane, but then he glanced sideways and saw me wiping tears from my eyes, and heard my voice trembling. Why was I so moved if it was all tripe he wanted to know? I had no answer to that, except to coin the worst of all clichés: I felt as if somebody had just walked over my grave. *Perfect analogy* he laughed. *It was me and I was driving not walking. We're all dead already,* he said, *-and it's pretty liberating once you realise it.*

If I'm dead already, does this excuse me from being killed by you? -I asked, a little apprehensively. *Relax,* he smiled, *you are in no danger whatsoever.* Strangely enough, it was round about then that he started speeding up again.

Where have you been driving us to? -I asked.

Same place I have been driving for the last few hours, he said, *the city centre, around and around, trying out different routes and sequences of turns. It's like a Chinese puzzle.*

And when will you have solved it?

Any moment now, I think, we will unlock its little secret, then its hidden mechanical heart will spring open. But first we must apply a little pressure...

He executed a series of sharp turns then began accelerating up a long straight avenue, his foot hitting the floor.

Look, -I shouted, over the rising sound of the engine, *-if you're not going to tell me who you are or explain what happened today then please just let me out. I'm not... impressed...*

Watch this, he said, the speed still climbing, bystanders beginning to notice,

-whatever happens, -he shouted *-I need you to keep watching the building at the end of this street... hold on tightly... keep your seatbelt fastened.. trust me.. you won't get hurt... this is the only way to get... your answers.*

The engine was whining, buildings and people and cars were flying by in a blurred kaleidoscope; only the street's end was clear; a concrete façade of an impenetrable bank building. I was terrified, and without thinking about it already screaming at the top of my voice. But I knew it was too late to try the door, that falling out would kill me anyway, that I had missed the moment, my only hope of survival gone. Yes, I was convinced then that I was going to die. As we neared the end, he went through two sets of lights and I even tried to put my hands on the wheel, God knows why, perhaps it was just instinct, but nothing swayed him. He was ice cold, immoveable, as he gestured with his eyes, and mimed with his lips again that I should look straight ahead.

We left the road and pavement at the street's end and the car arched through the air and straight into the concrete façade of the bank building. But at the very second of impact, where the first microsecond of some sickening crushing sound of glass or steel should have occurred, nothing happened. Absolutely nothing. It was hard to look at. It had gone against every mortal instinct I possessed but I had looked straight ahead at the thing that was about to destroy me. And nothing had happened.

Time seemed to slow down, there was a sudden silence cut only by an alien wailing sound which with some effort I then recognised as the sound of my own scream continuing, then trailing off. We were moving through the air, clear blue sky was in front of us for a moment, then I felt that we were moving downwards in an arc. A city slid back up into view; we were falling. A delayed sound of breaking metal reached my ears from behind us, then we landed with a crushing impact, the kind of dead-stop that judders your very bones, in the middle of a shallow fountain. Metal buckled, stone splintered, water leapt into the air then came back down to whip us, angry that we had taken its place. We were stationary again and, incredibly: very much alive.

He was reaching over me, undoing my seatbelt, seemingly moving in a faster timeframe, but perhaps this was just a symptom of shock. As we emerged into the rubble and saw the astonished faces, the familiar street scenery of an ordinary urban day, I realised for the first time that the weirdest things of all are the things we think are normal and take for granted. At first it was just a momentary feeling, but later I would learn to extend it, and here was my first revelation: I saw planet Earth and her inhabitants for the first time *as they really are*, as if I were an outsider, an alien, a new beginner. It was overwhelming, literally mind-blowing.

I reached the edge of the fountain – he must have half-carried me there, my arm around his shoulder. He was pointing back up at the broken railings on the bridge above; where our car had gone through. *You saw it didn't you?* -he said, brushing hair from my eyes -*the building disappeared, didn't it? The city altered itself in order to preserve us, and you saw it happen...?*

Yes, I muttered, still more than a little dazed, -*I saw it... it happened.*

People were gathering around us now, and chattering, reaching out their hands to help us.

Where are we now? -I asked. *They all seem to be talking in...*

Italian? -he asked, -*Well, we're still in the same city, our city, except...*

He clicked his fingers in front of my nose, and the people started speaking English.

-*except that this is my favourite district of it, I have a little bit more control here and...* -he hoisted me to my feet and began to lead me away, -*come on, I have lots to show you.*

He shrugged off the bystanders with a rapid barrage of excuses, then, pointing over their heads at an approaching police car, grabbed me and plunged into the Saturday crowds, took me on a sprint through and under and around as many people as we could find. By the time we stopped we were blocks away, and he had succeeded in losing us and any would-be pursuer.

We sat down at a street café and he asked the waiter for two vodkas and tonic. I picked mine up and threw it over his face. He seemed to enjoy this, and just ordered me another one. This one I threw over my own face. He laughed and ordered another two, and we both drank them, oblivious by now to the stares from the other tables. He apologised to the waiter, by way of an old joke: -*I'm sorry, my friend has a drink problem... she keeps missing her mouth.*

Then he insisted I follow him into the Saturday crowds again, for his next "lesson", and I wondered what could possibly top immortality. We walked for a while. He seemed to know where he was going, but also to be reading the people we passed as if they were weather fronts before a storm. He brought us to the edge of a road junction, one which bisected a pedestrian precinct. On either side of the road now were built up two crowds, one to each side, waiting for the lights to change. Taking my hand, he pushed and jostled our way until we stood at the very front of one of the crowds. *Look,* -he said, gesturing right then left, -*no cars are there?* Sure enough, the nearest were moving away, but still nobody was crossing. *Watch this then,* he said, and walked out into the road and began crossing it. From half way across, he turned his head slightly, and smiled to see that like the Red Sea after Moses: the two banks of people were now breaking up, the two halves starting to flow together.

I caught up with him and asked what point he was making. *But don't you see,* he gasped, *if there were no cars then why was nobody crossing? In this city, people jaywalk everywhere, but not there. Suddenly nobody could do it at that moment, in that place. Why is that?*

I waited for him to tell me. *Nobody wanted to be the first*, he said, *to be seen to be the first. In that situation whoever stepped out would have had the eyes of a hundred strangers on them, and that was unbearable to them, so I had to do it for them. It wasn't cars they were afraid of, it was individuality.*

I must have looked disappointed, or he read my mind and said: *I know it doesn't seem as important as surviving a car crash, but, believe me, the implications of what I showed you there are just as devastating, maybe more so. It took me years to recognise this phenomenon for what it was, even though it probably happens every day and nobody notices it.*

Then he drew me another example, even more mundane: *ever wondered why there is always the last one of everything left in the supermarket?* He led me into one, and sure enough it was true. He picked up the last loaf of white and spun around, saying: *Why is everyone so scared to pick this up? They find it almost impossible to take it, in case there's something wrong with it, even if it is completely perfect and wrapped and air-tight. It's the same thing, the terror of being the only one, an individual.*

Next, he said he wanted to show me the repercussions of this, *a lesson in fluid dynamics* he called it. He found a sign outside a shop, the kind of sandwich-board thing that sits on the pavement, one that said "20% off all Chart CDs", with a big arrow pointing into the shop doorway. Well, he looked around then just picked it up and walked off with it, moving rapidly. A block away, he found the entrance to a narrow cobbled lane leading off the main street. There was nothing whatsoever down this lane, except bins and rubbish, but he set the sign up at its mouth so that every shopper would see it pointing them in this direction. We waited and watched and nothing happened, and this seemed to please him. Then he said: *-Right then, now help me stage my next miracle,* -and he took my hand and made us walk purposefully down the first part of the lane, turn round the first corner until just out of view, wait for 5 seconds, and then march purposefully back. We repeated this strange ritual 10 times, and then began to extend the route further into the courtyard, further each time for another 10 circuits. And sure enough, after 5 minutes, something truly astounding was in progress: we were now merely a small part of larger human endeavour: scores of people, couples, children, families, were all pouring down this alleyway, walking around the courtyard, finding nothing there, and mildly disappointed, walking right back out again to re-join the passing crowds on the street. It was extraordinary, and yet strangely inevitable.

Despite founding this madness, we were now clearly no longer an essential part of it: it would now go on all day without us. Laughing, we stood in the middle, and watched the hopeful faces going down and the disappointed faces going back, all chatting, all self-absorbed. *And just think... -*he said exultantly, *-all that would be required is for communication to break out; for someone on the way back to warn the total strangers going in of what their fate will be! But it will never happen! This is what needs to change about the human species, or they will become extinct...*

This wasn't what I had expected, but I was mildly impressed as I ran after him again, leaving behind the human maelstrom of inconsequence that we had started. *But why are you showing me this? -*I asked, -*What has this got to do with the building you jumped off and the car we just crashed?*

Everything. It's about transcendence, a universal misunderstanding of the nature of consciousness, which needs to be corrected.

*And who's going to do that? Make that correction? You? -*I shouted, as we swam again through the sea of people.

He stopped and turned to face me. *No, you are. Not today, but maybe tomorrow.*

And what about you? Why not you? -I asked after him as he started off again.

No, not me, I'm afraid, he mumbled, almost absent-mindedly, as he turned to look upwards, *-because...I'm going to jump off that towerblock in about 3 hours.*

No, no, wait a minute, that was this morning. You did all that this morning.

Did I? You're a newspaper person, I'll bet you know what date it is every day, so what day is it today then?

The eleventh, I replied, *Saturday.*

Now check your watch, he said and went to buy a newspaper from a street vendor.

While I puzzled over why my watch said the tenth, he held out the newspaper to me, page after page, the same impossible date. My head spun.

Don't worry about it, -he said finally. *No doubt you'll dismiss it in the end as a "trick of the mind" or "deja vu" or something. That usually does the job, wallpapers over the cracks in your mind sufficiently for you to keep on stumbling forward.*

But not for you?

No, not for me, that's right, because I trust only my own observations, not group consensus, thus rendering me mad in the world's eyes, or the world mad in my eyes, or both simultaneously in a relativistic sense. It's a question of going our own ways, splitting apart...

You're losing me completely, I'm afraid. -I said, somewhat downcast.

Right then, let me show you mad, he said, *follow me.*

A block away, he gestured to me to watch as a man approached, running along the kerb line, looking back over his shoulder as if anxious to catch the bus that was trailing him. Leaving a suitable gap, we then jogged along behind this guy for a while, in fact for several blocks until the point was proven. *I call him Buscatcher, but, believe me, he has never caught a bus in his life, nor ever will. He just spends all day running towards bus stops and looking over his shoulder, in a state of terror that he cannot get to the bus stop in time, and indeed he never does.*

Now here's a good one, he said, *to watch while you get your breath back, this is Skywatcher. He can walk for a block or two, but, and here he goes now..., he must always stop and stare up into the sky with his mouth open for about 5 minutes at a time, perfectly still. God knows what's going on in his head, unless of course it's God that's talking to him. I once saw a group of children stand near to him and play at chipping pebbles up into his mouth when he was doing this. I think he just swallowed them.*

And this is Spinner, he said, as a tramp so dirty as to be almost pitch black brushed past. Every 3 or 4 metres, he did a full pirouette, 360 degrees as he kept walking. *-Some sort of alcohol damage to the canals in his brain that control his balance I think, to him this is easier than walking straight. He isn't even aware of it anymore.*

Ah now, this is Quantum Leap, he said, as a dishevelled character with bushy black hair swung past. We walked closely behind and listened to his incessant muttering, *-do you hear that? That's Physics equations, no really, this guy is a qualified scientist, PhD, respected once, now insane, lives in a homeless hostel with a room full of text books from which he hates to be separated. Apparently he thinks he is on the verge of a breakthrough in the laws of Quantum Mechanics and who knows, maybe he has broken through already and this is all that* *he's left behind of himself? Lives with junkies and winos, sleeps with Neutrinos and Higgs-Bosons.*

Bag-carrier! -he announced as a man with a fleet of polythene bags sauntered by, vaguely anxious as if heading home. -*Sometimes he can carry over a hundred at once, doesn't let anyone near them or he gets angry. I waited until he was drunk one night and went through them all. Nothing in any of them. He just seeks more of them out every day and carries them around for some kind of security. Maybe it's a compensation for his owning nothing in this materialist world: the bags make him feel safe and normal and purposeful, like they need him and they won't get to their destinations without him.*

Now, last but not least this is Litter-Lifter. This district used to be a village once, in the time of his grandparents, and in this spirit, perhaps, Litter-Lifter now continues to take personally every single piece of litter he finds on these pavements, no matter how small. To him, it is as if you have dropped a piece of orange-peel on his living room floor. Of course he must pick it up – it's automatic. So he spends all day picking litter up with his bare fingers and taking it to dustbins. If only every City Council could count on a local lunatic as diligent and useful as this one! Story goes he became homeless a decade ago after he became obsessed with keeping his own flat tidy. He took to locking himself out and sleeping on the park bench outside, just to stop himself from making it messy again.

OK, OK! -I interjected at last, -*What's the point this time?*

He looked at me blankly for a second, as if assessing me as another maddy. *One word...* he said, ...*Relativism.*

Or in Quantum Leap's case, Relativity?

Quite so! Their world's are real to them, got it? And unlike our next and final subject, their worlds pose no threat to

*other people – they are carbon-neutral, in the current parlance.
We should show them more respect in that regard, even learn
from them.*

As we walked a few blocks towards his next
demonstration, he told me two stories to occupy me. These
stories were both absolutely true, he said, and that they happened
to contain metaphors appropriate to what he was trying to show
me.

Parables then? -I asked.

*Yes, although before you ask, no, I am not Jesus or
Mohammad or Moses, you can make your own mind up as to
who **they** were. They wanted followers, but I want people to stop
following anyone.*

*Like Bob Dylan says: "Don't follow leaders, and watch
your parking meters..."* -I interjected.

Yes, I am familiar with his work, he said, *-but here are
the stories. Both belong to a time within living memory when
this city was often beset by thick fogs caused by all its chimneys
burning coal. These fogs were referred to as "pea-soupers".
One night, a man coming home late became caught up in a fog
so dense that he could literally scarcely see his hand in front
of him. He became completely lost and wandered for hours in
desperation until he chanced to run into a stranger who was
clinically blind. The blind man just asked him his street and
house number and then led him there, walked him home safely.
You see? The blind man was the only person in the city that night
who could see. To him the fog made no difference at all. So who
was the cripple in that situation?*

*Or consider this: can you imagine how a human face
or a human body must look to a new-born baby, to a mind that
does not yet have the knowledge to connect an eye or a mouth or
a hand to each other, to make them into something meaningful,*

into a human being? A baby must be truly terrified of what it first sees of this world, but therefore truly perceptive, not yet blunted by all the hackneyed assumptions and conventions that we heap upon life. How as adults, can we regain that insight?

OK, back to the fog. In similar weather, two long distance lorry drivers had been travelling up here from the south. One of them had hitched a lift from the other after his truck had broken down, and was now sitting in the passenger seat with his friend driving, chatting away as they drove through the fog and the traffic jams. The traffic jam ground to a halt at one point, and since this guy was now bursting for the toilet, he took the opportunity to just get down from the cab and jump over the nearby fence to "take a leak". He was never seen again. The fence was in fact the railing along the edge of the bridge that crosses into this city a hundred feet in the air. He fell through fog and darkness for a long time before hitting the river below. I sometimes try to imagine his mental state as he waits for the grass verge, then hopes there isn't one, then realises any kind of landing is going to be fatal. In the end he just wants to go on falling in blackness forever, replaying his life in his head. You see, you feel sorry for the guy in this story don't you? -because you're OK and you haven't jumped off a bridge yet? But you should feel sorry for yourself, sorry for all of us, because all of our lives end badly really, don't they? Given that we all must die apparently, then we are all falling through darkness, wishing it was a dream, hoping to infinitely postpone the inevitable, in denial, feeling foolish and stupid and ashamed about our fate. But why? Because we misunderstood the situation we were in, we made assumptions. But the man who jumps off that bridge intentionally, not by accident, how different is his fall? Maybe it's completely different. He dies just the same, but on the way down perhaps he feels no shame or foolishness.

I'm not sure I understand, I stammered.

That fall is your life. You have a choice about how to feel about it. Or to use another analogy "happiness is the way you arrange the furniture inside your head". Or let's look at it this way: cast your mind back to when you were a child, a baby. How did you first enter this world? Believing and accepting that you were going to end up as an incontinent pensioner with arthritis dying in a nursing home? Or did you trustingly believe that you were immortal, a beautiful perfect thing that was loved and cared for by everyone around you that could only go on blossoming like a flower, renewed magically every morning as fresh as the sound of the singing birds, never to age or decay? Can't you remember how powerful you felt before the terrible facts of reality first began to invade your mind as you grew up? It is as if you arrived here as a God, but must leave as a leper. You see? You were tricked, we have all been tricked. Like the lorry-driver's mate jumping over that fence, you entered life in good faith but have found yourself betrayed. Unless...

Unless what? -I asked, intrigued by the doubt in his voice suddenly.

Unless, what you felt as a child was right, that everything since is an illusion.

Before I could ponder this idea however, we had arrived at what he wanted to show me. It was just a man sitting in his parked car, asleep at the wheel with the radio on, but I knew by now that he would somehow turn this into more than it at first seemed.

He took my wrist and checked my watch, -*Right this guy's brilliant, my favourite maddy, I call him Mister Sad, although I suppose he must have a real name too. This is his dinner break, and his lunch break was the same. God knows what his colleagues used to make of it. He comes out here to eat his lunch, in his car with the engine running, so that he* can listen to the radio and keep the heating on in winter. He's been doing this for 20 years now. Think of the damage to the Ozone. He used to go home to his wife you know. They would have dinner together, watch a little TV, and then he would sneak out again to spend the night in his car. Eventually even that became too much of a burden, so he left her so he could spend more time with his car, or rather he just never came home one night. He still thinks he's a salesman, but in fact he has no job anymore. He was sacked 10 years ago, but still goes around all the office doors, saying the same things to the same faces, who give back the same forced polite smiles and make the same polite excuses. And nobody listens too closely anymore to what he's trying to sell them because they're not interested anyway. But if they did listen they might finally notice and find it strange that he never mentions anything specifically, neither product, range, nor brand, but talks endlessly and in enormous generality about the selling of something, exhausting the full range of available adjectives, something we all must need, indeed something we all use every day, but don't get the best of, don't get the most out of, something nobody wants and nobody wants to talk about, but that he must nonetheless attempt to sell to them. An existential salesman. People in the offices he visits see him approaching, make excuses, pretend to move jobs or retire or die just to avoid wasting time with him, but he meticulously cross-examines their receptionists for contact names and numbers. Back in his car, he reviews nightly his dwindling lists of victims, and battles to expand them, as if the mere maintaining of these lists were raison d'etre enough for his mission, his life. He is exquisitely mad, but continues to escape detection within a societal system fluid enough to contain him.

But what will become of him?-I asked

Oh, one day he will finally forget the subtle boundary between his own body and his car, and drive through the plate glass window of a hairdressers when he wants a haircut, or *demolish a public toilet to take a leak. But since innocent people might die in that scenario, I think we should help him now and superglue his doors and windows shut, what do you say? That way he can suffocate and starve to death inside before anybody notices. I'd like to think they'll bury him in his car too, like a Viking in his ship, or Pharaoh with his favourite slaves, going into the next life in style. Picture it: the headlights flashing and car-alarm sounding as the first clods of earth landing on the roof set off the motion sensors, the irritating sound gradually fading under six sweet feet of earth.*

He went into a newsagents shop and emerged a moment later with some superglue. Then he embraced me. And then it was that The Reporter and the Man From Nowhere kissed in the street, even as they stole Mister Sad's keys as he slept and sealed the parked car in which he would now be trapped forever. Indeed, the poor wretch woke up and panicked and beat on the window, the glass misting as the air grew stale, his pleading eyes resting on the strange couple outside who now, content with their random assault, lost themselves in each other, while his cries went unheard.

Time altered. The traffic around us sped up, night fell, the air was used up. The loss of ourselves became literal. We changed places, in our bodies and in our souls, and now I don't know anymore who is telling this story, still less who will ever read it. But I know it must be told, what else is there to do with such knowledge? -and then the rest will be over to you.

We led each other to the building opposite, a towering glass edifice, and inside: crossed its public lobby unnoticed. In the lift, once other passengers had left, we opened the control hatch with our fingernails and then a host of wires of various colours, writhing like malevolent snakes, made their way out and up our shirt sleeves and punctured the skin, sunk their teeth into us, making connections. My veins and arteries seemed to open up, I felt my lifeblood pump and ebb and flow into the grids of light and data that surrounded us on every floor we passed. The walls became glass. I saw the myriad lives, plunged in servitude and indolence at their desks, pitiful yet charged with strange desire, like wine-bottles in some priceless cellar. I felt as if there might be time in another life, to drink their memories, partake of each bitter flavour.

I pressed another button, or a button pressed me, like so many grapes, and the building got taller. I felt we needed another hundred storeys, so the machines made them like fermentation, and took us through them, pushing the earth out below, ever further from our feet. I could feel the stars around us in the blackness of space and I was reminded that humanity has really always been moving, falling or sailing, in this starry void without knowing, all our lives, that we are spacemen already.

At last on the roof, we ran out laughing until we saw the view from the parapet and that the Earth and the Moon had changed places. My new friend showed me what lay out below: the map of the labyrinth that no man had yet unlocked. We watched it changing: a street bent itself or closed or opened to divert an attempted escapee here, to contrive a fatal meeting there, or a marriage, to stitch and mend a silver fabric like a spider's web, which seemed to stretch like frost in moonlight unseen over everything. And beyond all this, where nobody could see it, the streets just ran out into desert, a barren moonscape, breathless beauty. Above this was our Earth, our imagined home, floating lost and forlorn like a fractured memory, an air bubble, a flaw in the glass of time.

While I was distracted, gazing down at the lava-flow of traffic, he pulled open his cuff and rolled up his shirtsleeve. I turned and I saw now that his whole flesh was black as night or rippling water and within it was moving a thousand cars and trucks, trains and buses, red and white lights in daisy chains, his veins and arteries were becoming motorways and slipways, roads and rails.

I stepped closer in morbid fascination, but he took a step backward against the parapet and lifted his right arm up and out until it mapped itself, found correlation with the glowing cityscape behind, then vanished. He then stepped forward with what was left of him, and with his left hand tore open my shirt. The buttons flew, but what the nightwind exposed below was no longer flesh but, again, the black velvet living cityscape of roads and cars. I gasped but he drew me closer and we kissed again. We could feel the movement of each tiny vehicle, the greater purpose of each route, the smaller spark of individuality, infinitely complex, that held each steering wheel, placed pressure on peddles, their wishes and fears, hopes and dreams, their warmth and chill, their blood and breath.

Even as he obliterated himself thus, he loosened every garment of mine also, both revealing and concealing our true nature, our apparent individuation, our actual sublimation, unification. We disappeared, but not before I asked him and he answered in one breath what this maze and prison meant: that it was the Creator's machine to build himself from pain again.

~

4b: Zagreus

...to build himself from pain again.

...he answered in one breath what this maze and prison meant: that it was the Creator's machine to build himself from pain again.

I finish reading and return the essay to its envelope in the drawer. I understand little of it. Still less am I able to accept the implications that it has been written by me, some time in the past. And yet I am vaguely exhilarated by the feeling of immortality that emerges in it. I look down at my bare arms as I sit at this desk. I watch the blood moving in the veins, the little muscles twitching from time to time, the sinews contracting. If I destroy this, I question myself: if I sever this contract with life on a whim, if I disrupt arbitrarily this system, cut through my flesh and bone, will it really re-establish itself, re-assemble on some further plane? I turn my eyes up to the mirror and our faces: mine and my reflection, break at last into a reckless smile. *One way to find out,* -we whisper, in wicked unison.

I complete my duties: I write down my understanding of the day so far, much of it hazy, finishing with this sketchy conclusion-

I think I see that inequality, although apparently absurd, actually functions as a kind of social etiquette. The poor, the crazed, the crippled, need the rich to feed them with their sprinkling rain of occasional coins, and to hold out to them the hope of alternative life, while the rich, more esoterically, actually require the poor as a backdrop to give them definition. If all citizens were well-off, then their wealth would appear as a mere fact of society, a given, as opposed to a statement of their personal achievement. Everything in the way they act and dress suggests that they want to believe that they are better than each other, a ladder of status of infinite rungs. But this ladder is too hidden, too fluid, in everyday life, for most of them to bear. Their self-esteem demands a much clearer constant reminder, of their superiority to somebody, of their supposed self-betterment. In fact, if the poor did not exist, it would be necessary for the rich to invent them, and visa versa.

I see also that motor cars are the prime totems of this status quo. These metal encasures, grotesquely expensive, serve as the hermit shells that isolate the commuters from truth as they scuttle to and fro like crabs on a riptide beach. If they were each forced to sit beside the poor and the diseased every morning on the bus, they might feel more inclined to remedy their condition. Perpetually stuck in traffic-jams: Cars are the jousting suits-of-armour of our unchivalrous age, inefficient, ineffective, vainglorious. They deliver us to the opposite of their promise: misinformed, insular, ignorant, impoverished, weakened, suffocated.

The Equality-Locality Paradox: the urge of most citizens to voluntarily place themselves on a scale of perceived affluence gives rise to an unexpected irony. The city becomes split into "good" and "bad" areas: many districts of varying "desirability" where houses are more or less ludicrously expensive. Those that "buy" these houses (although actually they mostly rent them from banks under the misconception known as "mortgage") end up paying such vast monthly payments for these houses that they frequently end up as impoverished in real terms, i.e. day to day cash, as the "scum" they are seeking to distance themselves from. Thus, an unconscious principle of equality acts unbeknown to the participants in the game. The link between this invisible sub-current and the human emotion formerly known as "conscience" is an intriguing but unlikely possibility, on which more research is needed. Similar effects apply obviously, to car purchase and the unnecessarily vast range of models and prices.

City As Stratification-Centrifuge: it is commonly presumed that the inhabitants of cities are more cosmopolitan and broad-minded than those from rural areas. Careful observation reveals an opposite effect, as yet largely undocumented. Like a large washing machine or mixer-blender, the city actually seems to split society into strata of like-minded groups: e.g. Those who like jazz music or folk music, Islam or Judaism, golf or White-Supremacy, dogs or anal sex, etcetera. Thus every member of each interest group is able to quickly surround himself with people of near-identical views who won't challenge his beliefs but rather reinforce them, setting in motion progressive fractures in the surrounding society as a whole. Thus in future we can look forward to ornithologist nail-bombers and trainspotter guerrillas: their occurrence is absurd but logically only a matter of time. Meanwhile in the sticks, the postman and the doctor and the village simpleton continue to have to talk to each other and show some respect and understanding towards each other's views...

I stand up and go to the window. Outside it is thoroughly dark now, and a million stars arc over it all, reflected, it almost seems, in a sprinkling of frost along the pavements. I hear the pumping of distant subterranean music, chorus of absurd drunken calls from the streets: chirping girls, and braying brutes of men, all of them intoxicated by something more than alcohol perhaps, a force that gathers them and drives them forward like flowers swaying and straining towards some hidden midnight sun, a black eye of sleep wherein all murmurs die, a forever-closing circle of sex, swallowing them all backwards. They blindly seek their own births, grappling in the darkness. But I know that gateway well, and that only in death can we re-cross its threshold, break the boundaries of our customary prisons.

I prepare to go to war. I open my cupboard and find a dozen identical black suits, no choices necessary. They are all the same size, my size. Putting one on, in mild amusement, I check the pockets of the others for clues. I suspect they have all been worn at some point, but meticulously dry-cleaned. Wait, I find an exception: a small piece of notepaper emerges from the inside-pocket of the seventh one along, bleached as if it has been through the wash. I unfold it carefully, and read these words in faded handwriting, recognisable as my own:-

There are only thirteen people in the world... but whoever notices this should try to forget it as quickly as possible. Not all knowledge is useful.

I discover that the nightclub is only two blocks away. As predicted, the bouncers on the door immediately recognise me and greet me as one of their own. They slap me on the back, not without warmth, but somehow tentatively. I read the signals.... Perhaps I am somebody not always predictable, an unknown quantity. Our tasks seem straightforward enough, I find no need to seek instruction.

The club is situated in an inconspicuous back alley, and yet the door is in the form of an enormous open mouth, sculpted from blackened cast-iron sheets: little black curls of hair even writhe over the chin and brow, made from bent mild steel bar. This is a laughing head of Bacchus, a classical sculpture. And the only light is a fiery red glow surrounding the head where it meets the wall, and emanates from somewhere deep inside its throat. We guard the door, the sculpture's teeth hover above us and below.

And one by one, quite arbitrarily it seems, we refuse and accept various groups of people who approach this entrance. They come up in all manner of dress: some outlandish, warlike, half-naked, others restrained, refined like uniforms, futuristic. But our rules for accepting them are as obscure as the rules that govern their sartorial choices. Only a fool would look for any meaning in it, but look they do, arguing with us, tearing their hair out, cursing as they walk away, puzzling over their imaginary shortcomings.

When my shift is done here, I swap places with a colleague and take up my post at a station further inside the club. Here, a cashier takes alarmingly large sums of money from the guests, while a colleague and I hand each of them immaculate white squares of fresh linen. These we then assist them with tying over their faces and heads. With a stylish slipknot secured with a silver chain to the back: we thus hood every guest completely and hand them over to an usher to lead them through large padded velvet doors into the main ballroom. They are suddenly pathetic as they are led: blinded by choice, willingly powerless.

I proceed to perform this task flawlessly, and yet, like the guests themselves I suppose, I find myself becoming increasingly curious about what lies beyond these dark purple velvet doors of which I catch only brief, and cryptic glimpses. As ever, I observe and store my thoughts for later analysis. I am surprised by the fervour, the anticipation, the cold but joyous sweat that seems to emanate from each guest as they reach the brink of being hooded, of surrendering their freedom, even their safety, to total strangers.

In time, again, a colleague arrives to change posts with me, and I move further in, like the guests, towards the throbbing heart of this complex.

Through the velvet doors I find the interior of a disused church, painted entirely black and dark grey, but filled with displays of primary-coloured lights. Beams of red, yellow, and orange: swirl and cut like swords through the smoky atmosphere. Clouds of dry ice billow from hidden sources. Wheels of green and blue lights, spin and change axes endlessly, on the ceiling. Now and again, governed by some random law of mathematics, all light departs at once, leaving the space in total darkness, before bit by bit the regime of violent colour and motion re-establishes itself again.

Strangest of all however, are the occupants of this domain, at tables and chairs, lined up at the bar, and dancing in crowds on the floor: groups of entirely sightless revellers, hooded in white, hanging onto each other for guidance, grappling blindly for alcohol, for conversation, for caresses, embraces, affection. Amazed, I observe now that the white cloths are just porous enough, made of some ingenious gauze, to allow the guests to pour drinks carefully through them into their mouths, to make out dim shapes and lights in front of them, to function, after a fashion.

Thus, they drink and caress, their sheeted faces becoming disfigured, unbeknown to each other, with stains of red wine and lipstick. Everywhere I move through the crowds, retrieving empty glasses, I see people groping and grappling, hooded faces pressed together blindly, kissing through the cloth, seeking each other out, seeking... something. And as if all this sensory deprivation were not enough; an enormous wall of sound is crushing everything, all life within the auditorium. Between each melody, a transition is cleverly contrived, so that almost no moment of silence is ever allowed to occur. Thus, wilfully deprived of sight and hearing, do these paying guests struggle against the odds to find each other and some amorous fulfilment.

One of my colleagues gestures to me, and lends me small white plugs, which he indicates I should lodge in my ears, giving me some kind of relief from the noise. I smile and thank him, or mime the words at least. He laughs demonically and points to a nearby corner where a guest has stumbled drunkenly too close to an enormous speaker, and now blood issues from both his eardrums, discolouring his white linen hood.

Before I can react, there is a tap on my shoulder. Another colleague pulls me over to a corner where he can shout in my ear until I hear him. There is someone at the back door asking to see me, he says he is some kind of relative with an urgent message, *although he looks more like a wino,* -this man sneers at me. So do I have a *"cousin Huey?"* His eyes widen provocatively. Realising of course, that I have no knowledge of how many relatives I may or may not have, I play it safe and follow his directions to the back door, moving mercifully further away all the time from the pulsing centrifuge of noise. I take the plugs from my ears, as a bouncer opens a door at the end of a corridor for me, and the cold night air floods in.

And here I meet the war-torn face of one of my brothers from earlier in the day: the grinning skull of one of the shadow people.

Malky -he croaks, and I correct him, and urge him to move further out of earshot, further back into the shadows, *William Gaunt* I say, *use only that name now.*

-*Ye said, last week, we could drop by here and ye'd gie us some spare tins mate, ye ken, booze ye had spare.*

I look into the bleak sockets of this grey skeleton, then think of the blinded sheep behind me, of their black-suited guardians who watch over them so cynically. The skeleton winks now, saying: -*ye said, ye'd huv some mental gear fur us, strong stuff like, mate, mental gear.*

I laugh, and pat him on the shoulder, an idea dawning on me, telling him to go back to the Necropolis and gather up all his friends and bring them back here. He shuffles off eagerly.

Back inside, my station has changed again, and I find myself posted at the next room: an inner chamber of this church of black light. Here I see that temporary couples, convenient fevered alliances, retire to caress each other in semi-darkness on soft black velvet couches with high backs and arms, which almost seem to swallow them with their comfort, like Venus fly-traps. The darkness is occasionally cut by sweeping blades of orange light in which I see the hooded faces pressed together, lips straining through the cloth. Hands exploring downwards, probing, clasping, searching desperately through their blindness, for identity, for clues amid the darkness and loneliness.

And I and my colleagues, like black crows hovering around carrion, we stand guard at the doors of these secret places, valves regulating the outflowing of human desperation, the short-circuit of sex. We moderate it. We allow it to happen. A drink split there, a step tripped over. We rush to assist the thankful blind on their journey into the pumping heart of night. I see now that this journey involves everybody, the whole city outside that I have passed through, all the saturday night paraders, the strutting half-naked children moving in sweeping crowds, searching, hunting down some indefinite prey. I see that they all seek this hidden heart, and tonight perhaps that heart resides here for a while, within these walls. There is one chamber left, a final room within the complex of *Zagreus*, an inner sanctum where the sound, the light, the feverishness may be even more overpowering, where perhaps it finds its closure.

The hour of midnight is struck. High on the wall in the high ballroom, the huge hands of an ancient clock turn over: survivors from a God-fearing former age, their tarnished iron still glimmering like the moon in this darkness. Now the doors to the final chamber are opened, a gong nearby is sounded.

Here in plummeting darkness we assist the blind to remove their clothes. The temperature is warm, the walls, ceilings and floors heated from behind. They are reflective glass, back-painted in dark red, while yet darker red couches and rugs fill up the space into which we lead the participants, naked except for their white hoods, whose chains we occasionally, discreetly tighten. Clouds of acrid dry ice fill the air, darkness tries to reign, resisted only by occasional unpredictable flashes of red, the random progress of laser beams slicing the air.

Looking on, just as I begin to feel nauseous in this snake pit, the writhing white blind flesh like lab rats, a hand tugs on my sleeve: a lost soul, drunk and disorientated. She asks me to help her, to tell her where she is, to lead her to the truth. Some switch inside me is suddenly flipped. I grab her by the shoulders and turn her to face the room of red mirrors. I unlock the chain to the back of her hood and unmask her. Her eyes widen and try to adjust to the scene. Lights sweep across the room and open up dramatic glimpses of writhing flesh, like maggots in a corpse.

She screams out loud, her open mouth echoed above by the wide eyes underlined with black shadow now melting down over her face like black tears. I turn her to confront her own reflection in the mirror, and she screams some more.

Somehow this noise even penetrates through the suffocating layers of pulsating noise in the space, and begins to awaken and galvanise the bodies scattered around: it is like a fire alarm being set off. I sense murmuring of panic and discomfort. I see people frantically reaching behind their own hoods. I turn and run from this scene.

I run down a long corridor, bumping past confused hooded figures, knocking some of them sideways. Blades of light sweep overhead, incising the foggy air. I hit the panic bar, and open the fire exit, to reveal a grinning gallery of skeletons: a band of comrades arisen from their living graves on the hill above the city, the city of the dead. Their mouths open in wordless joy, revealing toothless grins, the grey bristle on their wasted skin wrinkles in anticipation. Thirsty and hungry, with outstretched hands, I lead them. I usher them into the sacred rooms of the decadent rich, the young and bored, sated with the lavish excess of what these dead men have nothing of. They smash open the fridges. They pour bottles of whisky over their faces, the laughing mouths. They overpower, by force of numbers, the lurching, braying bouncers. They pour draught beer straight from the taps into their mouths, fighting to lean down behind the bartops. They laugh at the confused hooded crowds. They trip up and corner the occasional naked ones, moving in like hyenas. I throw open every fire exit and let the chill autumn air flood in. The pumping music floods out into the night, carrying in its inexorable wake, burying among its folds: the cries of the innocent, the blind, the confused. Nobody lives in the city centre anyway, who values peace and quiet. Who will bat an eyelid that tonight's cacophony should include among its polyphony the shrill noise of suffering?

Thus do the grey demons unleashed for a night, set about their white virginal prey: the unwitting living who gave not a thought to poverty or death. The skeletal hands bring chill knowledge to the soft, the plump, the pampered rumps of those who closed their eyes, who turned their faces from the moon, the flipside of the world they had created.

I take to the cobbled backstreets and leave it all behind me, the confluence of dark and light. I put my hands in my pockets, turn up my collar, and whistle softly into the night. Where am I going? To the river I suppose, to somewhere clean and renewing that might carry me to morning. The whole city still aches and boils over in its weekend ecstasy of amnesia and self-destruction. Wild singing issues from crowded late night bars, people stagger home in groups like troupes of unapplauded clowns. Endless queues for taxis stretch around corners like the twitching tails of dangerous serpents. Fights break out. Deep-fried food is disgorged from glowing booths of harsh electric light and poured like a petrol elixir into those who have lost life and sight, become robotic. Their limbs seem disobedient, like children again they struggle with their first steps, move quickly to avoid falling over, lean against walls for stability.

Further on, in the darker reaches before the river, I see couples struggling together in the dark as if trying to unlock something, grappling for the key to some mutual door. Harpies in leather skirts and boots strut and pout on street corners. Skeletons use needles in the dark, inject themselves with neon light, red fires light up their veins. I see them as if skinned alive, anatomical diagrams of sinew and muscle laid bare: they grin and leer from the shadows.

But nobody can touch me. The streets thin out as I reach the river, and the moon parts the clouds above to greet me. I kick off my shoes and sit on the cold stones of the quayside and bathe in the silver light of solitude. I make some notes in my sketchbook, my last observations, then toss it bitterly into the water. Pretending to look the other way, I see from the corner of my eye a dark figure downstream wade out and retrieve it, place the book hurriedly into a plastic bag. So the Keepers are still with me. I wonder how many of them followed me tonight, how closely they watched me, or influenced events? It is impossible to know for sure what they expect of me – or, if they are to be believed, what orders I myself gave them some time ago, which they still meticulously follow.

If I am caught in a game now, then perhaps it is only ultimately a game of my own making. And the answer to everything, the reason for it all if I need one, is just locked up deep down inside myself, if only I could reach it. But I may never remember, never recall what this is all about, although sometimes drifting in or out of sleep one senses it lying there softly, the reason, like a memory, like a pebble or a stepping stone underwater, lying just out of reach of your naked foot.

I stand up and take my clothes off. It is time again. To trade up and take a new hand of cards. I slide off the mossy quay and slip shivering into the freezing black water, drift out with the tide, lie for a while with my face to The Moon, searching for her in my memory, asking if she is my mother. But she says nothing, without even a tear in her eye.

Now I turn my face to the blackness, to drink the night dry, in sympathy with all the unanswerable thirst of everyone I leave behind me. And with them I dream of a shore where I might be washed up with my mouth full of sand and my ears turned inwards like spiral shells, intimate cathedrals: echoing to the distant hissing of foam, the music of the oceans. Listening for an answer.

~

3b: _Mussolini

...listening for an answer.

...my ears turned inwards like spiral shells, intimate cathedrals: echoing to the distant hissing of foam, the music of the oceans. Listening for an answer.

I look up now, disturbed, confused by these manuscripts brought to me in this candlelit room. Donna kneels in front of me by the fire. She has been watching my reaction to what I read and now she hands me a book of photographs, while Mussolini curls up on the dusty floorboards, flames throwing orange flashes of reflections in his shiny black coat.

The photographs show Donna with a man who she says is me, in various scenes, mostly holidays, climbing mountains, strolling by the sea. But then it occurs to me that I haven't the slightest idea what I look like.

What's wrong? -she asks, sitting up on one arm, leaning her face up towards me.

Do you have a mirror? -I ask, -*Did we have a mirror here? I need to know what I look like...* I feel my pulse quicken with a curious urgency and fear that I don't entirely understand. Donna stands up and looks around.

She goes searching and then, carrying a candle, returns to the room with a mirror in her hand. We sit together and look into it. I see that we are indeed the couple in the photographs. I feel a wave of relief pass over me. I run my hand over my face, exploring, flexing flesh and muscle, then gently, I do the same to hers. Her eyes are soft and brown. She has been sad and tired for a long time but now some deeper, buried glimmer is returning there. She smiles: -*Do you remember anything now then? Do you believe me, do you believe in your own life?*

I remember nothing. No people, no places. But I do however, remember some facts. I remember that Mussolini was a fascist dictator in World War Two. I remember that dogs live for a maximum of about sixteen years. I remember that the breath of a human being should leave a mist on the surface of a mirror...

Her eyes widen and she draws back, starting to shake her head: -*What are you saying David, I don't understand...?*

I take her wrist, and bring her gaze back to meet mine. -*That dog is a puppy, but he was a puppy ten years ago in that photograph, he hasn't aged a day. Neither have you or I. And our breath left no mist on that mirror a moment ago. But it's simple really isn't it? We aren't ageing, because we aren't alive anymore.*

You're mad...! -she says, grabbing the mirror back, lovingly spraying fog onto it from her mouth. -*You never did know much about dogs, he's a particular breed that...*

Stop, -I tell her, placing my fingers over her lips, -*I'm prepared for all that now, I know the way the rules change, but I've trained myself to overcome them. I know you will try to convince me that the flaws I see in the shape of things are an illusion. But I know what I saw. I recognise the structure of The Game when it shows through, and I won't conform to it.*

What do you mean? I don't understand any of what you're saying now! -she gasps, falling back alarmed.

I'm saying this isn't real, even if you think it is, genuinely believe it is, it still isn't. You're blinding yourself in order to buy happiness. You must decide to wake up.

You've gone completely mad David, how can I wake up? Pinch myself or something!?

Watch this then, -I say, and lunge forward to the fire. I lift a burning log from the blaze, by now glowing red hot, and hold it in my bare right hand. She tries to scream but I put another hand over her mouth. I watch the expression in her eyes slowly change until I know she has understood.

Her eyes shine blue, unearthly pure, as some strange new knowledge, never before met, flows into her being, inexorable, like ice.

But... but... you're not even burning... your skin...!

I pass the log to the other hand: it is unscathed. Gingerly, tentatively she reaches out and touches the skin.

My God... Oh God... it's not even warm...

With my other hand I start to crunch the log, and flames lick upwards, sparks fly out: a dust sheet almost catches fire, she beats it out. I return the log to the fire, and we face each other again.

Oh God, oh God... -She is saying, tears welling up in her eyes, -*What's happening? I'm frightened, this doesn't feel real anymore David... Help me.*

I take out another log, an even hotter one, and hold it out to her.

What?! -She recoils in revulsion.

Hold it, -I say, -*If you resolve not to believe, if you truly decide not to believe, to refute reality like I do, then pain, everything, will just go away. You're immortal. You know it deep down. You've always known it. Take the log. Touch the fire. It won't harm you. Trust me.*

We look at each other a long, long, time in the flickering firelight. The candles around us dance intermittently in various nocturnal breezes. Her dark eyes are like tunnels meeting mine: our souls line up and empty their contents into each other, into the space between which is no space, we vanish out of reality. Reality dies in us, reaches a conclusion it was always waiting for. Donna takes the fire.

The flames leap up between our outstretched hands. She looks up in wonderment, as the roof and walls deconstruct themselves backwards, tile by tile, stone by stone, the starry night sky coming through in progressive sections, the candles blowing out.

Mussolini moves backwards across the floor in slow motion, his head rocking from side to side like a broken toy.

Donna turns her head a little, catching sight of him. Before I can anticipate and act upon my next thought, she breaks one hand free as if to move to pick him up. I want to try to begin to mouth the word "no" but everything, the whole weight of the universe seems to be on my tongue, as if my timeframe is immeasurably slower than the events I am observing. Some powerful force breaks our hands apart, and a plume of orange red flame turning pink leaps up into the night sky. Donna spins off towards Mussolini. I try to move after them, turning around. In the process of speeding up towards normal reality, the following all occurs simultaneously in about four seconds:-

Donna runs towards what was the front façade of the house, now a blackened line of deconstructing rubble, falling sideways, picking up Mussolini as she slides downwards. From this point the flames now burning on her left hand spread rapidly in tiny tongues across her entire body destroying all her clothes and then turning all her white skin to brown, then black, then the dark mossy green of tree bark. As this is happening, she is turning and flying forward, now clutching Mussolini, but rotating again towards a vertical position with her feet moving foremost. Her feet make contact with the earth of the garden outside, and her limbs deform, attenuate, elongate, reach outwards and upwards, sprout branches and leaves, grow into a third yew tree perfectly aligned to the other two. Following after, struggling to speed up, I finally arrive at the foot of what is now a tree to find myself shivering there, arms wrapped around the trunk and foliage, tears rolling down my cheeks. Rain is falling softly on my head and shoulders, on the silent garden all around.

After a while I hear footsteps behind me, then a snout, some other dog, a large black Labrador sniffing at my heels.

Are you OK there? Is something the matter? Have you had an accident sir?

I slowly stand up, to find myself facing some stranger in the rain, in the ruins of a burnt-out house, in an overgrown garden.

No. I'm fine, thank you.

A middle-aged woman stands there under an umbrella, her eyes probing my face with concern and curiosity.

Did you…? Did you know them?

No, -I say, dusting down my legs, and preparing to leave. *I'm just interested in trees. Taxus Baccata...*

What? -She seems confused, wrong-footed all of a sudden.

Yew trees. They live a very long time you know. Longer than us. If only they could talk.

Yes... I suppose. I thought maybe you knew them, the owners. Perhaps you were a relative, he had a brother I think...

Reaching the edge of the garden, I see that she is preparing to leave also. I ask a question: *are you one of the Keepers?*

Keepers, I'm not sure what you mean, a gardener? Nobody tends to this place, as you can see, though I dare say someone will build a new house here soon. It's been over ten years now you know, since the vandals put the place up in flames... You are alright aren't you?

Yes, thank you, yes.

I turn to go, then remember something else; -*Oh excuse me, would you know when the last train is... back to the city I mean?*

She checks her watch. *About twenty minutes or so I think. Quite soon. You should be able to catch it.*

Now the sky is huge, the hedgerows dwarfed and humbled beneath it all, suburbia hunched in humility before the moon: nearly full, yellow and sailing amidst an eerie oculus of mist and haze. Cotton wool buds of clouds tumble off from it in multiple directions, amid an indigo deep sea of blue and black. The rain has stopped. I walk down this hill and climb towards the station on the next hill: where the silver rails of progress slice exquisitely across the top of the town with the steady precision of a surgeon's knife.

On the way I pass a thousand puddles, fragments of reality's broken mirror brought down. Overhead, perhaps I catch a few glimpses of enormous grey cogs turning, where the sky has fallen away: the celestial scenery straining to function. Through the windows of the water's still surface on the pavements below: I glimpse the figures and faces of the watchers, upside down, *Keepers* eyeing me knowingly from the netherworld, nodding at my trials and torments. Then a breeze picks up and I am spared their attentions, as each little microcosmic lake becomes a storm-tossed ocean.

Climbing the steps to the station at last, I take a deep breath of the chill night air. The waiting room is locked but still lit up. I am the only one on the platform. Below me, the whole suburb that was once a village spreads out, all the little roofs like heavy eyelids, plunged in sleep, together, side by side as unselfconscious as children. To know, or believe at least, that I once lived here, but to remember nothing. How can it be? But such a thing moves me, haunts me more than if I remembered a single detail. It's like a life I never led, a time that never was. What sweeter sadness could exist than the forgetting even of one's own life? What could that be, if not death's reward?

I hear the train in the distance. I sniff in the night wind, sweet and mysterious, bringing me news I will never hear of the glow of dawn beyond the distant horizon, of lost friends, forgotten conversations, unrequited loves, all the unfinished ends of threads of my life. Dreams that never quite happened, but could have and live on somewhere in limbo, bathing in the light of possibility, of desire.

I climb down onto the tracks and kneel like an athlete, poised to begin some incredible sprint, to run faster than anyone has done before. The moon looks down as the beautiful silver machine howls in anticipation of me, roaring down the tracks.

I break into a run and in just a few moments feel the removal of air behind me as I am overtaken by a power and strength greater than all men. It sings of the distances between cities, of the music of electricity flowing through wires across vast empty moors. Absorbing me, it tastes the bitterness of human yearning. While in return I attain mathematical perfection, supreme order beyond all emotion, accelerating to infinity.

~

2b: _Butterflies

...I attain mathematical perfection, supreme order beyond all emotion, accelerating to infinity.

I close the faded manuscript on my lap, where I sit by the window in the drawing room, on a summer afternoon. The chair creaks as I stand up. My feet echo on the polished floorboards. The glass door hisses as I carefully return the book to its place in the bookcase. I see no date on it, but it seems old and fragile. I did not understand most of it, but I am only ten years old. I enjoy reading books that I do not understand, and revelling in that mystery, that blissful confusion. What a pity it would be to entirely grow up one day and find the dreary answers to everything.

And now it must be time for me to go and follow my family down the road to the sea. The shadows have lengthened in the August field, under the hay bales laid out so harmoniously, each waiting for the farmer and the short journey to Winter storage.

I walk into the hall and, opening the glowing stained glass front door, step out into the lazy heat of afternoon. The crows wheel over the shorn fields, but even sound seems deadened at this hour, sunken in pleasurable lethargy.

White butterflies flicker by the hedgerows. I half-break into a run in anticipation. Leaving the house behind, I skip along the dry furrowed farm track to the sea. I move out into the impossibly wide flat expanse of other fields, golden crops swaying imperceptibly in the tiniest breath of wind. Overhead the blue sky is perfect and magnificent, criss-crossed by white vapour trails. At a bend in the road, I look back to see the old house, its ivy gable sailing amid the sea of gold – and, hidden somewhere behind it, the main road running from the village on northwards up this coast and past all the other scattered townships.

Last night, walking back from the village, my father placed his hand on my shoulder, to keep me safe as the last bus drove by. It was nearly sunset, and looking after the little red country bus, I marvelled at its lit interior where only one passenger sat, on the back seat, reading a paper. The unknowability of that passenger and their destination, the mystery of that moment and of everything that might come after, is with me still.

And now only one bend remains in this road, this dusty track, before it turns towards the sea, and each hedgerow either side will slide apart like magical curtains as the sand dunes begin, and I run to meet my brothers, my mother and father.

They will be young, as I will always remember them. My mother picking flowers and sea shells, my father hunting for crabs, my brother drawing pictures in the sand or making sculptures out of driftwood.

I turn that corner in the road, and I hear the roar of the sea beginning, beyond the rustling of the corn and of the dune grasses...

~

1b: _Switchback

...of the corn and of the dune grasses

A car door closes, and I am woken up abruptly. Bleary-eyed, I turn to look at you. You sit down and fasten your seat belt, laughing at my afternoon nap, reaching your hand out to switch off the car radio which now emits a blank wall of white noise, as though a transmitter has gone down, or the signal drifted.

Now we are driving around the harbour and I try to explain to you my strange dream, how there was a weird story on the radio, and it ate into my sleep, taking me down with it.

But you seem disinterested, your attention fixed on the road ahead as we climb the steep slope out of town, leaving this little fishing port behind.

Half a mile north, the road re-joins the lochside, following close to it, with only a border of thin birch saplings, like a bamboo plantation, between us and the low rocky shore.

The water is light grey and uncertain in mood, like the sky above it.

We pass an unusual sign: forbidding overtaking, blind summits for a quarter mile it says, a *switchback*. I look in the mirror. Behind us, two rural youths with the clothes and the car of disenchantment (a dilapidated *hot hatch*) immediately pull out to overtake and begin accelerating to pass us.

In front of us, the first blind summit falls away with magical immediacy to reveal its hidden sting: a fast sports car approaching from the opposite direction, incredibly close, less than thirty feet.

You gasp, almost cry out. The screeching of various brakes begins, releasing dust or smoke from the wheels or the road or both.

I become very calm, calmer suddenly than I have ever been in my life. It just flows over me.

I know what happens next, I say.

I know what happens now.

~

_Afterword

Nothing is dead but what has never been
The coloured past outshines tomorrow's grey
Besides whose formlessness it can display
The sequence of the effort and effect.

-Guillaume Apollinaire.

Dear Martha,

By now you will have been wondering for quite a while where I am or what became of me. Of course, those feelings are a lot like what Alexander put me through, and perhaps it is appropriate, even *salutary* as they say, that I should in turn inflict them upon you. You were such a fan of this sordid story, you and that creep Dundas in his dirty raincoat, maybe this is your ultimate thrill: to be made to live inside *Ultrameta* yourself while I run free, living the good life, moving between lovers like a bee among flowers, or whatever else your paranoia conjures up for you. It's certainly better weather where I've escaped to, make no mistake of that.

Let's get this straight, or clear I should say: I am not a lesbian. But during those three weeks in which we drove around the city and its outskirts together everyday: I began for the first time in my life to question and understand what the true nature and meaning of human desire might really be. How can so many million years have gone by and this issue still not be settled? The phrase *carnal knowledge* comes closest, granted, there is a seed of insight there which everyone is missing.

Don't get me wrong. I wasn't getting glimpses of your knees or peering down your front every time you drove. It was never like that, at least not until the last few seconds anyway. It was the discussions we had. The long searching ones in which you would ask me about how Alex had kissed me and what it felt like when he and I were intimate together. Desire has a spiritual component you see, and it was the poetry you were conjuring up, that we both conjured up as we talked about Alexander Stark, that turned gradually into obsession and love.

My heart began to leap with excitement, my cheeks blush, each morning when you pulled up outside in that pale blue metallic sports car of yours. I thought at first it was just talking about Alex that was exciting me, that we were bringing him back to life somehow by visiting all those places he had been and standing there together imagining the atmosphere, or talking to witnesses who remembered something he had said or done.

The unspeakable strangeness of it all, it unnerves me even now: to stand in a never-before known place where someone you loved once went in secret and did or felt something desperate without you, years beforehand. Oh, how can I express it? But I know you understand. The sense of sweet hopelessness, of dislocation and yet strange focus: a sense that there is a love there that crosses time and place and reconnects you to those events and that person. But I don't need to tell you do I? This is what you are feeling again now, for me now as well as Alexander.

How we wept together after finding the *Reverend John* and finally persuading him to admit that Alexander had employed him. He lived again in that man's incredible memories of him, and after he left us, the way you embraced me and then kissed me on the forehead to stop my tears: perhaps that was the moment when I first loved something in your eyes, or the beautiful way your hair falls over your soft little elfin ears. I began to see it then: how unbearably perfect you were, how I envied the way God had made you and I wanted to learn more, to learn everything about you until I could contain you in my mind in totality as God would do. And there is desire right there

I think: I have just defined it. Funny how you have to creep up on those things.

Then we were on the road again, and travelling ever backwards to try to uncover the centre of the story and the seed that had first grown into the madness in Alexander's head until it sent him out into the world seeking to challenge the very borders of life and death. I wondered if it had been September the 11th 2001: how much the television coverage had obsessed him, his deep-seated intuition that maybe the *jihadis* were onto something, that they like every other religion: had a fragment of God's broken vase in their hands and were cutting themselves on the edges, that they were right that death was not the end and that they could approach it fearlessly with momentous consequences.

You took me to that hidden stone-age monument on the hills to the north overlooking the city. I had presumed it didn't exist, had thought it was just a fantasy to serve some obsession of Alexander's about pagan blood sacrifice. But when we stood there together in the September mist I saw you shiver with the chill disquiet that perhaps there was some truth in his mad speculations: that our ancestors had understood better than us how life was distributed among our many bodies, that we are not the separate individuals we appear to be, but portals for something invisibly shared.

It was after that, returning to the car and seeing how shaken you were, that I first kissed you full on the lips. It was so natural, like a memory from a former life, that I literally seemed to wake up a moment later as we both blushed and I scrambled for my keys and started the car. But for the rest of the day, the memory of the heat of your lips was burned into the back of my mind and hidden there, a secret treasure that I would only dare to return to late at night, in the seconds before I went to sleep.

We never did work out what had happened to that nightclub singer, did we? Although we spoke to people that remembered her, heard a recording of her incredible voice. She had returned to Turkey or Morocco or wherever she was from, and how could we ever pursue her without the language. And then there were those photos that suggested she had jumped into the sea off Athens when *Interpol* had boarded the ferry she was on that summer. And her face in the police files was strangely familiar, like someone you had seen all your life and yet not looked at, an enigma concealed within the familiar.

The house in the wheatfields was your idea. I had always puzzled over that section in Alexander's letters: the meaning of the strange child in the room full of books, although of course I had my suspicions. You had spoken to his parents about it and armed with the knowledge that this was a holiday house they had stayed in when Alex was a child: suggested we travel there together and rent it for a week.

How we shivered over those ghost stories, eh? That was it, that was where it happened of course. You and I alone together in that beautiful stone villa among the golden fields by the sea, as the late sun fell bleeding to the ground. Of course we couldn't sleep in different rooms, and as we undressed in front of the full-height mirror, I saw from your manner that, although a little shy and quivering with strangeness, you too felt the subconscious need to let the other person see your body.

I saw suddenly that we were about the same height, our hair length and colour not so different. In front of the mirror in the growing twilight I saw at last that we were two halves of the same equation you and I, or perhaps two thirds: the remaining jigsaw piece being Alexander Stark, the ever-present, ever-absent one who came to life between us when we were together.

Hugging close for comfort, I asked you for the hundredth time how Alex had made love to you and how it had made you feel, and our hands whispered across each other's skin, conjuring Alex out of the darkness. But now this was our triumph, nature's triumph, although so many people call these things unnatural:

very quickly Alexander left us, became unimportant at last, as we both saw that what we had always loved about him was not him at all, but our versions of him, how we were with him.

I had always loved the thought of you kissing his neck, and wrapping your legs around him, comforting him – that long white body of yours, so soft and lithe. We kissed each other's lips and our hands moved, soothing, exploring. I kissed your breasts and your back and your legs and your knees as Alex must have done, loving with my eyes and hands every inch of you, and desiring you so completely that I wanted to be you.

We were two halves made whole, perfect mirror reflections. Our skin in moonlight: the bruised flesh of peaches cupped around a wrinkled stone of memory, of absence. My face pressed between your legs was like the last plea of a blasphemer who has turned away from every other door of knowledge in this wretched puzzle of a world. Here I was, immersed in your sweet smells and pleading with the creator to take me back through this door from which I came and re-birth me now in the image of my beloved Charlotte Stark, the perfect apple of all my desires.

And this time: for once, God answered. I woke early before the first light of dawn and looked at myself in the mirror. I had changed places with you, a simple, beautiful sleight of hand. Now I saw how Alexander had done it, where Himeropa had got to. I wept as I caressed your exquisite face in the mirror, and put on your pants, your dress, delighting in the sweet aroma of your body all over me. Now at last I had attained the ultimate goal of all desire: to become its own object.

I took your banks cards and passport and driving licence and ran out and jumped into your car and drove for a week. I've let a few men enjoy your body since, I must confess, but don't worry, I wasn't cheap. I'd like to give you a return address so you could tell me about you waking up without me, but that would be uncharacteristically stupid wouldn't it? Instead, I intend to go on enjoying my own imagining of that scene: the first morning sunlight cutting through between the drawn curtains, you waking up with a fuzzy head and your alarm at finding the bed empty, your happy guilt and disbelief at remembering what had occurred between us: a good deal more than you think as it happens.

I picture you in your white dressing-gown running onto the beach and staggering along over the sand and the rockpools, barefoot, hair in disarray like a madwoman, running towards something: the south, the sun, the future, eternity, me. And the fragments of sky reflected in the rockpools are like mirrors that you'll come to eventually, tiring, slowing down, sobering up.

And you won't like what you see.

Yours truly, with love,

-Charlotte S.

_Appendix

I stand amid the roar
Of a surf-tormented shore,
And I hold within my hand
Grains of the golden sand-
How few! yet how they creep
Through my fingers to the deep,
While I weep- while I weep!
O God! can I not grasp
Them with a tighter clasp?
O God! can I not save
One from the pitiless wave?
Is all that we see or seem
But a dream within a dream?

-Edgar Allan Poe.

M E M O *(inter-departmental)*

Dear Sirs,

As duty officer in charge on the occasion of the fatal road accident that occurred at approximately 2.15pm on the afternoon of 12th September 2012 on the first bend of the A83 Tarbert-Lochgilphead road, I was first on the scene and attended to the dead and wounded, until the paramedics arrived. Some days later, as standard procedure, I passed the personal effects of the deceased, one Alexander Stark and his wife Charlotte to the Strathclyde CID as part of their investigation of the facts surrounding the case.

It is with some surprise and indeed anxiety that I have recently heard bizarre rumours, some even reported in the *Tarbert Times*, to the effect that my name (although I had never met the late Mr Stark) and description and an account of the events of the accident were somehow contained within the manuscript found in the glove compartment of the crashed car.

I was not aware that the late Mr Stark was a novelist, still less someone reputedly with occult powers to divine the future. Irregular though it seems (the circumstances are hardly normal at any rate) I would request that I be given copy or at least sight of the said document or the relevant pages thereof, in order to put to rest the understandable disquiet and curiosity that my family have been subject to over the last week during which these outlandish claims have emerged.

Yours faithfully,

-Inspector Walter M Dundas
Strathclyde Police, Lochgilphead.

322

The Wilderness (by Madame Mortadore & The Clouds) : copyright

every morning hard to rise
but who to challenge, who to blame
that every day turns out the same
the weight of sadness on my eyes

the nightclub music playing loud
drowns everything we loved or fought
coupling without words or thought
nowhere more lonely than this crowd

open the door and try some more
I feel the sun upon my face
don't want to join the human race
don't let today be like the day before

the television soap is on
it tells us how to think and feel
makes fiction of what once was real
community and family life long gone

the daily panic, constant noise
greed and impatience, a gripping vice
the streams of traffic; frozen ice
the human soul has lost its voice

children daren't walk to schools
unbridled freedoms have their price
choice degenerates to vice
we live in fear, not fear of rules.

(behind my face there's empty space)
there is a wilderness inside me
beautiful and open, calm and cool
where nature grows and blossoms
magnificently free of every human fool.

(behind my eyes the future dies)
there is a wilderness inside me
an undiluted, unpolluted place
with no fences and no houses
magnificently free of every human face.

Ultrameta

By Joy Hendry

If even the author tries to tell you he understands this novel fully and definitively, he's lying, or at best plain wrong. *Ultrameta* is of an order of fertility and complexity, of ambiguity and mystery, of weirdness and such incredible diversity that not even God (if He exists) would have all the answers. That's what makes it such a challenge and an exciting, even a dangerous journey in prospect for the reader. *Ultrameta* is so 'stappit fu' of meanings and possible significances that it can't be pinned down – cannot even pin itself down. So fasten seatbelts … prepare for a rough ride into the unknown but all-too-well known, the predictable and the unpredictable, the banal and the extraordinary.

Douglas Thompson sent me the title chapter of this book on 19 April, 2005; it was returned the following day with some editorial suggestions, which were implemented immediately and the story bounced back onto my desk by return of post! (Damn!) I accepted it on 17 June of the same year (unusually quick for me, I have to admit) with an acceptance letter which said: "It's a strange piece, and none of us are sure we understand it. But after much head-scratching we've decided we can't turn it down. Very odd! … All very Lanarkish." It finally found its way into print in July 2007. It would have been sooner but for endemic problems this side, but there was also a long process of editorial back and forth between Douglas and myself, working together to get the piece just right.

I vividly recollect one rainy Saturday afternoon working on the final editing and formatting of 'Ultrameta' and feeling intensely agitated about many things which just weren't quite right, and was overtaken with the desire, an overwhelming urge to get my hands in the mix, which resembled a lush, if explosive and slightly imperfect sultana cake. The writing was so genuinely remarkable, so accomplished, so different and yet so readable – and yet not quite 'there'. A protracted correspondence followed, of proofs, comments and arguments (all very good-natured) backwards and forwards, until a mutually acceptable version was finally arrived at. For me this was a rewarding and stimulating process; I don't know how it was for Douglas and have always felt it impertinent to ask; I don't know how far the process influenced the considerable work that has taken place between then and now to reach the finished product. Lying behind this impulse was a commitment, unquestioned on my part, but inexplicably strong, based on the feeling that here was something very special, extraordinary, even – which is why I am keen to write this.

Ultrameta introduces us to what might be an entirely new concept: that of the serial suicide, a frightening prospect if you consider today's Middle East. What if … no, exactly, you don't want to go there. Logical concomitants of that include reincarnation, multiple identities, the possibility of time-travel, historical simultaneity and no doubt much else. And so on to life in all its multicoloured, multitextured but sometimes very dirty tapestry, death of course (the universe – etc!).

Moving from 'Ultrameta' (the chapter) to *Ultrameta* the novel, I found that a strange and intriguing individual episode had mushroomed like an atomic bomb into a fully-worked out monograph which reminded me forcibly of Alasdair Gray's *Lanark* – in one book instead of four. A key element is time: our hero, Alexander Stark, an apparently happily-married professor of English at Glasgow University, is mad (though beware, in madness is, almost always, more sanity than any one individual can bear). He disappears for years, supposedly suffering from amnesia, and the novel comprises a series of very odd letters, written in his own fair hand, which his wife Charlotte, receives periodically from – well, goodness knows where – but these letters all appear to come from *other* individuals, and all involve the death of the central persona. So Stark may be mad, he may, or may not be all the characters concerned (Fraser Finch, William Gaunt, David Thin, Icarus, a Roman General, a Druid priest, the dying artist Giovanni Piranesi, a charismatic Italian singer Hamira Mediora – and others) – we don't know. Hamira is especially fascinating: she carries a virus with a difference – one which infects everyone who falls under the sway of her magnetism and hypnotic singing with a compulsion to face and tell the truth with often fatal consequences. But Thompson writes so persuasively that the different worlds of all these characters become very real indeed. And all these worlds, vividly described, lead us by the nose to ask fundamental questions about the world we live in here and now.

Stark has come to inhabit Ultrameta, defined in the novel as the City of the Soul, and, if souls exist at all, surely they know not boundaries of either time or space. Who can say that one soul cannot inhabit another?

I can't offer definitive interpretations or categorisations of this book, and don't want to. It isn't science fiction, though there are elements of science fiction there in retrospect. To Icarus, for example, the world of 9/11 is indeed science fiction. *Ultrameta* is like a literary tardis, transporting us to all manner of worlds, from Ancient Greece and the Roman invasion of Britain, to a post-modern landscape of glass and metal – and a great deal in between. The television features strongly, helpfully providing glimpses of other times and places right on cue … And the characters range from Greek demi-gods to Glasgwegian thugs.

Ultrameta is multi-genred, if anything. There are powerfully horrific elements, scenes gory and wretched enough to satisfy anyone with an appetite for these things; the grotesque is there in abundance, the Gothic too. Crime-fiction is a strong thread throughout. The Stark case quickly becomes obsessive for detective Walter Dundas and journalist Martha Lucy, their investigations providing the foundation for a long-standing affair. They discover, to their and our confusion, that there is indeed empirical evidence for a great deal of the material in Stark's missives, gradually building up over the course of the novel a suspense about, not so much 'whodunnit' but 'what'sitallabout'. Will they, and we get an answer? Read the book and find out! But there's more even to that single element: the nature of the quest lifts our two sleuths into metaphysical realms and dilemmas, bringing to mind the soul-searchings in McIlvanney's *Laidlaw*.

What about fantasy – well, it's there too, reminding me at times of David Lindsay's *Voyage to Arcturus*. Pushed to shove, I'd call it a genuinely metaphysical novel with its roots in the kinds of questions explored in the likes of Hogg's *Confessions of a Justified Sinner*. And Stevenson's *Weir of Hermiston* and, of course, *Jekyll and Hyde* gone multiple rather than double and let loose in a time-machine.

This bears pause for thought: many people claim to have multiple personalities (I don't believe it's helpful to regard this as 'a disorder' and their experiences shouldn't just be dismissed as lunatic). I have a friend, an American academic, who 'came out' as 'multiple' about 20 years ago. Once she overcame the social opprobrium (being rejected by many of her so-called friends when they learned about 'the other' – not to mention coming to terms with it herself) it's been a blessing, indeed a gift. I remain rather proud of myself that when the 'other' revealed herself to me, my instinctive response was: "How exciting!" Indeed it has been and is: the other draws, paints, acts, writes poetry, which the academic can't, and has a quite distinct personality of her own – even her own voice.

It isn't a new thought to me, but maybe part of what Douglas is getting that is that to experience this wonderful, bewildering and sometimes awful world we need much more than one self. Or perhaps that quite naturally we are many 'selves' in one, which training, education, society, the world as it is 'run' today kills off, one by one, leaving only vestiges lodged in a 'primary' persona. No one of these many 'selves' can exist on its own and therefore each must be killed off once its had its fling, but in Stark the need to explore these areas of his psyche, his nature, his personality, is so powerful that he has no choice but to 'let his demons out' and tumult towards their individual destruction under the watchful eye of The Keepers. Significantly, each different chapter, each different 'persona' is narrated in the first person. There are many ways in which Stark is "The Inhabited Man", a concept explored towards the end of the novel. Perhaps the ultimate goal is to throw away current restrictive notions about 'the self' and admit to a vision much broader and deeper, and to work towards a society which allows our many selves to integrate gently together without doing any of them violence. And that the ultimate aim is for each integrated being able to say, like the inscription found by Dundas and Lucy on a sarcophagus in Glasgow's Necropolis: *Et in Arcadia Ego*. Louis Macneice's masterpiece: 'Prayer Before Birth' stirs in the recesses ...

But then, what about the historical layers? What about the political layers? (An awareness of the political situation of Scotland through the millennia is strongly present and you notice in scenes from the past the seeds of the present. Indeed, I see this novel as part of Scotland's current and ongoing drive to take her place in the international community of post modern reality.) Perhaps oddly, associations most powerfully evoked for me were from folk song: Leonard Cohen's 'Suzanne' whose gentle musings contrast sharply with the sharp, violent images of Jaques Brel's searing 'The Port of Amsterdam', Dave Goulder's reflective 'January Man', Cyril Tawney's eerie 'Sally Free and Easy – that sort of thing ...

And of course it may finally be also an autobiographical novel. There are frequent flashbacks to what appears to be Stark's childhood, mainly describing a rural setting, the family's country escape, walks by the sea – and later visitations to a father-son reunion before death, and one suspects that, however far fetched the mediations throughout the novel might become, they locate back in Thompson's own background, especially in the relationship with his father. The father/son motif, mirrored by the struggle between the old and new, especially the latter's need to destroy the former, recurs constantly. Icarus must account to and for his father, Daedalus; it's Piranesi's son who is inescapably adjured to bear witness, to tell the world his father's stories and insights – and so on. If you accused Douglas Thompson of being Alexander Stark, I wonder how forcefully he could deny it! This rural idyll of childhood memories, and the rural setting of chapters describing the Roman struggle against the Picts, stands in sharp contrast to the many chapters dominated by urban 'reality' and technology, as if they stand on two opposite sides of some psychic abyss.

It's both an Odyssey and a Nostos – an attempted inward journey to the home of the soul based on an outward journey into dark and uncharted yet all too well charted waters. One constantly recurring theme is the relationship of the old to the young, both in human and historical, factual terms. Stark isn't alone, but under instructions from the mysterious Keepers. The Chief Keeper (the only one named) is the Reverend John says to Stark (aka William Gaunt at the time): *"... all that is required of us ... [is] to bear witness"*. And Stark in his many identities, capable of experiencing such an astonishing range of 'reality', has been given the hair shirt with 'Witness' in bold letters front and back by said Keepers, and is unable to remove it. At no point does he know who he 'is' unless somebody else tells him. Knowing who he is is not his job – yet! Maybe someday ...

And, if anything, the novel is asking us to explore our own multiplicity, our own full capacities, to become Witnesses ourselves – with the Government Health Warning via Hamira: "The amulet around my neck reminds me of the price I have paid to live in truth, the missing jigsaw piece, the memory of my beloved children [from whom she is now forever estranged]. For each person the price is different, for most the sacrifice is too great."

So, Who Are They? The Keepers? I think there are many thousands of possible answers but I'll have a stab at one: they are whatever drives the human race on in the pursuit of genuine personal identity and integrity, and of much wider truth, honesty, knowledge, the good life – maybe even the Garden of Eden. Maybe they could even be the clouds drifting across the novel's many skies?

"Nature has spoken to me and I have understood," Hamira says. Maybe Thompson's trying to find a way to open the floodgates so that we can listen to what Nature has to say. In a novel bursting with significant quotations, one apparently low-key one really hit me. At one point, when still a young child of 10, walking with his father on a beach on a beautiful summer's day and overwhelmed by the beauty and grandeur of it all, his father says, simply: "I know, son, I know ... "Sometimes your inside just gets too big for your outside." Stark goes on to reflect: "Then perhaps I guessed for the first time what I know now: that the body falls away like the skin of an orange, peeling as the hot sun rises in the sky of our hearts. Fear nothing. We are found, we are all found, and nothing is lost."

It is, of course, for history, the critics, the literary pundits, the reading polity and above all time to judge the ultimate quality and worth of this novel. I can only heartily commend it to you as a unique experience. You can read it at many levels, dig deep for parallels, references, associations, significances, unpick its imagery, reflect on meanings and significances large and small. Let your imagination go to town and enjoy the riot. Or you can take it on a much simpler level, as if jumping into a little boat on a vast sea which is the beautifully composed language of the novel, its poetic rhythms, its sonorities and sensitivities – and, indeed, its sheer driving force, and just see where it gets you. Be swept along with it on this strange, sometimes disturbing but certainly magical mystery tour of the extremities of human experience – without trying to interpret or explain – and discover which shore, or shores, it casts you up on. You will certainly be stimulated, enlightened, and wiser, for the trip.

-Joy Hendry
Edinburgh
May, 2009.

"Ultrameta wears its classical influences on its sleeve: stories include settings like Roman Britain and Greek myth; the organization recalls Dante's inferno, even with Vergil-like guides on the journey; chapter names are often Latin or Greek(ish) words. It also buys into the Ancient Greek notion (found in Hesiod, for example), that humankind is in decline from an ancient ideal (in which this collective (un)conscious was known and understood) ...The book is many-layered and challenging ...it hangs together well, though, and it's fun to go back from the finish and re-read, seeing connections where they weren't apparent before..."

-Hugh Cayless, The Future Fire.

"...Think Borges or Italo Calvino with shades of Dickens. ... good books are almost always like this, like some elephant felt at by blind men--one feeling its trunk, another its side, a third its tale--each calling it something different, each getting a different sensation from it. ...Out of all the books I have read from this year, from small press to large (and I do read a lot), I would say this is certainly one of the two or three best. Read it."

-Brendan Connell, author of "Metrophilias"

"This is a fascinating journey into other realities, other times, other personas. The story, or stories linked by subtle threads, takes the reader into a literary maze. The ideas overflow the narrative, but the structure is precise (like a maze).

I found the whole experience (because that sums up what it is) absolutely compelling. I don't pretend to understand everything here, and am sure the book deserves a second read, but the prose sparkles, the images sear the imagination, and the reading experience is very much like an adventure into the many lives, genders and guises of Alexander Stark, the central character(s).

The book is described as 'a fractal novel,' explained on the back cover as 'the secret structure of life itself.' All I can say is, read the book for the multi-layered experiences, for the adventure and the narrative excellence..... but do not hope to understand everything. Wonderful!"

-Trevor Denyer, -Midnight Street.

"If you thought Cloud Atlas was a little too conventional, Ultrameta may be the book for you... Identities and realities are constantly shifting in Ultrameta. Multiple characters return home with amnesia and start reading through their mysterious notes. The letter from Charlotte to Martha placed at the end of the book is a world away from the one at the beginning to which it's replying. Even the novel's structure cannot be relied upon to stay the same: the chapters don't all flow neatly into the next; and the second chapter in a pair isn't always a direct continuation of the first. There probably isn't a definitive interpretation of what's going on in Ultrameta, but that hardly matters when the ride is so intriguing ...But it's the entirety of Ultrameta that impresses the most; there's nothing else quite like it, I'm sure."

-David Hebblethwaite, Follow The Thread blog.

"Douglas Thompson has created something which feels quite unique... at once powerful and challenging... Part fantasy, part horror, there is no denying the power of the prose.

On the most surface level you can see a story of a man living many lives, but like Thomas Pynchon, James Joyce and Samuel Beckett, what you see on the surface is but a reflection of the immensity which is hidden beneath. Really, I don't throw those names around lightly; I really was that impressed with the novel, this represents a new form of literature for a new century.

If the review appears short then maybe a new form of criticism needs to be employed, for my part I was just blown away. There are few book which clash imagery and ideas in such a perfect union as Ultrameta. If this isn't a modern classic, then there is little justice in the world, which would be an irony considering the content of the book."

-Charles Packer, -Sci-Fi Online.

"...so astonishing and so astonishingly good, indeed brilliant, that it is totally worthy of comparison with Lanark. Nothing is ever entirely new in literature, but this novel comes near to it, as gripping as it is disconcerting, with enough different goodies in the larder to keep a family going for a nuclear-shelter decade...

...In short, a fantastic novel in both senses of the word, which includes, but also goes way beyond, entertainment, casting as it does an insight on modern urban life... And most important of all, it is a bloody good read, with not a single page that doesn't satisfy, excite, amaze, or even simply mystify (but in an intriguing, challenging manner), the reader in some way..."

-Steve Redwood, author of "Fisher of Devils".

"...The remarkable thing about this book is that despite the experimentation, the eccentricity, and the frequent changes in point of view, tense, location and time, it's exceptionally readable, each carefully crafted sentence going down like hot chocolate laced with brandy ...both frightening and exhilarating. By turns cynical and idealistic, liberating and claustrophobic, this book is entirely entertaining and highly recommended."

-Stephen Theaker, Dark Horizons.

"...one of the strangest novels I've ever read... the quality of the writing and the surreal and intriguing stories caught my imagination. This is one book I'll be keeping for another read – at least."

-Anthony Williams, -British Fantasy Society.

Lightning Source UK Ltd.
Milton Keynes UK
UKOW05f1145230713

214227UK00001B/21/P